Praise for Timothy Janovsky

"*The (Fake) Dating Game* is an utter delight, chock-full of all my favorite tropes. Game show antics, idiots-in-love, and a healthy dose of steam, this book swept me off my feet. Sexy as hell, with Janovsky's trademark wit and charm, this book is everything I want in a romance novel!"

—Alison Cochrun, author of *The Charm Offensive* and *Kiss Her Once for Me*

"Janovsky (*New Adult*) returns with a playful yet heartfelt romp through grief and new love set against the backdrop of reality TV.... The result is fun, fast-paced, and full of feeling."

—*Publishers Weekly* on *The (Fake) Dating Game*

"Janovsky (*New Adult*, 2023) is an inspired choice to help Harlequin launch their new Afterglow imprint since he has a real flair for delivering sensually descriptive love scenes with steam to spare and a gift for crafting characters with whom readers can readily connect. Pair this with a fun game show setting (think *Supermarket Sweep*) and a story line that is both humorous and thoughtful in its exploration of the grieving process, and readers are the real winners!"

—*Booklist* on *The (Fake) Dating Game*

"Fans of the fake-dating trope and game shows will find a lot to like here. Holden is a sympathetic narrator, and readers will happily root for him as he learns that while there are no quick fixes for grief, opening up to the right people can make all the difference."

—*Library Journal* on *The (Fake) Dating Game*

Also by Timothy Janovsky

The (Fake) Dating Game
You Had Me at Happy Hour

Visit timothyjanovsky.com or the Author Profile
page at Harlequin.com for more titles.

ONCE UPON YOU & ME

TIMOTHY JANOVSKY

Recycling programs for this product may not exist in your area.

ISBN-13: 978-1-335-57496-1

Once Upon You and Me

Harlequin Enterprises ULC
22 Adelaide St. West, 41st Floor
Toronto, Ontario M5H 4E3, Canada
www.Harlequin.com

Printed in U.S.A.

For those in search of that fairy-tale feeling...

This book contains discussions and depictions of divorce, biphobia and a parent living with MS. Please take special care while reading.

Much love,

Timothy Janovsky

One

ETHAN

ONCE UPON A TIME... the large, hand-painted, wooden sign that greets guests visiting Storybook Endings Resort—a jewel of the modern Catskills—should read.

After many chilly winters exposed to the persnickety elements of upstate New York, though, the sign has been dulled by rot and wind, mold and ice, so at most distances it reads *O PO A T ME.*

Oh, poo at me, if you read it aloud with a specific cadence and tone, the one Ethan Golding perfects now with his head of maintenance and longtime friend Gabriel Esteves. They snicker at the sign that they're about to replace.

Snickering is simpler than attacking the hurt feelings whirring like an out-of-control chain saw within Ethan.

This billboard-sized hunk of wood has been welcoming people far and wide for nearly a decade. Every year, post ski season, the resort gets tended to in the way one might tend to a boat they hope to take out into open waters at the very first buds of spring. *De-winterizing* is what Amy Lu, Ethan's erstwhile wife and current boss calls it. From their odds-and-ends budget this year, Amy has chosen to erect a backlit, plastic sign in place of the original, handcrafted wooden one.

Ethan needs more than two hands to count off the number of odds and ends he'd have prioritized over this one, but these days, getting an idea in edgewise with Amy Lu is like fly-fishing without a license, reckless and utterly pointless.

Ethan and Gabriel rove around to the other side of the sign, through the newly coming-to-life grass, taking pictures as they go to commemorate what will no longer be. The chain saw goes berserk in Ethan's gut as he recalls putting this sign up for the first time—laying the timber wood frame, digging the holes for the posts, setting up the lighting.

With the look on his daughter Samara's face when she saw the finished sign for the first time, one would've thought Ethan had achieved a feat of magic. Reviews of Storybook Endings Resort have called it enchanting and timeless and a little slice of magic in the heart of the Catskills. But Ethan is no magician, because for the first year after his divorce he tried every trick in the book to make Samara and Amy reappear, and nothing worked.

The south-facing side of the sign fared much better than the north. *AND THEY LIVED HAPPILY EVER AFTER…* It's the final message families see when leaving the resort. Those words mean nothing to Ethan as he reads them now. His eyes are drawn down and to the right, toward the insignia he couldn't avoid if he tried.

Storybook ENDINGS Resort.

That yellow logo is branded onto everything within a twenty-three acre radius, from the pens at reception to the hand towels in the bathrooms, even the white fleece quarter-zip thrown over Ethan's flannel. An emblem that says, "Anything that's *ours*, stays."

Well, not Amy.

Five years ago, she was wearing the same exact fleece on the day she served him the divorce papers. They were not a surprise in the slightest, but the upset and disappointment came as if they were. Flagrant and sharp. Then, she rolled her medium-sized suitcase, which also had the resort logo on it, out the front door of their lovingly crafted, English-style cottage. Ethan built the place with his bare hands for their family. It's set back on the property and ensconced by balsam trees that are bright green in the summer and always coated with white, powdery snow in the winter.

Amy would've stamped the Storybook Endings logo on those tree trunks too if she could figure out a way to monetize their scent, sell them to the devotees who visit once, twice, sometimes five times a year.

Crunch, grr, cruunch. The horse-drawn Cinderella carriage rolls along the path on their right. It's Sunday, which means the Bannisters' wedding weekend has come to an end. Vows exchanged, drinks had, and a final brunch of eggs benedict eaten.

The white, pumpkin-shaped contraption invades Ethan's peripheral vision and plunks down the gravel with Paulie, the teenager from the town horse stable in a costume top hat and tails, at the reigns. Seated cozily inside, Zanib Bannister née

Schroff and Owen Bannister cuddle close on the plush white seat with a sparkly blanket draped across their legs. Their foreheads press together in a private moment of sheer bliss.

Alongside Gabriel, Ethan pastes on a smile and waves his cupped right hand in a rolling motion, as all employees are trained to do. The pomp is all second nature to him because Storybook Endings is a premier wedding destination. With cabins enough to sleep an entire extended family and a barn that can be transformed for a classy ceremony and immediately turned over for a rustic, farm-to-table reception, the resort has solidified itself as a mainstay for those who want sweeping Disney vibes without the Orlando tourist-trap price tag or the creepy dark rides.

Now it's not just dark rides Ethan finds creepy; it's the marriage act altogether.

Up at the top of the hill, the wedding party stands near "The Castle." It's an all-purpose lodge with a jewel-toned facade that makes it look like it has a drawbridge and stained glass windows and a turret. Cramped together in various types of garb—dressy casual has lost all meaning these days—the guests chatter and wave off the happy couple as the carriage disappears around the curve of the road, which is artfully concealed by the exacting brush.

Before he hired Paulie, Ethan often drove the coach himself.

At the end of the drive, the coach will stop, the couple will be escorted into their waiting hybrid crossover with their luggage already stowed in the trunk, and they will drive off into the metaphorical sunset. In reality, by nightfall, they'll be making love in Turks and Caicos, and statistically speaking, by year three, they'll be considering separation.

That same pervasive cynicism is illustrated when, as soon as that carriage clears sightlines, the waving, fawning mass of Bannister-lovers immediately drops the act. Postures falter, smiles fade. Lined coats get thrown on over dresses with small straps and low necklines. Ties get loosened or torn off altogether.

Everyone is noisily concerned about checking out or getting home in good time or who should take the rest of the seven-tiered cake with them. One elderly woman says, "No more weekend destination weddings. I'm too old not to sleep in my own bed after dancing that much."

"Out with the old, in with the new," says Gabriel, clapping his gloved hands together, ready to get to work. Now that the party has cleared, they can replace the sign in peace.

"Soon enough you'll be saying that about me," Ethan gruffly jokes, pulling his own tan workman's gloves from the worn back pocket of his trusty, boot-cut Levi's.

Gabriel, four years Ethan's junior with brown skin and broad shoulders, slaps him on the back and squints against the mid-March sun. "Cool it with that talk. Forty is the new twenty-five."

"In a few weeks, I'm going to have a sixteen-year-old daughter," says Ethan. "*Sixteen.* I don't feel twenty-five. I feel ancient. I can see the crypt opening and beckoning me inside for a long, overdue slumber."

That feeling expands from his mental state into his joints and shoulder muscles as he and Gabriel lumber with the heavy wooden sign, releasing it from its frame and setting it down on a tarp they've unrolled on the grass.

"If you're ancient, then I'm pre-ancient, and I refuse to believe that. It's all about mindset," Gabriel says after they've hauled down the back side.

"My mindset is—let's get this done as quickly as possible so I can make sure checkout is going smoothly," he says, all business.

They go to the shed near the lodge and haul out the high-density urethane sign that Amy had custom made and transported there. It's a thick, rigid hunk of plastic but practically weightless.

"This crap is really going to withstand next winter?" Gabriel asks.

"Longevity has never been Amy's top priority," Ethan says, then immediately wished he hadn't. Good thing he couldn't see Gabriel's face, which was hidden behind the sizable sign between them—otherwise he would've been shot with a firm, judgmental glare.

"Why couldn't the original sign just be touched up and refinished?" Gabriel asks after a beat.

"Good question." Ethan wrote the same sentiment in various replies to the original e-mail from Amy's latest assistant, Taylor Frost. All are still unsent. Either because he doesn't want to ruffle Amy's feathers or because he finds Taylor's e-mail contact headshot rather fetching. The photo showcases Taylor's brown hair that falls in beachy waves, his wide, toothy smile, and skin so sun-kissed it makes his russet brown eyes look like the gemstones in a bracelet Ethan once bought Amy for an anniversary.

Ogling a picture of his ex-wife's personal assistant feels too much like a personal low point, so he gives Taylor no further excuse to invade his inbox with Bruce Springsteen "Dancing in the Dark" era good looks.

"More cost-effective, I guess. It's waterproof, and it won't bow. From what I've gathered, the sign-making company will easily be able to replicate this a dozen times over for 'brand consistency.'" Those two words carry the overwhelming stench of disdain on them.

"The Texas location got this, too?" Gabriel asks. They climb their respective ladders in perfect sync, tool belts donned, ready to affix.

"The Texas location has had it since they opened." Ethan lets out a grunt as he weasels the new sign into place. "Blame them for our extra work."

"How are things looking with the California location?" Gabriel asks. The light tone belies the weighty topic.

Ethan huffs through his nose, which causes his trimmed dirty blond mustache hairs to tickle his upper lip. He's had a full beard since he was eighteen, yet he's never gotten used to the way his facial hair behaves. It refuses to be tamed or grow at a reasonable pace. His clippers deserve a break for their frequent, reliable service. "Beats me. I don't get cc'd on anything anymore, which is fine."

Not that he needs to spell this out for Gabriel. He was there through the divorce when Ethan sold away his right to the title of co-owner. All he wanted out of those arbitration sessions in sweaty conference rooms with wilted salads was joint custody of Samara and to stay on as general manager of the original location of Storybook Endings Resort, the place he's called home for nearly a decade.

Storybook Endings started as a small spark of an idea, a place for Samara to live out her full-scale princess fantasies. He never dreamed it would turn into a success or a legacy. Both of which he's working hard with his therapist not to begrudge. Because his wife ran off with the success and his daughter who is now "too old for princesses" wants nothing to do with the legacy.

Gabriel struggles a bit, trying to get his side of the sign straight. "If we know anything about Amy, it's that if she wants something enough, she'll make it happen."

"Ain't that the truth?" If only she had ever wanted what Ethan wanted. A queen who held court for the visiting masses, a princess who thrived within the confines of his kingdom, and a finite happily-ever-after, like the sign says.

But signs lie.

So do fairy tales.

And life goes on.

Bang, ba-bang. With two final, vigorous hits of Ethan's hammer, the new sign hangs firmly in place. Ethan and Gabriel meander back to inspect their work.

In the unobstructed sunlight, it appears much shoddier than the wooden sign still lying on the tarp, but on overcast days or at night in the landscaping lights, the difference will barely be noticeable. "Oh, you repainted the sign out front? How lovely," the regulars will say on their return visits to the resort this summer. Ethan will stand behind the reception desk as he always does, smiling and nodding and not going into detail about how everything is being upgraded and standardized and automated.

If he doesn't watch his words or his step, he fears he'll end up just like the sign. Replaced with a newer, cheaper make and model.

Gabriel goes up to the sign, fiddles with the lower right-hand corner.

Ethan's eyes zip, once again, to the logo inscribed there. It occurs to him, for the first time, that the word *endings* in the business's logo is underlined and bolded, so it reads "Storybook *Endings* Resort."

The swooping, magenta lettering—now untarnished and vibrant—mocks him. He tugs at the tall collar of his fleece so the cool wind hits his overheating neck.

How many logos had they considered from the marketing firm before they settled on this one? Their divorce was practically forecasted there this whole time. He lets loose one of those quiet, mirthless laughs he's grown accustomed to.

How many endings had he endured recently?

Five years ago his marriage ended, and five months ago his thirties ended.

Now he'd just like this workday to end so he can go watch a Spielberg movie on the couch with his Newfoundland named Nana, eat a personal cauliflower crust pizza with extra cheese and nurse a beer or two before bed.

"You coming to the brewery tonight?" Gabriel asks as they begin to clean up. "I met this guy through the snowmobiling group I'm in. He just moved up here after the holidays. He said he broke up with his long-term partner and needed a new start. He's going to join the usual bunch. I think you two would really hit it off."

"Why? Because he's also dated a man?" Ethan asks. He always gets prickly when people try to set him up, like he's some lonely sap who needs a significant other to make him interesting.

Gabriel tips his head and glares up at Ethan. "No, because it's impossible to get you out of the house these days and he's a fun, outdoorsy guy who seems nice."

"This nice-seeming guy's name is…?"

"Kurt."

"Age?"

"Forty-six."

"Job?"

"Jeez," Gabriel cries. "You gonna want his shoe size, too? His social security number? I don't know. I've only spoken to him twice. You're not hiring the guy. You're getting a drink among friends, and he'll be there, tagging along. You can ask him all these questions when you meet him tonight at the brewery."

Ethan usually avoids the brewery, which is housed in an old, converted firehouse in town. It's not the mostly burned-out jukebox that seems to only play Willie Nelson, nor the life-size Betty Boop statue that holds the chalkboard menu right up next to her ample, sculpted cleavage that keep him away. It's not even the slight waft of burned rubber that always seems to hang in the air there. It's that he and Amy and Samara used to eat and drink there—on credit—when they were new in town and just starting Storybook Endings Inn (the resort part came later with surprise success and expansions).

Ethan's skin slicks at the thought of sitting beside some forty-six-year-old snowmobiler named Kurt in a booth that's haunted by the memory of his family unit, unbroken.

He's lived Once Upon a Time...and learned his lesson about Happily-Ever-After. Trying again now, at his age, in this town, well, it seems childish.

But Gabriel's looking at him, shaking his head, waiting for a response, and there's no way Gabriel will believe he has other plans beside walking and feeding Nana, so he says, "One drink."

"One drink is all it takes, my friend," Gabriel says, clapping Ethan on the back. "One drink is all...it...takes."

Two

TAYLOR

At 4:30 p.m. in the west parking lot of La Jolla High School, Taylor Frost sits in the driver's seat of his bluish silver used sedan waiting for his boss's daughter to be let out of school. His trusty surfboard remains affixed to the roof. Waking up before his alarm and a clear, beautiful forecast meant he couldn't pass up the opportunity to shred some waves before work.

A cool mid-March breeze floats through his open window as he reads his boss's bio for the sixth time, scouring for typos. Even one misplaced comma makes Amy Lu upset, so he circles back for a seventh go.

Amy Lu, a proud Chinese American woman in business, has become a major player in the hospitality industry, winning numerous awards, grants and other accolades. The rising hotelier began her career by cofounding the Storybook Endings

Resort in Calico, New York, a charming respite in the Catskills that gained popularity online with whimsy and charm. She is now the CEO of Storybook Lodgings, the company that has turned the original Storybook Endings Resort from single location to chain. With two thriving locations, the original and one right outside of Dallas, Texas, and one set to open on Lake Tahoe later this year, Amy is looking for partners to help expand her vision and operation on the West Coast and beyond.

This bio is going in front of investors. Big suit-and-tie types who have the capacity to flood money into the business that Amy can immediately put toward the necessary finishing touches on the dream California location. And as her personal assistant for the last three years, Amy's dreams have become Taylor's dreams.

Partially because his (long-term, so-close-he-can-taste-it) dream is to get a full-time position in hospitality at one of Amy's locations.

He sips from the iced green tea latte sweating in his cup holder and pointedly ignores the fact that his current job is only hospitality adjacent. When he first saw the job listing for Amy Lu's assistant, he jumped at the opportunity to apply, and after several intensive interviews and a lengthy trial period, he scored the gig.

At first, he assumed this would be more of a ground-floor position. Going to the locations. Assisting where needed. Learning the ropes of the business while seeing smiles on the faces of luxuriating guests.

That's not at all what greeted him on day one. He practically spent an entire twenty-four hours stuck in an AC-less room undoing the mess Amy's previous assistant left behind.

Amy Lu's day-to-day is more big picture. So big, in fact, that he only ever sees the forest, never the trees. Illustrated now by an e-mail crashing into his ever-flooding inbox from a photographer out near Lake Tahoe. The first photo attached to the e-mail is of a forest. Edge to edge green. Overwhelming in scope.

The photographer was tasked with taking aerial shots of the resort grounds for the website update. Amy wanted some dreamy photos to go along with the press release and reservation link, so Taylor found, vetted and hired the best candidate. The second attachment on the e-mail is a sweeping shot of the cabins and the pool and the sandy volleyball courts from above.

At least there's a bit of beach along with the swath of forest in this one. Something new to lure and appease Taylor's eye.

For a moment, he gets lost in the image, fantasizes about moving up north to help launch this brand-new business venture. That daydream gets squashed as soon as the doors to the school clamber open and a rush of teens spill into the parking lot.

Samara Golding moves among them. She inherited her father's towering height and her mother's jet-black hair. She walks with the bounce of a still-fifteen-year-old but has the heavily done cat eye makeup of a soon-to-be sixteen-year-old. Taylor knows this in-between well. He ferried five younger siblings through the plentiful awkward stages of adolescence.

Samara flops into the passenger's seat and immediately reaches for the aux cord. "You have to hear the new Olivia Rodrigo," she says, already scrolling through her music app.

"I added it to our shared playlist this morning. I don't know if you saw it."

Taylor spent half his day unburying himself from an e-mail mountain, so he'd missed the notification. He rarely got a second to check his personal phone in the afternoon. "I didn't, but now I'm excited. How was photography club?" he asks, throwing the car into Drive as the pronounced electric guitar wobbles through the speakers.

She adjusts the camera bag in her lap so it doesn't get jostled in transit. "Great. Can you take a left? I'm starving. I want In-N-Out."

The house is five minutes away. In-N-Out is thirteen minutes in the opposite direction, a route that's always punctuated with pesky traffic. But Taylor's growling stomach decides for him. Once again, he forgot to eat lunch because he was too wrapped up in a whirlwind of responsibility.

"Mr. Larkspur loved my portraits of you," Samara says as they traverse down Soledad Mountain Road. Taylor agreed to model for her a few months ago after she mentioned he could use one of her edited photos as his professional headshot. "He says you make a good subject."

Taylor laughs. "Does he?"

"Duh." This has been an ongoing topic since Back-to-School night in September. Amy sent Taylor in her place and Samara's photography teacher took a distinct liking to Taylor. "Is it an age thing?"

"No, it's not an age thing," Taylor says, remembering the flutter of attraction he felt when the early-forties, tan-skinned man chatted him up after the session where he discussed the advanced photography syllabus and showed some students' work from previous years. "It's a time thing." Taylor dedicates his life to Amy Lu and Samara Golding. To his roommates and his siblings and the surf. Men rarely find their way into that cluttered snapshot.

Samara whines when they pull into the drive-through lane at In-N-Out instead of parking. Taylor tells her Amy's expecting them back ASAP. She huffs, but happily accepts the fresh-cut fries slathered in sunflower oil when he hands them to her. She puts the Olivia Rodrigo single on a loop since they were barely listening on the ride over. By the time Taylor parks outside the Beach Barber Tract rental with its large southern magnolia taking up most of the front yard, he practically knows every lyric.

Once inside the single-story house, Samara races with her food to her bedroom, eager to edit that day's shots. "Don't forget to do your homework, too," he calls after her. Some days, he feels more like her older brother than her mom's employee.

Amy's in the third bedroom, which she turned into her home office, decorated with her signature colors—crimson, gray and white. She sits behind her glass desk, laptop open, desktop monitor on, phone pressed to her ear. She's wearing a bright red blouse, a pencil skirt, and her jet-black hair is parted down the middle, hanging in shiny, straight tendrils that stop right at the crests of her petite shoulders. Her calculated mouse clicks can be heard out in the hallway.

Taylor waits outside, as he always does, until she looks up and gestures him in. One time, he made the mistake of bypassing this formality and accidentally overheard his boss saying some racy things to her recent boyfriend that he still wishes he could scrub from his memory.

"Okay. Great. I'm glad you understand the urgency. I appreciate your willingness to get this right. I'll have my assistant on it first thing. You're a gem. Take care." She's setting her iPhone down on the desk, a hard-won smile catching on her face. "Did you see Silvan's e-mail?"

"Yes," Taylor says, pulling his tablet from his bag. This tablet is his lifeblood; his whole career exists inside that terabyte hard drive. Amy's everything—dietary restrictions, coffee orders, family birthdays, address book, etc.—can be pulled up with a single tap of the electronic pen on the ten-inch screen. Taylor treats it the way some might treat a family photo album, with reverence and gentle care.

"Well? What did you think?" Taylor is about to speak when there's a ding from Amy's phone and, probably having forgotten she asked a question at all, she starts typing out a response to someone else while speaking to him. "I thought the angles of the photos were off, and the lighting wasn't right. I need him to go at it from a higher elevation, which means another pricey helicopter rental, but what can we do? I'm going to fly up north to go out with him and grab the shots we need for presentations and the website. The sooner we have the right visuals, the easier it will be to onboard new investors."

"Understood." Taylor launches every airline price tracker he has downloaded. "When do you need to be in by?"

Amy's head is still down, thumbs moving at the speed of light. "This Friday, returning next Wednesday."

Taylor doesn't need to reference her calendar. She's now double-booked, but he won't phrase it as such because the bookings are his business. It's his job to make her days as effortless as possible. "Excellent. Should I reschedule our travel to upstate New York for Samara's sweet sixteen preparations, then?"

One of Taylor's largest duties this year has been preparing Samara's birthday bash. She and fifteen of her closest friends will take over the cottages at the Catskills Storybook Endings to make friendship bracelets, roast s'mores, play laser tag, and have movie screenings. The three-day, two-night trip will end with a proper party in the barn, which will be turned into a glimmery dream complete with photo booth, cake pops, and dance contests.

Overseeing the booking of flights and accommodations for sixteen precocious teenagers was a challenge, but he grew up in a big family, so corralling the uncorralable is a skill he's fine-tuned his whole life.

Amy purses her lips before saying, "No, you go ahead as planned. Move my ticket to Samara's flight."

"Will do." Taylor's insides do a strange dance. He hasn't traveled anywhere on his own in years. He barely even gets privacy in his three-bedroom apartment because when you're the lone single person living with two couples, you're last in line for just about everything.

"Book me in first class," Amy says.

"On it." He finishes writing out his notes, seven tabs already open and loading. "Should I reschedule the inspection of the Catskills location you had planned for before the party? Maybe for the end of the week?"

"I trust you can handle that for me. You know my standards well enough by now," she says. It comes out so blasé that he almost doesn't register it as an exciting compliment. "Make note of anything that you think is amiss. I'll check it out when I arrive and make proper provisions to fix it moving forward. Does that work for you?"

A swelling sense of responsibility rises high through him like a particularly good wave to surf on. Maybe this is the ultimate test to see if he can live up to her lofty expectations for full-time resort workers. A true position is so close he can practically reach out and grab it. "Absolutely."

"Good," she says with a hand wave. "I'll expect my travel itinerary by EOD."

"On it."

"Is that for me?" Amy asks, eyeing the bag of In-N-Out he'd set down upon entering. "You really do think of everything." She stretches her hands out in greedy thanks.

He hadn't thought to order her anything. In the last three years, Amy has eaten fast food in front of Taylor exactly once. She took the burger off the bun and didn't even finish. She hates the way it makes her feel, but perhaps the stress of the California location is weighing on her so much that she could use the comfort. Far be it from him to deprive her of the greasy, savory goodness. He yields his belated lunch despite his furious stomach.

His hand is on the door handle when Amy says, "Oh, and please e-mail my ex-husband about the change of plans. Better from you than from me."

He's certainly heard that refrain before. "I'd be delighted to."

On his walk back to the kitchen, those silly words bang around inside his brain. *Delighted to?* As Amy's personal assistant, he's expected to adopt her stance on the people in her life. It's not that she doesn't like her ex. It's more that she begrudges him for having to chase her aspirations solo. For leaving her with no choice but to pack up and explore greener pastures for the business they birthed together.

That's the story Taylor's been told. It's gospel truth to him. And every time he thinks of it, he shudders.

Taylor operates under a firm "family first" policy. He doesn't understand how someone could be so selfish and stubborn as to let his partner and daughter move far, far away when they needed him the most. It's unthinkable.

Which means, when he settles down at the breakfast nook in the open-concept kitchen, he swats at the slight titter of attraction that crops up as he pulls open his e-mail browser and keys in Ethan Golding.

Taylor has a type. Tall. Broad. Bigger than him. Outdoorsy. Guys with facial hair and eyes that have *seen things*.

The photo of Ethan attached to his e-mail contact is new-ish and checks every damn one of Taylor's boxes. Ethan's dirty blond hair refuses to stay in place despite there being signs of product in it. He has a well-groomed beard that suits his squarish jaw, and a body like a brick house—sturdy and bulky and warm-looking.

Nope. No way.

If Taylor's learned anything from Amy's cautionary tales, it's that business and pleasure do not mix. Any sort of attraction he may be harboring for Ethan Golding is fatuous and fleeting.

To avoid considering this any further, Taylor sends off a very polite e-mail to alert Ethan of the schedule changes, puts on Samara's playlist and then compares first-class seat options for his boss's upcoming excursion.

Three

ETHAN

From: TaylorFrost@StorybookLodgings.com
To: EthanGolding@StorybookLodgings.com
Subject: Re: re: re: Schedule Change

Dear Ethan,
The Snow White cottage will do just fine for me for the week, and thank you for complying with my request for late check-in. I should arrive to the resort shortly after 6 p.m. eastern time.

I will be busy with preparations for Samara's party, so I will mostly be out of your hair except for when we do our walk-through inspection. I have been entrusted with the task and appreciate the entire staff taking care as to treat it with as much importance as if Ms. Lu was in attendance. I look forward to meeting you on March 22nd.

Warmest regards,

Taylor Frost

Personal Assistant, Amy Lu

There's something condescending about the way someone could write such a coldly formal e-mail, have the last name Frost, and still have the gall to sign their e-mail *warmest regards*. This e-mail has all the warmth of the arctic tundra.

Granted, when Ethan got the e-mail, he was mostly relieved. No longer would he be squared with entertaining his ex-wife for an entire week without their daughter as a buffer. Putting Amy up in one of the guest cottages while he walked back to their old family cottage every night to make dinner for one would've been weirdly ravaging.

In the intervening years, their fractured family has met in neutral locations for small vacations and long weekends. But having her back here without Samara, after so much has changed between them, well…he doesn't think he'd even know how to talk to her. Most of their communication as of the last few years has been through this guy. Taylor Frost. A cute face paired with icy verbiage.

Gabriel sidles up to the reception desk after fixing a burned-out light bulb in the foyer and says, with the stepladder under his right arm, "Kurt would really like to see you again."

Ethan is thankful for the reprieve from tapping his fingers anxiously against the welcome desk, awaiting Taylor Frost's arrival, but regretful that his friend has chosen *this* topic to break the spell with.

"I don't think that's wise." One drink with Kurt was all it took for Ethan to decide that dating isn't for him.

Last week, everything seemed to be going well with Kurt, the decently handsome used car salesman with fetching salt-and-pepper hair, until the rest of the group went to go play pool in the back room. If they had never been left alone, Ethan might've entertained another outing with Kurt, but when the conversation veered toward their dating histories, the whole night went to shit.

"Ah, yes, I remember Gabriel said you were married," Kurt mused, pouring himself another drink from the sweating pitcher on the table between them. "Remind me again, dead or divorced?"

Ethan tried to mask his shock over this man's bluntness. He appreciates a person who cuts to the chase in a conversation, but he physically had to take a second and a sip of his beer before he responded. "Uh, divorced."

"Ah, yeah. It's coming back now," he said. "I got out of a long-term relationship recently, too. Only engaged, though, on my side. What was your husband like?"

"Wife, actually," Ethan said, refusing to sound sheepish even though he easily forecasted what was coming next.

Squinted eyes. Check. *Passing confusion.* Check. *Slightly open trout mouth.* Check. *And then: "Have you been with…guys?"*

Ethan domed both hands around his beer glass. "I have."

"So you're…?"

"Bisexual."

Kurt's nod came too slowly to read as acceptance.

To his credit, he didn't say what other men of his age have said to Ethan before. *Is bi a real thing? You just want it both ways, don't you? I'm not sure I could date a bi person. You really should've put it in your profile.* Ethan's heard it all before.

Dating in upstate New York for a divorced, bisexual, fat,

single dad who just turned forty with very little fanfare is not sunshine and rainbows, storybooks and sunsets. The past five years have been a montage of awkward conversations, shitty beers in shittier bars and slow head nods from guys named Kurt.

Gabriel bristles, setting down the stepladder. "What? Why not? What's wrong with him?"

"There's nothing wrong with him," Ethan remarks unconvincingly. "We're just not a match." He grabs a pair of scissors from the drawer to his right and snips off a stray thread from the purple-and-gold flannel he's wearing. A Christmas or two ago, Samara gave it to him as a gift, and even though the hem of the right sleeve is fraying from being worn and run through the wash so often, he refuses to get rid of it. It reminds him too much of his daughter whom he misses with every fiber of his being.

"Where have I heard that before? Oh, yeah. You. About the last few people you've gone out with. When even was the last time you went out with someone before Kurt? A year ago? Two?" Gabriel says a little too judgmentally for Ethan's liking. Just because Gabriel has an awesome, successful, lawyer wife doesn't mean everyone needs to be perfectly partnered. "You're never going to find a match with that attitude."

"Maybe I'm not looking to find a match," Ethan says, steadfast.

"If you're not looking for a match, then who's going to light your fire, Mr. Golding?" Gabriel asks, voice leaden with overwrought innuendo.

"I'm perfectly capable of lighting my own fire, thank you very much."

"Mherm." Ethan and Gabriel both startle from the sudden presence of another person in the reception area.

As soon as Gabriel steps to the side, Ethan is face-to-face with Taylor Frost. Those russet eyes are even more arresting in real life, drawing Ethan in at an alarming rate. Trying to preserve his cool, he looks down, which is by far the worst move he could make. Taylor's lean frame is wrapped up in a colorful, tie-dyed sherpa hoodie and gray sweatpants, so form-fitting and thin that Ethan can practically see every line of Taylor's underwear.

Hold on. Is he even wearing any underwear?

"Sorry to interrupt," Taylor says.

"Welcome to Storybook Endings," says Gabriel when Ethan remains silent for a beat too long.

"Thank you," Taylor says, voice like jam being swiped across toast. Smooth with a slight crunch.

"I'm Ethan Golding," he says, finding his words albeit the most obvious ones. "It's nice to meet you."

Taylor drops his purple bag by his feet to meet Ethan's outstretched hand. The cold of Taylor's palm is a shock and exacerbated by a few stylish silver rings—one on his forefinger, one on his middle finger, and one on his pinkie. Ethan imagines at least one of these is a gift from Amy. That's how she's always gained favor—through tokens. Ethan wasn't materialistic, but clearly Amy never read that book on love languages.

"Same here. Good to put a person to the e-mails," Taylor says, oozing a laid-back friendliness that jars Ethan.

Unlike his last name and his hands, Taylor radiates hotness. Yes, in his looks, but also in his demeanor. His posture is lax, his dark brown hair is mussed and longer than it is in his recent e-mail photo, and he moves as if suspended in a pool of water, an effortless glide.

"Let's get you all checked in. Would you mind giving me your ID?" Ethan asks, reverting to his welcome wagon script.

Taylor's hands pat at the pockets of his sherpa, then his sweatpants, before rooting around inside his suitcase. A look of confusion wriggles onto his face as he mumbles his way through something. "I had it in here. Then, I stopped to get gas for the rental car, which I parked down in the lot at the front gate—" He meets Ethan's waiting eyes. "Must've left my wallet in the glove compartment."

The full day of travel has clearly made Taylor tired. Forcing him to walk all the way back down the hill to the parking lot and get his wallet would be cruel. Ethan's inspected the face on the e-mails enough times to know Taylor's not some sort of imposter. Unless he has an evil twin come to tear Ethan's life asunder…

"Let me just…" Taylor turns with his bag toward the door.

"No need," Ethan says swiftly, uncertain where this forgoing of policy is coming from. "We can handle all that tomorrow. Tonight, we can just get you settled."

Relief wisps across Taylor's brow. "Thanks. Before we do that, is there a restroom you can direct me to?"

"Through there," Gabriel says, pointing toward Knights & Knaves, the resort's bustling game room.

Taylor disappears through the faux stone arch masking the doorway.

"Are you blushing?" Gabriel asks when the wooden door has swung shut.

Ethan scowls. "No. Why would you ask that?"

"Because your cheeks are red."

True, there is an inconvenient heat on his face that he can't blame on standing under the vent. "I'm not good at regulating my temperature. Between the heat being on and the cold draft blowing in from the door, my body doesn't know what to do." He strips off his puffer vest and sets it under the desk.

"Maybe your body was responding to something other than the temperature," says Gabriel, whose eyes saucily chart a path back toward the bathroom door.

"Can it, Esteves. Don't you have a bed frame to fix?" There are always work orders piling up around here. A decade of wear and tear takes a backseat to funneling money into new locations, apparently.

"I wouldn't if this place weren't so damn romantic." Gabriel clears his throat and shakes his head. "When the new booking website launches, make sure there's a check box that reads 'I understand that banging like jackrabbits is strictly prohibited on property beds.'"

"Mherm."

Ethan stops short of hanging his head this time. That embarrassed blush is back with a mutinous vengeance. Taylor's timing couldn't be worse.

"I'm off," Gabriel says, hoisting the stepladder back up. He turns to Taylor. "Enjoy your stay."

Taylor thanks him, holding there in the foyer, uncertain, with his phone clutched in his hand.

"Go ahead and sign the guest ledger." Ethan produces a heavy, leather-bound book from its perch under a purely decorative glass case. He makes a show of blowing off pretend dust like it's an ancient thing, when really they rotate them out by season. From behind the desktop, he grabs the trusty pot of ink and the feather quill and passes both to Taylor.

"Neat," Taylor says as he writes his name in tidy cursive. *Who knew good penmanship could be so attractive?*

To avoid that internal question, Ethan turns away to grab the key to the Snow White cottage off the ornate wall of hooks. "Let me show you around."

"Oh, no, I can carry that," Taylor says.

Ethan's already come around the desk and scooped up Taylor's suitcase with ease. "Nonsense. Allow me."

Ethan may have denied his own blush earlier, but there's no mistaking the pink coloring that sweeps across Taylor's cheeks and makes Ethan's stomach wildly flutter as they exit The Castle side by side.

Four

TAYLOR

While Samara might say otherwise, a photograph can't fully capture the true nature of its subject.

This is the first thought that crosses Taylor's mind when he sets his sights on the original Snow White cottage. It has a roof with a thatched appearance, hearts carved into the shutters and an arch of lush greenery over the rounded front door. Here, Taylor's wholly ensconced in the poured-over stories of his childhood. No photo, no matter how good, could've prepared him for how instantly at home he feels, like he's pressed between the pages of a well-loved book.

Photos also had not prepared him for Ethan Golding in the flesh beside him. As they approach the cottage, Ethan details the resort with the appealing enthusiasm of a wise, practiced narrator. Even more appealing might be his giant-like stature. At six-foot-two, Taylor is not used to looking up at others as they speak. He relishes the sensation of being dwarfed for once.

Dwarfed. Too fitting for where they are.

"This is yours for the week," Ethan says, gesturing for Taylor to go on ahead.

Inside, the walls are a pale yellow and the ceiling is a powder blue. To his right is a kitchenette that features a microwave, a retro-style fridge in poison-apple red, and a charming teapot. The surfaces are clean yet the air smells earthy, in a good way. Rich and a little smoky.

"It's lovely," Taylor utters. It can't be larger than three hundred square feet, but he's used to economical. To having the walls close and barely any floor space. He likes it that way.

"As you can see, there's a small sitting area, a reading loft up that ladder, and an *evil* queen-size bed." Even if the line is scripted and Ethan probably says it to all the guests, Taylor can't help but smile at the spontaneous-sounding cheesiness. "The bathroom is through those doors. The fireplace in here is gas, but there's a wood-fired hot tub and a fire pit outside should you care to use them."

Taylor widens his eyes and flares his nostrils. "Me no make fire," he says in a ridiculous caveman impression he learned from some cartoon he watched with his brothers when he was a kid. The fairy tale environment is already making him playful.

The slightest of smirks tugs on the right corner of Ethan's mouth. "It's not hard."

"That's what my older brother told me when he convinced me to sign up for the Boy Scouts. He went on to be an eagle scout. I never earned a single badge," he says with a laugh.

"Never?"

"Not one. I picked up a few skills, but badges weren't important to me like they were to my brother. I spent more time helping him earn his since he cared a lot and wanted that full sash. Yet I still went to every meeting. Can you believe that?" he asks, rolling his eyes at his younger self. "Thinking about it now, I almost definitely had a crush on our troop leader, so maybe that had something to do with it."

"Maybe." Ethan nods, almost as if he's closely considering this. "I could teach you now. It's never too late to learn."

Taylor peers at the bed overlaid with a tree-patterned quilt, which has a deeply enchanting allure. He's spent the last who-knows-how-many hours cooped up on a plane and then cramped in the front seat of a small rental car. He's been throttled and bumped and jarred from an upright half-doze while listening to Mitski. Now he'd like to sink into a mattress and stare at the ceiling, however, this man—who has, what, five inches on him, maybe a little less if his work boots are to be accounted for—is gazing down at him and raising a questioning, nearly hopeful brow. Damn, he wants to know what those steely blue eyes look like with firelight dancing in them.

"Okay. Can you give me ten to get settled?" Taylor asks, miraculously more alert than he was seconds ago.

"I'll go grab a bundle of firewood and meet you back here."

Ethan's absence frees up some space in the well-laid-out cottage. Not much, but still, Taylor takes his purple suitcase to the bed, unzips it and sprawls out—his stuff and himself.

This is more *his* than he's ever had before. He grew up in a crowded home, lived in a crowded college dorm and now shares an apartment in Encinitas with more people than should be allowed on a single lease. Two-hundred-and-twenty square feet all to himself is downright luxurious.

He takes his tan toiletries bag into the bathroom. His hair is matted down at all weird angles and his sweatshirt still has in-flight pretzel crumbs clinging on to the fabric. Not exactly the first impression he was envisioning.

After shucking his layers and kicking them across the floor with his bare feet, he turns the hot water on in the shower and rinses off. It enlivens his senses. The body wash in the holder affixed to the tile wall is fragrant with citrusy notes. He recalls being cc'd on Amy's e-mail threads about the new supplier—a boutique brand that has something to do with goats and the environment. The details are foggy, but Amy was so spectacularly happy when they secured the partnership that they went out to an expensive lunch to celebrate. Those good days at work make all the hectic, stressful ones worth it.

Standing naked and wet before the sink, he looks into the mirror-mirror-on-the-wall and half expects to see a hovering, green face ready to tell him who is the fairest of them all. He towels off before slipping into his warmest layers.

Outside, Ethan wears a beanie. He has a plaid blanket tucked under one arm and a pile of logs under the other. At his feet, there is a collection of pine needles, bark and some gnarled twigs. "Ready?"

They start with the small pieces that make up the bottom of the pit, what Ethan refers to as the tinder. "The fire icon on the Tinder app makes a lot more sense now."

Ethan lifts a brow. "Never used it."

"Never?" Taylor asks. Maybe it's an East Coast quirk. On

the West Coast, most adults, regardless of age or relationship status, participate in swiping culture.

"Never. I wouldn't even know what to put in a profile on one of those things."

"It's never too late to learn," Taylor says, a cheeky echo of Ethan's own words from earlier. Aware he shouldn't flirt like this with his boss's ex-husband, he still gets brief pleasure from the exchange. Especially when Ethan angles away to hide his reaction, which Taylor can tell by the slight shake of his wide shoulders is a good-natured chuckle.

They move on to the kindling. It's stacked smallest to largest in a pyramid shape, leaving room for the inevitable fire to breathe. Taylor takes this as a reminder for himself to breathe, too. Leaning over the fire pit under the stars with his shoulder brushing Ethan's makes his chest feel small and shy. Like if he exhales too audibly, words like *I think you're ridiculously handsome* might appear in the cloud of his breath, like the caterpillar from *Alice in Wonderland*—a story that is well represented at this resort.

Ethan hands Taylor a long-stemmed match. The rasp of the match against the box sends a satisfying prickle down Taylor's spine. Ethan adds some more kindling until he sustains the flame and it becomes a squiggly dance of orange and yellow against the darkening night.

"A wood log or two should do the trick now," says Ethan. Taylor adds those and then they stand back.

Taylor holds his palms up to the warmth. "Guess you were right before. You are perfectly capable of lighting your own fire."

Ethan sucks in his lips and shakes his head. "I'm sorry you walked into that."

Taylor waves a newly-warmed hand dismissively. "Please. I thought it was funny."

Clearing his throat, Ethan turns back to the Adirondack chair behind him and passes Taylor a blanket. "For you." Taylor accepts the blue, checkered wool-blend. "I brought over a bottle of red wine, too, as a little welcome gift. I know I always enjoy a drink after a long day of travel."

"How sweet. Thank you." This is a work trip and yet Ethan is treating him like he's a valued, returning guest. He supposes that's just the Storybook Endings way.

Ethan's shoulders fall forward in something resembling a shrug. "You'll find glasses inside should you want it. I won't keep you."

Did he say glasses? Plural? Might he…

"Have a glass with me?" Taylor asks quickly. He's not ready for Ethan to go, and drinking alone is no fun. "If you're free to."

Ethan glances over his shoulder as if consulting with someone unseen. "Oh, um, sure. Thanks."

"Good. I'll need you to teach me how to put this fire out later." Taylor proffers the explanation to put Ethan at ease. To set right his intentions. His perfectly friendly intentions.

"I'd be glad to," Ethan says. "Okay if I go inside and grab the glasses?"

"Oh, I can do it."

"Please, allow me." Ethan's large, calloused hand splays in the center of his chest. What does his heartbeat feel like against that palm? Is it a slow, unfazed rap or a hastening titter in response to Taylor's offer? Honestly, he's not sure which he'd prefer. But he's certain which would be less compromising. He's out here for work, *not* pleasure.

Ethan comes back holding two full glasses by their stems. Taylor isn't used to being doted on. He's made a career out of being the doter. A turn of the tables may be just what the doctor ordered.

The first sip of the decadent red Ethan gifted him raises his internal temperature to a relaxing place. Under this blanket, beside this roaring fire, within Ethan's calm gaze, he's not sure he's ever been cozier. "I didn't expect it to be so cold out here. It's spring."

"In name only," Ethan says. "We've had snow this late in the year before. Thank God there's none in the forecast, though. It's a hassle to deal with, and with Samara's birthday coming up, I don't need to be worrying about the weather on top of everything else."

"Of course," Taylor says, taking a sip of wine. It's weird, now that he considers it, that he spends more time with Samara as Amy's assistant than Ethan does as her father. "I've only been to the East Coast maybe twice in my life and both times it was for summer vacations with my family."

Ethan nods. "You, um, mentioned an eagle scout brother. Is he your only sibling?"

Taylor is heartened Ethan's been listening so intently. "Far from it, actually. I'm one of seven kids." In a family that large, his voice often got drowned out. And with his job, he tries to be a soft, unimposing presence as best he can.

"Seven? Wow, really?"

"My parents are deeply in love, go-with-the-flow types who don't believe in birth control, so..." Taylor says.

For a time, he thought their laid-back relationship was madly romantic. They were the epitome of a couple that takes life's blessings day by day. But now their carefree ways might have more to do with deep-seated immaturity rather than firm beliefs in destiny and fate. Like they were constantly playing roulette with finite resources—limited number of rooms in their modest house, limited amount of money coming in from their ever-changing jobs. Not that Taylor or any of his siblings ever went without, but they often had to make do. Menopause finally put a stop to the constant question of whether their family would be expanding that year or not.

Ethan is quiet for some time. Taylor isn't sure what to make of the silence that is punctured every other second by a crackle from the fire. Many people over the years have pitied Taylor for being in a family ripe for the reality show treatment, but he wouldn't trade his siblings for the world, even if his relationship with his parents leaves something to be desired.

The wine and the warmth from the fire only serve to make him drowsier. He swirls his wine around in his glass and looks longingly back at the cabin. "It's funny you put me up here, actually. My mom sometimes refers to us as her seven dwarves."

Ethan chuckles throatily at this, while wearing a smile that casts an amiable glow. It rivals the fire between them. "Which one are you?"

"Doc," Taylor says. Then, after a long pause in which he can tell Ethan is waiting for him to go on, he adds: "I'm the second oldest, so I was the one the kids came to when they got a paper cut while working on a school project and needed a Band-Aid or had a cold and needed someone to make them soup and turn on the humidifier."

"What about the Eagle Scout in the family? Isn't there a badge for stuff like that?" Ethan asks.

"Owen? Yeah, he didn't stick around after he turned eighteen," Taylor says, chest growing tight.

"Did you ever consider being a doctor?" Ethan asks, clearly sensing a need to skip over the Owen comment.

The question is surprising, yet not unfounded. Still, it makes Taylor bristle a bit as he shakes his head. "My parents aren't big believers in modern medicine. They prefer home remedies, herbal stuff. They're hippies like that. So, no. It never even crossed my mind like it does for most kids when they consider the big options like president or astronaut. I don't think I'd be smart enough for all that anyway. I just like taking care of people."

"Hence being a personal assistant."

"Yes, *hence*." Though, personal assistant is only a way station, right? Sure, he's been in the role for almost three years, but Amy promised him advancement and with the new location...

At the bottom of his wineglass, Taylor lets out a huge yawn. He's already so comfortable around Ethan that he doesn't want the night to end. His body refuses to move even as he struggles to keep his eyes open.

"You might've been Doc as a kid, but you're looking more like Sleepy right now," Ethan says with a gentle playfulness propping up his words.

"It's been a long day," Taylor says.

"Why don't you go in and to bed?" Ethan asks.

Taylor swallows the sudden truth, that he's too enraptured by the way the firelight fox-trots across Ethan's face. It creates new shadows in interesting places. Ethan's got such a sharp, square jaw beneath that full beard. And his eyes are deeper set than Taylor had imagined.

"I'm comfortable here," Taylor says, poorly fighting off fatigue.

"I think you'll be more comfortable in bed," Ethan says. "I can see to it that this gets put out. I'll just need to sit out here for a bit longer until it dies down."

"Oh, I'd appreciate it… Thanks for the wine and the lesson," Taylor says, maneuvering the blanket around to his back and hoisting it up onto his shoulders. The warmth from the fire, closer now, infuses him with boldness. Taylor locks eyes with Ethan across the flickering flames. "And thanks for the nice conversation."

"My pleasure." Ethan wears a fetching close-lipped smile. "I hope you sleep well."

Taylor stifles another massive yawn. "I know I will."

Soon, he's proven correct when, after brushing his teeth and changing into a pair of shorts, he nestles under the covers and drifts right into dreamland, knowing that a striking, burly night guard is right outside the door, tending to the last embers of the fire and providing Taylor a newfound, bone-deep comfort.

Five

ETHAN

The next day, the empty bottle of cabernet sauvignon sits at the top of Ethan's recycling bin as he makes himself a sandwich for lunch in the kitchen of his cottage. Set back in the trees, less than a mile from main camp at the end of a curving mulch path, is the abode he built with his bare hands for him, Amy and Samara.

It was supposed to be their forever home. But forever is the stuff of fiction.

Eyeing the empty wine bottle, he's filled with images of Taylor from last night and the unexpected fireside bonding they did. Heat generated between them that had nothing to do with combustion.

Bringing the bottle of wine along with the kindling was a half-formed gamble. Getting chummy with his ex-wife's personal assistant isn't exactly the way he should've spent his Friday night, but there was something in the way Taylor didn't quite match up to the person Ethan had generated in his head that had him wanting to linger longer, inspect closer. Much like the fire, Taylor was languid, warm, effortless. Three qualities Ethan is in short supply of.

It matters little as he throws the crusts of his bread into the compost bin. Doing this always makes him feel like a child, but his preferences are his preferences and he's enough of an adult to know not to deny them. There's no need to suffer through the food parts you don't like when apple skins, coffee grounds and bread crusts make such perfect compost. What doesn't nourish him can nourish the earth.

"Arf," says Nana, sitting patiently on Ethan's left. She's a seven-year-old Newfoundland named after the Darling's dog in *Peter Pan*. Amy had adopted her and Samara had named her, but she'd always been Ethan's. Bonded to him from day one without reservation or, in some cases like when he's using the bathroom, boundaries.

"Sorry, Nana. Didn't forget about you." It's a lie. While momentarily recalling Taylor's sharp jawline—made sharper by flickering orangey firelight—he'd completely forgotten that his best pal was even in the kitchen with him. Chances are he'd have been so lost in his hyperfocus over the surfer-lite smoke show residing in the Snow White cottage that he'd have tripped right over Nana.

Such is life having ADHD as an adult. Most people think ADHD is reserved for disruptive kids in middle school classrooms. Those people would be wrong. He got himself into therapy after the divorce. He was resistant to it for ages until Amy suggested couples counseling, which led them to the conclusion that they were good business partners and bad life partners. Despite knowing this, he took the divorce as a brutal rejection and a moral failing on his part.

Leaving his sandwich behind for a second on the counter beside the sink with its charming window that looks out on the myriad of balsams, he goes to the hooks by the front door and gets Nana's harness.

It's a dark blue mesh with the Storybook Endings logo on it. On her back, there's big, yellow embroidered lettering that says: *NANA. I'M FRIENDLY. PETS WELCOME.*

"It's a to-go lunch kind of a day, Nana," he says, opening the door for her to go outside and pee while he fetches his lunch and thermos.

Just outside the front door is usually a lush garden fit for frolicking fairies and other mythical woodland creatures. No English cottage would be complete without one. After last frost, it's a spectacle of lacey blue Russian sage, Thriller lady's mantle, tea roses and boxwood. There's even a stone birdbath and a rock path that leads around the house to a peaceful bench where Ethan likes to sit.

Today, humidity hangs over the resort like a guillotine. Morning has given way to a cloudy afternoon with a storm on the horizon, which means most guests are sticking close to their cottages or are probably inside The Castle sipping coffee at How Do You Brew or playing games like Ping-Pong or foosball in the Knights and Knaves rec room.

Midbite of turkey, cheese and spinach with a squirt of mayo on rye, he contemplates where Taylor is. Has he hit the ground running on party preparations or is this a Saturday of rest? Probably the former.

The Taylor from last night was likely a fluke. You don't exist in Amy Lu's orbit without being a frantic workhorse, right? That's why Ethan often felt like Pluto, demoted in Amy's solar system.

In the distance, Taylor appears sprawled out on the sun porch in a rocking chair, wearing another pair of gray joggers, another hoodie and, this time, tall knit socks with Birkenstocks.

Nana, who is usually very reserved with the guests because of her training, bounds right up to Taylor with her tail wagging a mile a minute.

"Oh, hello there, Nana," says Taylor as if they're old friends, setting the book he'd been reading down on the small, circular table beside him. The title indicates that it's a book about wildlife in Northern California. "I was wondering when I was going to get to meet you."

"You know about Nana?" Ethan asks.

"Of course. Samara's shown me tons of pictures. Growing up I always wanted a dog, but we didn't have the space or the money." Taylor gives Nana scratches right behind her ears, which are her sweet spots. Her right rear paw goes a *thump-thumping* against the wooden boards of the porch and her mouth hangs open, tongue lolling to the left in happiness. Taylor's face mirrors hers. The sweet sight is almost too much for Ethan's boarded-up heart.

"Right. Sleep okay?" Ethan asks, rubbing a hand through his beard. It's his nervous habit. He has no reason to be nervous other than the fact that he spent half his night wondering how Taylor and Amy maintained a professional relationship when they seem so different. He supposes Taylor's just been adopting Amy's demeanor and aesthetics to better serve her.

"I slept like a log," Taylor says with a free smile.

"That's good."

"I almost never sleep in, so when I woke up at eleven a.m. I was shocked, but well rested. There's nothing on the Samara-party agenda today, so I'm relaxing and not thinking about work." His eyes wander to the cover of the book he set down before. "Okay, that's a lie. This is sort of work. As you know, the Lake Tahoe location is set to open this summer, and I'm unfamiliar with the landscapes and wildlife there, so I figured I'd do a little *light* reading."

Ethan laughs because the book looks to be at least six hundred pages. Nothing light about it. "Sounds like a good use of your time."

"For sure. I'm preparing for a cutthroat interview process," he shares. "I'm hoping there's a spot on the staff for me at that location."

"I didn't realize you were looking to leave Amy," says Ethan, only registering after the fact how odd that sounds.

"Oh, not leaving. The assistant position was always meant to be temporary. At least that was the impression I got. The business has exploded since I onboarded, though, so I understand advancement has taken a backseat to making sure Amy is taken care of," Taylor says with a level of maturity Ethan doesn't think he could share. If he were promised a bigger job and had been languishing away in the same post for almost three years, he'd probably be irked all the time. But he supposes he's been in his role with the resort for significantly longer and change is simply not in the cards for him.

He wants to say something to that effect—say *more* in general like Taylor seems to do so easily—but fears if he does, he'll find himself in the rocking chair on the opposite side of the table. Soon he'll be engrossed in another telling conversation with this personable personal assistant when he's supposed to be working. "I'll leave you to your reading."

Ethan starts inside when Taylor jumps up and says, "I grabbed my wallet from the rental earlier. I had to get my phone charger from there this morning. You can make a copy of my ID now, if you're not too busy."

The all-staff meeting he's running isn't for another hour, so he waves Taylor inside with him. Nana curls up in a spot in the sunshine on the far side of the porch, knowing she's not supposed to go inside.

As they pass through the coffee shop, Ethan asks Camille, one of the baristas, to pass him a small plate for the remains of his sandwich.

Behind the reception desk, Ethan wakes the desktop and starts up the copier. Taylor fishes into his pants pocket for his wallet. The movement of the thin fabric causes *other* things in the vicinity to move as well.

Lord. What is he feeding that thing?

Off-kilter now, Ethan forces his eyes back to the computer screen while reprimanding words bang around within his head. Having a glass of wine with his ex-wife's employee is fine, but imagining his ex-wife's employee's dick is not.

Even if Taylor's freeballing is dickstracting…

Distracting!

His whole body is clammy from the embarrassing fodder his brain is overflowing with.

"Here we go," Taylor says, sliding his ID across the counter.

"Thank you." The two words come out as a strangled whisper. He tries to clear his throat—make it sound natural—but Taylor's birthday turns the clearing into a full-blown coughing fit. *Christ, twenty-seven?* Of course there would be an age gap but thirteen years seems more like an age gulf, and *thirteen?* An unlucky number at that!

"Are you okay?" Taylor asks, reaching out and placing a comforting hand on Ethan's wide, fur-coated forearm. The electric touch only makes Ethan's coughing fit louder and more uncontrollable. "Do you need me to get you some water?"

"Fine," Ethan croaks, able to collect himself. "I'm fine. Thanks." He tips his head toward the sandwich as if to say *Bread, huh?*

Taylor's eyes stay fixed on the plate. A small grin plays on his lips. "No crusts?"

Ethan reroutes his gaze to the computer. "Don't like 'em."

"Neither do my little brothers. I used to have to cut them off their sandwiches when I made them lunches. I swear I could've made at least three more sandwiches with the amount of crust I threw away each week."

"I compost," Ethan says almost curtly as he saves Taylor's ID in the proper reservation file. "For gardening. It's good fertilizer."

"You garden? I love gardening," Taylor says. Ethan senses an invisible cord between them that gives a quick tug. "I love being outdoors. There's nothing like getting your hands down and dirty."

LORD.

Maybe it isn't better that Amy's not here after all. At least her presence would be a constant cold shower every time he imagined Taylor soaking in the wood-fired bath beside his cottage, imagining various cuts of swim trunks he may or may not have packed.

When stressed, Amy is prone to snap. And nothing stresses Amy out more than opening a new location, and nothing would make Amy snap more than finding out Ethan was harboring sexual thoughts about her personal assistant.

The last thing Ethan wants is snapping. Because even if he's no longer her husband, he is still legally her employee and her coparent, and her strictures impact his life to a high degree. She's the one Samara lives with full-time. She's the one he needs to answer to when he wants access to his precious, intelligent, almost sixteen-year-old daughter.

Taylor Frost is a siren to which he will turn his head and plug his ears. Aside from the walk-through inspection later in the week, there's no reason Ethan needs to cross paths with Taylor. Taylor will be busy putting together Samara's party. Ethan is in the midst of peak spring break season. The resort is booked up completely, and there's another wedding soon. With so many guests milling about, there will be plenty of places to hide.

"Enjoy the rest of your day," Ethan says with a firm sense of finality as he hands Taylor his ID back.

Six

TAYLOR

Did you know Lake Tahoe has its own version of the Loch Ness Monster called Tahoe Tessie? Taylor types to his sibling group chat as he lies in his queen bed in the Snow White cottage. His book is splayed open on the quilt beside him, untouched for the last thirty minutes.

It's hard to focus when Amy's gone silent and Ethan's gone cold.

His boss *and* his boss's ex taking up space in his brain is a mind-bender.

Amy's silence is to be expected. As per the itinerary, she's in the air somewhere over central California right now on her way to the campground they've retrofitted into a resort. A perfect location with its own storybook-style lore! He screenshots a photo of what Tahoe Tessie might look like and sends it along in the group chat.

Faith, his sister who's currently pregnant with her first kid at twenty-four, chimes in first: **Ew! I don't like the way it's looking at me through the screen.**

Todd, who is closest to his age, adds to the thread: **Read the news articles I send you all for a change @Faith. There's scarier stuff in that sea you're always letting your kids swim in.** Todd is a bit of an alarmist and a conspiracy theorist and Taylor has him muted on all social media to preserve their sibling relationship as best as possible.

Faith married rich—a tech wunderkind—and they have this gorgeous house in San Francisco that Taylor's only seen in pictures. Getting away from work is nearly impossible these days. That's why he should probably be enjoying these bits of rest and relaxation by doing one of the many leisure activities available to him on this expenses-paid work trip, but putting on clothes and getting up feels like too much effort, especially after he tried to go out on one of the hiking trails and found this East Coast humidity and the stirring, buzzing bugs to be deeply unpleasant.

Scientifically impossible but she looks cool! That's Finn, Taylor's youngest brother who is in college studying marine biology.

A text notification in a different thread opens. It's from Sasha, the second youngest of the Frost family and the sibling Taylor's closest with. She's in her fourth year of an intensive program to become a physical therapist, which is really testing the limits of her ADHD diagnosis. She's constantly itching for change.

Tell me you're not bored already that you're sending fun facts in the family group chat, she writes.

Staring up at the timbered ceiling, he fishes around in his

brain for a good excuse. The only one biting at the baited hook is that he doesn't want to run into Ethan again. Last night, over a lesson and a glass of wine, he thought they'd fashioned a nice rapport. Then, after a mildly awkward conversation on the sun porch, Ethan went all resort-manager-stern. Had he said something? Done something to upset Ethan? If he did, he can't recall.

Puh-puh-puh. Rain rapping against the window and a distant roll of thunder provide him exactly the convenient excuse he needs.

It's raining so I'm stuck inside, he says. **Plus! it's late! I'm three hours ahead, remember?**

As the minutes pass before Sasha responds, the rain grows harder. A sudden gust of wind makes the cottage creak. He's thrust back to stormy nights in childhood when Todd would suggest a living room sleepover. Taylor had graciously given Todd the attic that Owen, their oldest sibling, had converted into a tiny bedroom when he turned fifteen and then vacated promptly after turning eighteen.

Even though Todd was thirteen and probably too old to be scared of a little lightning, Taylor always obliged. He'd grab their camp sleeping bags from the basement and corral his younger siblings into the living room where he'd read stories from their collected *Grimm's Fairy Tales* book and supervise microwave s'mores.

He's lost in the sound of the wood groaning and the rain mounting when his phone pings. **It's Saturday night! Go out and get some!**

The only some I plan to get is sleep! he writes, even as his mind and muscles protest. He's been lying in this position for too long and even though the mattress is comfortable, it sags a bit in the middle, making his lower back hurt.

In the kitchenette, under the window, he grabs the electric kettle fashioned to look like a vintage teapot. From a basket in a cubby, he grabs a bag of green tea, waiting for the bubbling of the boiling water to join the night symphony surrounding him. A newfound isolation sweeps through the room, even though he's only maybe ten feet from the next cottage.

Could you be more boring? I'd love to be anywhere but at the library studying for my anatomy exam. The next text comes in whip fast. Is there at least a bar at the resort? I'm sure it's crawling with hot dads.

Upon reading the words *hot dads*, Taylor gets a flash of Ethan capably lighting the fire outside his cottage last night. Ethan looked immensely climbable in his distressed jeans and soft-looking flannel shirt. He texts back, I don't sleep with guys with kids!

Who said anything about sleeping?

Taylor chuckles to himself as the kettle clicks off. He pours the hot water into his off-white mug, watching as the tea steeps in swirls of color. A clap of lightning goes off like a camera flash; a closer roar of thunder rattles the cabin.

Weren't you the one who said going out there solo was your chance to let your freak flag fly?!

While high on weed gummies and binging Netflix with Sasha last week, he may have said something to that effect, but that was before he arrived here. Before he saw how remote this place is. Before he realized that you can't have unregistered guests on property. Before he learned the nearest guy on Grindr is two miles away!

I decided not to pack my freak flag because this is a business trip.

Once again, he's overrun with images of last night. Sitting across the fire from Ethan as they talked and sipped. Nothing about that felt like business. Like work or stress.

Yet this afternoon, at reception, when he handed Ethan his ID, Ethan's aura changed from mossy green to muddy brown. Last night, he kept thinking. *How could someone like Ethan end up with someone like Amy? They're polar opposites.* Then, Ethan said, "Enjoy the rest of your day" with such a tight-lipped resolve that Taylor couldn't shake the feeling that he was in Amy's presence. *I suppose you can't be married to someone for as long as he was with Amy without absorbing some of their qualities.*

He takes his tea over to the small table that folds down from the wall and scrapes the chair up from beside the roaring gas fireplace. He boots up his laptop and checks in on Amy's flight to find it running on time. Good. He'd scheduled her trip down to the hour and even the slightest delay could've hindered this important session.

His fingers jump to text her and inquire about the in-flight meal he painstakingly special-ordered from the airline. Her list of dietary preferences is long, and even so, Taylor has them memorized. He knows which foods to avoid, which to order, which to substitute, which make her sleepy and which revitalize her. The same goes for drinks.

Funnily enough, this morning (or early afternoon was more

like it, by the time he willed himself out of bed), as he stood at the counter at How Do You Brew, he ordered a medium whole milk latte extra hot. *Wait, what?* He hasn't drank cow milk in years, and the caffeine from regular coffee gives him the jitters for hours after.

"Sorry," he'd said. "Please forget that. I'm so used to ordering for my boss. A matcha latte with oat milk if you have it."

The wind picks up, rattling the window pane over the sink. The rhythmic patter on the roof sounds like a tap dance ensemble doing a show up there. "Guess I really am in for the night," he says to himself, more than okay with that. He double-checks the windows are secure, locks and latches the cottage door and queues up an action movie.

The grainy quality of the Chris-starring film—Hemsworth? Pine? He doesn't know the difference—matters little because the explosions and sirens wail in discordance with the storm raging on outside and lull him to sleep. Chaos has always been calming, until—

Crack.

Who knows how much time elapsed? The movie must still be going on.

Smash.

Did he hit the volume controls in his sleep? The room is unmistakably louder.

Whoosh.

A channel of cold air whips at Taylor atop the covers. He sputters awake, sensing dew drops on his face. He's not usually a drooler. Perhaps his dream made him cry? He wipes at his cheek only to be hit again. His eyes shoot open.

The window beside the bed on the back side of the cottage

is missing an entire corner. Shards splay out on the floor. The better part of a hefty tree branch sticks in through the pane like the arm of an intruder. Wind and rain slash through the flaps of the thin curtains.

Taylor slams his laptop shut and moves it away from the incoming pour. Careful not to step on any glass with his bare feet, he races for the other side of the cottage where his suitcase is slapped open. He finds socks, sandals and his bright orange raincoat, which Sasha always says makes him look like a personified traffic cone.

Locating the map Ethan handed him yesterday beside the kitchen sink, he flips to find the emergency maintenance number. It rings and rings but ultimately nobody answers. *Crap.* He searches frantically for some way to stop the elements from coming in, but has no luck.

Frustrated and out of options, he throws up his hood and treks out into the woods.

Seven

ETHAN

Nana is the first to respond when the rapid knocking at the front door sounds off.

She springs into action from her position at the foot of the bed and races ahead with a bark.

Ethan, bleary-eyed from intermittent slumber, is slower to react. Wearily, he throws on his robe, slides on his slippers and, out of an abundance of caution, grabs the baseball bat he keeps resting beside his bed. It's 2:30 a.m., and he never gets visitors.

Between Nana's barking fits, Ethan calls, "Who is it? Who's there?" His voice emerges as gruff and as intimidating as possible even though Samara says when he does that, he sounds like a teddy bear with a head cold. Because his hands are clammy with sudden nerves, his grip on the bat is loose and swaying. Things are not going well.

"Me!" he hears beneath the din of the storm that is ripping through the forest. The weatherperson in these parts said nothing about winds like this, though Ethan did forget to do a second weather check earlier in the day like he usually does. "Tay...! Plea open...! Hello!"

Certain he's not to be met with a murderer, he drops the bat and flings open the door. Taylor stands in the flickering porch light looking like a waterlogged traffic cone. His feet must be freezing. His tall white socks are muddy and slicked to his skin.

"What's happened?" he asks, pulling Taylor into the warmth of his cottage.

Through Taylor's hiccupping breaths, Ethan can make out, "Branch...sleeping...broken...roof." Those words in quick succession paint a clear enough picture. Suddenly, he gets a flash of a task on his to-do list for the last few weeks: *trim branches near Snow White cottage.*

"Shit. Are you okay? Are you hurt?"

"I'm—I'm ah...fine?" It's clear he's shaken up by what happened.

Ethan doesn't know what comes over him. Before he can question it, he's pulling Taylor in for a hug that he hopes quiets his frantic inhales. He must've run here. And he's freezing to the touch. Ethan doesn't know this man well, and he's far too aware of the very few layers separating the two of them in this moment, but the hug is what Taylor must need because as soon as Ethan rubs a hand along his quaking, wet back, Taylor's breath evens out to a seminormal tempo. His muscles unclench beneath his reassuring palms.

He fits so well here, in my arms.

That floating, sumptuous thought is enough for Ethan's

sense to kick back in. Begrudgingly and far too sluggishly, he pulls away.

He can't even care that Taylor is dripping all over the place and tracking mud through his living room. He brings him straight to the kitchen, sits him down in a chair and crouches in front of him.

Taylor inhales slowly through his nose and exhales even more slowly through his mouth. "Sorry. I got frantic after I couldn't find anyone at The Castle. I remembered you saying you lived just north of the cottages, so I used the compass on my phone and found the path." He pulls his wet phone from his pocket and tries to wipe the rain off the screen with his damp hand. Ethan grabs him a paper towel from the holder by the sink.

"Did you try the emergency maintenance line?"

"Nobody picked up. I'm really sorry. Stuff is getting ruined."

Gabriel is going to get a stern talking to tomorrow. He's probably forgotten to leave the ringer on while sleeping again. "You didn't cause the storm. I'll go inspect the damage. I'm sure it's nothing that's not fixable. But first, let me get you something dry."

"Oh, no. I'll only get wet again when we go back," says Taylor, sniffling and brushing the rain droplets away from his bloodshot brown eyes.

Ethan shakes his head resolutely. "You've had a night. Please, stay here and get warm." With that said, he turns to prepare the teakettle before racing down the hall to his room to change. From the closet, for Taylor, he grabs a fluffy towel then dithers over which clothes to bring him. Taylor will swim in everything he owns. Oh, well. Something big and dry is better than something clingy and sopping.

Taylor thanks him when he hands over the folded pair of sleep pants with a drawstring and an old T-shirt from his college days. "I'll be back. Make yourself at home. I'll try to be quick. Nana, behave while I'm gone, okay?" She plops her butt down right next to Taylor as if planning to guard him with her life. "Good girl."

With a heavy-duty flashlight in hand, Ethan charts a direct course through the trees toward the Snow White cottage. Screw the path. This way is quicker. Even if somebody blindfolded him and forced him to wear noise cancelling headphones, he'd still know the way there. His internal compass is finely tuned.

The culprit is, as expected, that blasted branch he'd told himself he'd get around to trimming. It's been jostled off the tree and it crashed into the cottage, clipping the roof and breaking the window.

There's a shed with emergency tools camouflaged by landscaping and set back in the trees from which he pulls a board, a hammer and some nails. This is the best he can do at this hour and in this reckless, battering weather. He times his hammer hits to the persistent thunderclaps to avoid disturbing the other guests who are, hopefully, sleeping peacefully through this frustrating ordeal.

Inside the cottage, he checks out the roof situation. A steady plunk of droplets fall from the ceiling. Using the bathroom towels, he tries his best to wipe up the rainwater. From under the kitchen sink, he grabs a metal bucket and sets it beneath the drip.

Once the storm has passed and daylight breaks, he and Gabriel can replace the window after a trip to the hardware store, but the roof is a nonstarter. He'll have to hire out. This cottage is going to be out of commission until he can get it fixed, and if this storm did damage like this all over the county, then it could be a while before his trusted contractor can come out.

He stalls inside the Snow White cottage, loses a bit of his initial adrenaline rush as realization washes over him.

All the resort cottages are booked solid for spring break. There's nowhere to relocate Taylor, except Samara's old room in his place.

Ethan flops down in the chair beside the table, takes in a bit of the warmth from the electric fireplace and really considers this. Since Amy and Samara left five years ago, he hasn't had any overnight visitors at Casa de Golding, as Gabriel would call it.

No family, no one night stands, no one.

There is something special and inexplicable about his home that he is unwilling to share with others. A deep part of him feels if he opens the door to a hookup or a date or even a friend, they might upset the delicate balance he's built in the absence of the two major loves he's had thus far in his life.

But what choice is there now?

He can't leave warm Taylor out in the damp cold.

TAYLOR

As Taylor's second cup of tea this evening brews and the storm slams itself against the side of the house, he struggles to tighten the drawstring on Ethan's flannel lounge pants. No matter how hard he pulls or how strongly he knots them, they still sag dangerously south of his hip bones. This is one of the perils of not wearing underwear. Going commando has always felt natural to him—he's never been one of those gay men obsessed with designer briefs—but now he's concerned he's showing off a bit too much.

Taking the mug to the table, the pants nearly slide right off his slender frame, causing him to trip and spill his tea all over the floor. As if this night weren't already a mess. Nana *arf, arfs* in dissent.

"Sorry, I'm trying my best."

Once he's cleaned up after himself, he trots down the hall and enters Ethan's bedroom. The space is all dark wood and old lamps and dusty framed pictures on the bedside tables. Samara's youthful face covered in Popsicle residue at a Fourth of July party pokes out from behind a stack of hardback library books—a collection of historical biographies.

A lazy, paddled ceiling fan *click-click-clicks* over the king-sized bed, causing tiny neon Post-it notes to flap from their random spots around the room. They say things like: *Buy carpet cleaner* and *Change sheets first of the month*. The crimson duvet (a remnant from Amy's time here, surely) on the bed is messily flipped back.

Taylor's not sure what comes over him, but he places his palm on the exposed cotton fitted sheet. Ethan's body heat still sizzles there. The momentary, spine-tingling thrill gets usurped when Taylor's pants slip again.

Growing up the way he did and living the way he does now, privacy does not come naturally to him. What's his was yours and hers and theirs. Which is why he has no qualms about going into Ethan's already-open closet and fishing for a robe.

Nothing is where Taylor expects it to be. Dirt-flecked boots are sat on the top shelf. A leaning tower of folded sweaters is seconds away from spilling across the floor. Wrinkly T-shirts in every color of the rainbow next to a plethora of flannels are hung on metal hangers that screech against the rod.

He has to rustle around quite a bit. He wants something that Ethan probably doesn't wear much, if at all, so he's not desecrating something he loves with his precarious pantslessness.

Aha! There in the depths he finds a red-and-green checkered fleece robe that looks significantly too small for Ethan's build. Taylor shrugs it on. This must've been a Christmas gift at some point. It's impeccably comfy against Taylor's chilly skin.

Once that's squared away, he hunts for a dryer. He'd left his wet clothes hanging over the lip of the tub so they'd drip into the basin and not all over the floor, but there's no way he can walk back to the Snow White cottage without pants in this storm. He'd be Marilyn Monroe over that subway grate, completely exposed to the elements.

In his search, he stumbles across a second bedroom. It's a place half-stalled in time, completely on-theme with the resort.

While the twin bed has an IKEA frame and a gray duvet laid across it, the wall behind it features an intricate mural. On one side of a rippling body of water is a kingdom, on the other is a tower, down from which a braid of golden, glowing hair falls. Lanterns light up the purply night sky above the scene.

This must've been Samara's room, and even though she hasn't lived here for five years, Ethan's preserved much of it. In the corner, there's a pop-up castle play set. The bookshelf is overstuffed with Judy Blume and Disneyfied fairy tales. He wonders, if he opened the drawers of the dresser, whether he'd find some of Samara's old clothes and toys, ones she's outgrown. But he doesn't test that theory.

When he turns back around, Nana sits in the doorway, staring disapprovingly at Taylor. What's that saying about dogs growing to look like their owners? It's eerily true in this case.

"I'm a snoop. I know. I'm sorry. I'm leaving." He shuts the door firmly behind him on the way out. Nana, clearly appeased by the apology, follows closely behind him like a protective shadow, which he finds comforting and chiding at the same time.

The combo washer-dryer sits stacked in a mudroom of sorts near the rear of the cottage. He throws in his clothes; the rattle of the garments flopping round and round reminds him of how Amy described this cottage to him when he first started working for her. She'd made it sound like a hovel. Now, having traipsed through it, Taylor couldn't disagree more. This place is homey in all the right ways with touches so personal no highly skilled interior decorator could come close to replicating them.

Ethan should be back soon, so Taylor busies himself with boiling some more water and setting out a second mug. Surely Ethan won't want him to leave right away upon returning.

Nana must have a sixth sense for Ethan's arrival because she's waiting beside the door before Taylor even hears the key in the lock.

He hopes he doesn't look too ridiculous standing there in Ethan's T-shirt and robe with no pants and two mugs of tea like some sort of weird welcome party of one.

"So it appears—" Ethan goes as still as a statue when his

eyes land on Taylor in the light. Something about the laser-like focus of Ethan's gaze makes a heat crop up on Taylor's cheeks, fiercer than any he's felt before. "Where did you find that?"

"The back of your closet. I hope you don't mind. The pants didn't fit." Taylor swivels his hips to make the belt on the robe dance, so Ethan knows what he's referring to. It's only after the fact that he remembers he's not wearing any underwear and the flaps don't overlap that much. The heat on his face doubles in intensity.

Ethan loudly clears his throat, probably embarrassed *for* Taylor. "No, it's fine. I should've gotten rid of that ages ago. That's not mine. That is—*was*—Amy's."

Mortification is a monkey throwing its feces at Taylor's face. Not only has he ended up looking like freaking Winnie the Pooh in his boss's ex-husband's house, but he's also managed to put on his boss's old robe to cover his unmentionables. Damn, his job is weird, and he's majorly messing this up.

Ethan bypasses whatever discomfort he's experiencing. "I boarded up the window, but there wasn't much I could do about the roof right now. I'm sorry for the inconvenience but it looks like you'll have to spend the night here." Ethan is clasping Taylor's purple suitcase by the handle. "I didn't grab everything. Just left what was still in it and zipped it up. I didn't want to go through your things."

The robe becomes a leaden cloak of guilt. Taylor didn't have the same courteous thought when he went searching for suitable clothing thirty minutes ago, but perhaps he should've. Maybe Amy's robe has dug up emotions Ethan had purposefully shoved to the back of his messy closet, and now here they are, flaunted out in the open on an unsuspecting model.

"Thanks, that's super kind of you. I really don't want to impose, though," he says, already uncomfortable. Staying here under this roof would only exacerbate the tightness in his chest.

"No imposition at all. There's a second bedroom here." Taylor tries not to make it obvious that he's aware. That he padded around in it, wondering why Ethan hadn't turned a room clearly made for a toddler into something befitting of a nearly sixteen-year-old. The teen Taylor dropped off at friends' houses and went birthday-present shopping with. She's strikingly mature for her age.

"I made you some tea." His arms have grown tired of holding both full mugs, and he doesn't know what else to do or say.

"Thank you. I'll have that shortly. I'd like to bring this to the guest room and clean up in there a bit, but please start in on yours. There are some cookies in the pantry if you'd like them."

Far be it from Taylor to pass up cookies, even if he's still queasy with unease. When's the last time he ate today? He finds the box of mint Milanos and a plate to display them on. He sets the teas across from each other on the wooden kitchen table and grabs coasters and napkins. It's like he's playing house in this unfamiliar kitchen with a large dog watching his every move.

Ten minutes later, Ethan settles across from him wrapped in a plush robe and slippers and says, "Sorry I'm not in the best mood right now."

"Don't let me keep you up if you want to go back to bed," Taylor says, worried he's overstepping by merely breathing in this place.

"Oh, no, I'm pretty awake now. All I mean is that I was

supposed to clip those branches a week ago, and it slipped my mind. What happened tonight could've been avoided or ended up so much worse." Taylor can almost visualize the different anxiety-inducing outcomes running through Ethan's mind like a movie.

"It's all okay now, right? You've got a roofer and a window person?"

"Of course. It's more that I like to be prepared for these sorts of things. Sometimes ADHD wins."

Taylor immediately flags the shock that crosses Ethan's face over sharing his diagnosis. The closet organization makes much more sense now. So too does Amy's constant refrain of, "Ethan's horribly unfocused. Always lost in his own head." *Does Amy know about Ethan's ADHD?* If she does, her callous words dampen Taylor's opinion of her.

To normalize talking about mental health, as he's always tried to with his siblings, he says, "I'm not sure you're being very fair to yourself. ADHD is a part of your unique brain. I always tell my sister Sasha that if you treat your brain like a villain it's going to act like a villain. Treat it like the world's coolest sidekick."

"That's quite perceptive." The embarrassment brushed across his cheeks melts away, replaced by gratitude.

"Thanks."

"You sound like a good brother."

"I try to be." Taylor leans forward in his chair, sensing the conversation about to slip into the easy rhythm it had last night beside the fire. "Do you have any siblings?"

"Two brothers. One younger and one older."

"The middle child, huh? I don't think I'd have expected that."

"Why not?"

"You have caring oldest sibling energy."

"Just because I'm the biggest sibling doesn't mean I'm the oldest."

"Oh, sorry, I didn't mean—" Taylor wishes he could retract the words like one of those sticky, slappy hands he used to win out of the quarter machines at the mall.

Ethan appears unruffled. "Unlike my ADHD, I do treat my body like the world's coolest sidekick. I keep it healthy and in turn it does everything I need it to do and sometimes more."

Taylor fiercely masks his intrigue over that *and sometimes more* comment despite his mind coloring in a pornographic image of it. He's already staying in this man's house, wearing this man's clothes, drinking this man's tea. So many professional boundaries are being crossed that his mind thinks dirty little fantasies are okay when they're not. "I hope I didn't offend you," he says finally.

"Not at all. It's a habit, I think. Getting ahead of it conversationally. I'm fat. It's not dirty or wrong. It just is. There are times when it sort of scoots out of my mind like earlier when I handed you those pants. I forgot waist sizes were a consideration." He laughs to himself. "Sorry for that, by the way."

"Don't worry. I'm comfortable." As he says this, he crosses his legs and tightens the robe belt. The last thing he needs is Ethan dropping his napkin and accidentally getting a free show. But the word *comfortable* has another meaning, too.

After Taylor's deep, peaceful sleep last night with Ethan

right outside the door, a slight fear had cropped up in him that tonight's slumber would be more restless.

Sure, the symphony of the forest would be playing right outside, but Taylor is used to people noises. To footsteps and closing doors and hushed conversations and teakettles whistling too early. He's never slept somewhere solo. He's actually quite relieved to not be staying in the Snow White cottage tonight. If the window shattering hadn't woken him, he's certain by 4:00 a.m. he'd have been wide-awake and wired, disquieted by the stillness. Here, he'll sleep comfortably. If he can get over feeling like an interloper.

And if he ever gets to sleep…

Because the Milanos get replaced, the teacups get refilled and their conversation ebbs and flows until morning light threatens to break through the dwindling storm.

Eight

ETHAN

"Three days?" Ethan bemoans into the phone.

"Maybe more. The damage is widespread throughout the area. I'll make it as soon as I can."

That's the last thing Ethan wanted to hear this morning. The resort is one giant mud puddle. Leaves and branches clutter the walkways. It's going to take all day to restore order.

Samara and Amy arrive in a week. Samara's friends the day after. Nothing less than perfection is proper for his princess's sixteenth birthday. His heart aches each time he thinks of her. He will work overtime to ensure there's not a single hiccup so they can enjoy their fleeting time together.

Gabriel stands nearby, nervously inspecting the damage.

"All right, Lee. Thanks for letting me know. Shoot me a message when you can." Ethan shoves his phone into his pocket,

Amy's imagined disapproval already loud in his ear. "Let's get the tarp, I guess."

Gabriel, a chatterbox usually, remains quiet as they head to storage. Ethan feels a little bad for how hard he laid into him this morning over the emergency line situation last night, but in the cold light of day the roof damage does look much worse than he had originally concluded. Just because they're friends, doesn't mean that he isn't still his boss.

Though, as they lug the tarp and tools back to the cottage, he realizes there was little more Gabriel could've done last night that Ethan didn't. Regardless, an answer and a fast response from Gabriel would've saved Taylor having to run through the entire resort straight to Ethan's door looking like Mr. Darcy in that movie version of *Pride and Prejudice* Amy made him watch a million times.

So maybe that's where his disgruntlement lies. As they position the ladder up against the cottage and he drags the heavy plastic polyethylene sheeting to the roof, he considers that maybe his harsh words weren't coming from a place of boss-like anger, but emotional fear.

Fear that he enjoyed drinking tea and eating cookies and talking with Taylor too much. Fear that he liked hearing Taylor moving around on the other side of the wall before he went to sleep. Fear that he could get used to someone else filling his home with laughter and lightness and… Whoa, he's getting ahead of himself. Which causes his boot to slip slightly on the rain-slick surface.

"You okay up there, Ethan?" Gabriel calls to him before summiting himself.

"Fine, just be careful when you get here."

Gabriel uses a broom to sweep away the debris. Branches and leaves leap off the sides of the roof, parachuting back to the ground where they belong. "Look, I'm sorry again."

"Don't sweat it. I'm sorry for how I acted this morning. I didn't get a lot of sleep last night." He organizes the two by fours they're going to nail down the tarp with and makes sure the plywood is the right size for the hole they're covering.

"Where did the assistant end up sleeping last night?" Gabriel asks.

"Samara's old room."

"You had an overnight guest?" A near delighted shock prances across his face.

"I didn't have much of a choice." Pointedly, he drills the thick piece of plywood into the roof. The vibration of the drill rolls through his entire body. He's always his most clearheaded when he's working with his hands. Tools feel like an extension of his power.

"I see," says Gabriel. "Makes sense why you didn't get a lot of sleep then."

"Watch it, Esteves," he says, standing. "I got him settled, we had some tea and we stayed up talking. That's it. Nothing else happened. Why would you insinuate something else happened?"

"Hey, I didn't say anything about something happening. You said something about something happening."

"Now you're purposefully confusing me."

"I don't know. Alls I was thinking when I said that was that maybe you weren't into Kurt because you prefer twinks..."

Ethan chortles at this. The laughter rumbles through him

and nearly throws off his balance again. "Twinks? Where did you learn that word from?"

"Kurt taught me. I had no idea gay guys had so many sub-genres."

"Genres? We're people, not movies," he says. "And you know I'm bi."

"Yup, a bi bear. I got the lowdown. I know the lingo."

It's impossible to stay mad at Gabriel for long. He's too affable. "Unroll the tarp."

Ethan moves to the far side of the roof on the other side of the peak. There's no damage to the front, but if they don't do this, water is likely to drip down and inside the walls. Mold would be a nightmare to get rid of. He takes his edge of the tarp and his first two by four and rolls it up before fastening it.

"You're telling me you don't find the twink assistant cute?" Gabriel calls from the other side of the roof. He's bolder now that they're not face-to-face. Ethan isn't within distance to nudge him for being nosy.

Not that he'd have the presence of mind to. He's overrun with images of Taylor in Amy's old Christmas robe last night. The flaps precariously close to splaying open. "Cute or not, he's off-limits. Especially while he's staying under my roof."

"Bless you!"

"What?" Ethan asks, confused by the non sequitur. "I didn't sneeze."

"Oh, my bad. Thought you did," says Gabriel earnestly. "Since you're obviously allergic to the idea of fun."

Ethan rolls his eyes and shakes his head before getting back down to work.

★ ★ ★

A half hour later, after he's sent Gabriel off to fetch the wheelbarrow to clean up along the tree line, he lets himself into the Snow White cottage.

It stands exactly as he left it last night only much quieter and, if he's honest, slightly drabber than he remembers. The Snow White cottage is, much like the welcome sign, in need of a face-lift.

It was part of the original design for their fairy tale oasis. Initially, Storybook Endings was only the barn, seven cottages and the pond. It wasn't until a profile in a major magazine and some TV coverage naming them one of the best summer destinations that a tourism boom swept up their small business. With the influx of capital, they were able to buy the land on the opposite side of Sunshine Road and expand exponentially—The Castle, the grotto and the heated pool.

Motionless now in the center of the room, he contemplates what life may have been like had that first domino of success not fallen and caused him to lose the life he always pictured for himself. He's not certain he would've ever fully explored his bisexuality, nor would he have gotten his late-in-life ADHD diagnosis.

The ghost of Taylor's voice from last night sweetly haunts him. *If you treat your brain like a villain, it's going to act like a villain. Treat it like the world's coolest sidekick.* It's almost unimaginable that someone not-yet thirty could be so insightful.

His attention is grabbed by the sound of a family walking by the cabin, chattering loudly. They sound happy that the storm has passed, and they can enjoy their trip again. This makes him smile.

Thankfully, the dripping from the roof has ceased, but the bucket is full. As he hoists it up, some shards of glass twinkle in the overhead fan light. Forgetting that he took off his gloves, he reaches for them only to end up slicing the palm of his hand.

"Fuck," he shouts, dropping the glass and the bucket, creating a brand-new mess for him to attend to. Right now, the only mess he concerns himself with is his bleeding hand. There are no shards in the gash that he can see so he grabs one of the hand towels to wrap himself up before swiftly heading home. He's got a first aid kit in the bathroom.

For the last five years, he hasn't had to knock unless Samara was visiting, so as soon as he's through the front door and down the hall, he doesn't hesitate to enter the bathroom. The lock's been broken for the last six months.

Surprise thumps him back hard into the door when he's met with Taylor Frost's toned, naked body stepping out of the steamy shower. The towel rack is far enough away that there are whole seconds between the intrusion and any option for modesty.

Don't you dare look down.

The chiding does nothing to stop his uncooperative eyes from tracking several beads of water racing from Taylor's Adam's apple, down through a light patch of chest hair sitting between two rounded pecs, and straight toward a cock more hung than Ethan has seen in porn videos.

Ethan twists around and fumbles with his nondominant hand to grab the doorknob. "Sorry!" In the process, the bloody hand towel falls. Christ. He scoops it up, scrambles out.

"Is your hand okay?" Taylor asks, sounding concerned and not the slightest bit self-conscious.

Ethan's heart is in his throat as he stumbles away from the scene and back to the safety of the kitchen. His hand stings from how hard he's clutching the towel to it now. There might be no glass in there, but he's probably getting little filaments in the wound, causing mini spikes of pain.

The hot water takes a minute to plunk out of the kitchen sink. There's a sharp sensation that shoots up into his fingers as he cleans the wound. He pushes through until Taylor speaks behind him. "Let me take a look at your hand."

"It's okay. I've got it." Ethan's embarrassment causes his voice to shake. He hopes the back of his neck is not as red as his face definitely is.

"Are you sure? I'm the one holding the first aid kit." When Ethan collects himself to turn, Taylor stands there in shorts and a T-shirt, holding up the white box with the red cross on it. In his other hand, he's got a bottle of rubbing alcohol. When Ethan told Taylor to make himself at home, he really took it to heart. There's something comforting about how he has seamlessly weaved himself into the household without needing to ask.

Ethan coaxes himself into a chair at the kitchen table and allows Taylor to clean up his wound. Taylor is gentle, lightly dabbing at the cut with an alcohol-soaked cotton ball. "It's not that deep. My brother got a worse cut in the same place once from shattering a vase when we were kids."

"Guess you've had a lot of practice when it comes to expert care," Ethan notes, feeling a tingle race down his spine. It's been a while since someone he doesn't pay, like a doctor or a barber, has tended to him like this.

"You have to wear a lot of hats when your parents aren't reliable and you're the oldest sibling in the house," he says.

"I thought you said you had one older brother?"

Taylor tenses and doesn't look up to meet his eyes as he places a square of gauze over the cut. "Owen, yeah. Like I said, he left when he was eighteen and I was fifteen. He and my parents never got along. I don't think he ever quite forgave them for having six kids after him."

"Did he not get along with you and your siblings?" Ethan asks as Taylor unrolls the wrap he's going to bind the wound with.

He shakes his head. "It wasn't that. I think my parents assumed he'd be the leader of the house when they weren't around, but maybe he was too introverted for that. A loner, really. The idea of family was poisoned for him. He retreated from us and then left us and then I became the de facto oldest."

"That must've been tough," Ethan says as Taylor turns his wrist into a mummy.

"Sure, but it also made me resourceful. I developed a lot of skills I wouldn't have otherwise." Taylor smiles without meeting Ethan's eyes, twisting the wrap on a diagonal and then horizontally around the back of his hand. "Is that too tight?"

"No, it's perfect." Ethan attempts to stay as still as possible. Unwelcome goose bumps dot up along his arms. Good thing his forest of forearm hair masks them.

Taylor continues doing figure eights with the gauze until he circles back to the wrist and secures it with a pin. "Hold up your hand like you're doing the pledge?" Taylor pinches Ethan's finger.

"What was that for?" Ethan asks, watching as red coloring returns under his fingernail.

"To make sure your circulation was still good. You learn a lot when your family doesn't believe in ER visits and your siblings are prone to accidents." He sets the supplies back inside the plastic container. "Good thing I was here." Overly intimate and yet somehow entirely natural, Taylor rubs Ethan's knee, which causes a bolt of lust to shoot up and into Ethan's groin.

"Yeah, good thing." Ethan catches his breath. "Speaking of you being here, the roofer won't be able to come out for a few days."

"That's rough," Taylor says.

Ethan nods. "The guest room here is yours if you want it, but I understand if you'd be more comfortable at the inn in town."

"I'm perfectly comfortable here as long as I'm not in your way."

"Not at all," Ethan says, pleased by the response. A smile climbs onto his face. "That's settled then."

"Awesome," Taylor says, flashing his own cool smile. "Is there anything I can do around here to help out?"

Ethan thinks for a second. "Do you like meat?"

Taylor's eyes nearly bulge out of his head.

Oh, no! "Gosh, what I meant to say was, do you eat meat? Are you a meat eater? You're not a vegetarian or vegan or—"

"I eat meat," Taylor says quickly, almost as if he's hoping Ethan will shut up so the awkwardness clouding the air dissipates faster.

"Great, good," he says. "I have burgers I could grill up for us tonight. I was just thinking I'll need a little help with the spatula." He waves his capably bandaged hand.

"Just call me your right-hand man."

Was Taylor playing into the accidental flirtation? Ethan's dirty mind twists with thoughts of a task he does avidly with his right hand, and it has absolutely nothing to do with flipping beef.

Nine

TAYLOR

The town nearest Storybook Endings is called Calico, like the cat.

On calls with Ethan, Samara chatters while Taylor half listens in, sending e-mails from the island in their kitchen. Sometimes she says things like, "How's life in Cat Town?" And then she laughs like she's watching her latest comedy-obsession on Netflix.

The name is not the only thing catlike about this town, Taylor observes, as he strolls down the slightly curved sidewalk, like that of a tail, between the florist and the bakery. The pace of life here seems leisurely. Meandering, maybe, is more like it. Matching the speed of the Delaware River flowing right beside the main shopping district and the pace of the few people ambling past him.

This morning, Ethan gave Taylor one of the old quarter-zip Storybook Endings employee fleeces to wear. Taylor's grateful for it now as he moves closer to the water and a chill whips up. The weather is as unpredictable as everything that has happened here thus far.

He passes a bustling antique shop, a vintage-looking movie theater, and a brewery that appears to have been a firehouse in a past life. He can't help but be utterly charmed and wonder why Amy made this place feel like an inescapable prison when the West Coast is overrun with fitness nuts and woo-woo cult crazes. This is slow yet simple. No shine. No gloss. Just natural beauty.

Not thinking too hard about all that, he enters the bakery and is greeted by the alluring scent of powdered sugar underpinned by chocolate. Dangling down from the front window is a pride flag, which puts Taylor at ease. This isn't one of those bakeries he's constantly reading about in the news.

The baker is a short, brown-skinned, balding man who, when told who the cake is for, beams. "Sixteen? Already? I remember when Samara was no more than five. She had a penchant for my sugar cookies. Where has the time gone?"

A warmth seeps through Taylor's chest. It must be nice to have a small community like this. To watch the local children grow up from behind a display case filled with the sweetest treats.

When Taylor's finished his delicious complementary cake samples and they've completed the order form, he snaps a picture and texts it to Samara. Strawberry filling still?

Samara instantly responds. Can we do chocolate mousse instead? Just found out Maya's allergic ☹

You got it! I'll make sure there aren't any strawberries in

the breakfast selections either at the resort while you're all here, Taylor writes back after making the change and exiting the bakery.

Ur the best! <3 Have you heard the new Billie Eilish song???

Taylor hadn't realized she'd dropped one as a surprise. Popping in my earbuds now!

Let me know what you think! Hope ur enjoying *cat emoji* town

The rest of his day is busy. He collects decorations, party supplies, props for the photo booth and local artisan goods for the welcome baskets he's going to place in each of the cabins the girls will be sharing. His bags hang heavy with rose petal soaps and homemade popping candies in all the colors of the rainbow.

By the time he's checked off his to-do list, he's starved. He completely forgot about lunch. The cake samples must've been enough to tide him over, but now he's hankering for a real meal.

On his way back to the rental car, he passes a Vietnamese restaurant. A man hurries through the door with a container of takeout, and Taylor gets a waft of peanuts and spices. One sniff is enough to make his stomach sing. His feet perform a sharp U-turn.

Inside at the counter, he's delighted to find this place is run by a Vietnamese immigrant who moved from New York City with her husband. Food with a history and a story is always so much tastier. Maybe that's the same way he feels about Storybook Endings. A resort with a lore is more comfortable than a chain hotel with no hallmarks in a major city. The more personal an experience, the more memorable it is. At least to him. And boy, has his stay at Storybook Endings Catskills already gotten *personal*.

As he looks over the menu, he decides he should grab food for Ethan as well, but he doesn't have Ethan's private number. He doesn't want to call the resort to find him, so he uses his personal assistant skills to make his best guess at what meal Ethan would enjoy.

Upon returning to Ethan's house, he finds Ethan hunched over in the door of the fridge, searching for something. There is a *Jack and the Beanstalk* comicality to the sight. Appliances appear minuscule compared to Ethan's enticing, towering stature. Taylor's gaze lands squarely on Ethan's round, perky backside tucked into light-wash jeans as he bends to inspect a low shelf. Assumedly tantalized by the scent, Ethan straightens up and peers over to where Taylor stands.

"I come bearing gifts," Taylor says, pretending he hadn't just been drooling over his boss's ex-husband's ample ass. "And by gifts I mean Vietnamese food."

"From Nga's place?" Ethan asks, his misty blue eyes brightening. There's a ring of darker blue around the edges that Taylor is becoming fast familiar with.

"Yes, she's lovely, and if the food is half as good as it smells, I'm going to be in heaven."

Taylor quickly helps Ethan set the table. They sit opposite each other like they did last night and unpack the brown paper bag together. Ethan freezes when he pulls out his pho noodle with braised chicken bowl. "How did you know my order?"

"As a personal assistant, you take note of things. Last night, your burger was basically a hockey puck, not even a hint of red in that thing, so I figured the rare beef was not the right choice, and Samara has a mild soy allergy so I figured there's enough of a chance you would too so that ruled out tofu. This was the last option," Taylor says, overly pleased that he's surprised Ethan like this.

"Wow. You're good," he says, popping the top off the bowl.

"I also asked Nga," he says quickly under his breath and then fills his mouth with jasmine rice. He doesn't need to see Ethan's smile because he senses it radiate from across the circular slab of wood between them.

"Honesty is a rare quality these days." Ethan's a master with chopsticks, using them to pick up some noodles. Somehow, he makes slurping look sexy. Taylor gazes down at his own meal to avoid looking too long at Ethan's lips that are perfectly framed by his beard. The fantasy of those dark blond hairs brushing across his smooth skin. *Ooh.* There are few greater pleasures in this life than kissing a man with a soft, supple beard.

Not *this* man, though, of course. This man is someone to share a roof and meals with. Nothing more or his career is as good as toast. Burned toast at that.

"Were you a personal assistant before you became Amy's?" Ethan asks.

"No, I was looking for jobs in hospitality. The opportunity opened up to be Amy's assistant, and I figured it was as good a way as any to learn about the business from the inside while picking Amy's brain," he says. "I've been following her career for a while now."

A puckering overtakes Ethan's face. Taylor fears he's said the wrong thing, but then Ethan says, "She's built quite the empire."

"Not without help she hasn't," he says to spread the compliment out a bit more without naming Ethan directly. From the conversations he's had with Amy, she painted Ethan as "stubborn." She said, "He wanted nothing to do with success or franchising because 'uprooting was out of the question for him.'"

It makes sense now that Taylor has seen Ethan in action. But he doesn't think stubbornness is the heart of it. Ethan is a necessary resource in the habitat he's built here. Ethan's arms are like sturdy, strong tree branches and his torso is a generous, aged trunk. It's as if the ground here has claimed him as part of the ecosystem. Digging him up and trying to replant him somewhere else probably wouldn't work.

"Why hospitality?" Ethan asks, seemingly ignoring Taylor's previous statement.

"Similar reasons to yours," Taylor says, adding more house dressing to his bowl.

"Oh, I never wanted to go into hospitality," Ethan says, face all serious.

Puzzled, Taylor says, "But you did all those interviews with Amy back…" He doesn't really know where he was going to go with that sentence, only that this doesn't jive with the Ethan from the magazines and the photo essays. He definitely won't bring up how attractive he found Ethan in all those spreads.

"I always wanted to own a business—that much is true. Amy and I cycled through many ideas over the years we were together. It wasn't until we had Samara that opening something fairy-tale-themed came to us," he says. It's as if a curtain of memory falls over his face, like Taylor is looking at him through a lacy pattern. "Samara was ravenous for Disney movies and picture books about princesses. We couldn't keep up. Every day she was obsessing over a different princess."

"I can relate," Taylor says, reminiscing upon his childhood fascination with the illustrations in the Grimm's complete story collection his parents kept around the house.

"We floated taking her to Disney World, but she's never liked rides. They always make her sick. We figured that would be a waste of money. We kept saying, 'Wouldn't it be nice if we had some place close that's magical but more outdoorsy?' This land had been in my family for a while. I think my grandfather always had dreams of starting a farm, but when he passed, he left the deed to my dad and—"

So enrapt, Taylor barely registers that his phone is ringing. It's not until Ethan says, "Are you going to get that?" that he looks down and sees Amy's photo taking up half the screen. The peaceful hold this conversation and meal had on Taylor shatters instantly.

"Gosh, I'm sorry. Yes, I should. Hold that thought."

Taylor races away from the table and into Samara's old room. Why's he breathing so hard?

Standing in the midst of the princess-y pinkness, he wonders how much he should divulge to his boss. Does she need to know he's staying here and why? Amy is big on allegiances. As a woman in business, she kind of has to be. To her, you're either with her or against her. Ethan's position on that continuum vacillates day by day. If she learned of Taylor's newfound connection with her ex-husband, she might get the wrong idea. Which is maybe also the right idea given how intimate their conversations have felt?

He doesn't have enough time to figure this out because there's nothing Amy hates more than being sent to voicemail. Except maybe idle pleasantries.

Prime example: "Taylor, they're sublime! The photos are everything I've been dreaming of," she says, not stopping for a breath between sentences. She possesses too much control to need to.

"That's fantastic," he says, sounding perhaps too chipper.

"Am I catching you at a bad time?" she asks.

His stomach growls, angry he had to leave behind that delicious food, now growing cold. His mind growls as well, upset to have lost the pleasurable stimulation that is listening to Ethan's deep bass voice regale him about his career.

"Did I lose you?" Amy asks. "I know the service can be spotty up there."

"No, I'm here. You were saying about the photos?" His mind flashes to Ethan's headshot from the Storybook Endings website, counts the number of times he mooned over it. He still can't wrap his head around how much more attractive Ethan is in person. Ethan's good looks have regressed Taylor's hormones to puberty levels of wonkiness.

"Oh, not just the photos, but the progress. Taylor, buying a legacy resort was the right move. Given the existing structures, the facades and frames have been much easier and quicker to install. Everything is way more on track than I ever expected," she says.

Taylor matches her enthusiasm as he says, "I'm glad to hear it's all going well."

"I'm sending you the picture proofs now. Just keep them between us until we've got the new test site up and running. Don't say anything to Ethan," she says pointedly.

"Ethan? Why would I say anything to Ethan?" The reverb of his voice has a distinctly defensive tone to it. As if he could broadcast his attraction to her ex-husband more.

"Because you're staying at the resort he manages?" she says slowly and cuttingly.

"Right," he says, palming his forehead. "Of course. Mum's the word."

There's a tenuous silence. "Are you sure everything is all right over there? You don't need me to fly out, do you? I'm entrusting you with this." That shiny promise of advancement from his first interview with Amy dangles in the balance of what he does and says next.

"No! I have everything under control. I just spent all day so focused on Samara's party preparations that I needed a second to reset and eat is all," he says, evening out his tone.

"Eat? Oh, with the time difference, I didn't even realize. It's dinner. Taylor, you should've said something. You really need to be more assertive. Go eat. Be on the lookout for my e-mail," she says.

Taylor's relieved to be off the line, but annoyed with himself for not speaking up about his new sleeping situation. It would mean little to Amy if he charged a few nights' stay at the Calico Inn on his business card if he explained. He's almost positive it would be preferable to shacking up with her ex, but...

Well, the roof and window will likely be fixed way before Amy and Samara's plane even touches the ground. There's no reason she needs to know about this temporary arrangement. Why upset her? That upset could blow back right onto Ethan for his carelessness regarding the tree limbs. He's not in the business of getting anyone in trouble.

Besides, he's selfishly enjoying Ethan's company, which is what makes him leave his phone in the bedroom and return to the kitchen to continue their meal. Only, when he arrives, Ethan is gone. His food has been cleared, and his utensils are sitting in the sink.

So much for hearing the rest of that story.

Taylor gloomily finishes his lukewarm dinner alone.

Ten

ETHAN

It's not until the next day, as Ethan's approaching the leaf-dusted shed where he keeps the archery equipment, that he remembers his hand. Still injured. Freshly wrapped. How's he going to teach like this?

Nobody else at the resort has the skills to lead this workshop. Panic bubbles up from his gut as he struggles to slide the first of many targets out into the grassy field with his good hand.

It's too late to cancel. There are chatty guests cresting over the path already. Kids are racing away from their parents, excited by an activity to let off steam.

"What'll we do, Nana?" Ethan asks his companion, stumped by this conundrum.

That's when, among the gathering crowd, Taylor appears. His hair is curling up at the ends. He must've showered and left his hair to air dry. At least Ethan wasn't around to rush in on him again.

Truthfully, he's giving Taylor some space since Amy's phone call interrupted their dinner last night. Amy's ringtone broke the inviting spell he was under. The hot, decadent Vietnamese food satisfied his cravings, and their conversation made him forget the very clear-cut reasons he can't fall into anything with Taylor. His job and his age are nonstarters.

Last night, snuggled up with Nana in bed, he spooled back through the conversation and realized just how much life experience he has on Taylor and just how far away from his Amy-induced heartbreak he's gotten. Opening himself up to the charms of the twink staying in his guest room and living off his ex-wife's payroll would undo years of hard emotional work. Not to mention give Amy new reasons to think ill of him.

But there Taylor is, standing on the edge of the clearing, waiting for the beginning of Ethan's class. And Taylor seems ready and willing to jump into almost anything.

"Hello, everyone. Thank you for coming out today for this afternoon's archery lesson," Ethan says to the group. Miraculously, Taylor is wearing sneakers instead of his usual socks and sandals, which means he can participate. Without asking, Ethan announces, "Unfortunately, I had a bit of an accident over the weekend, so Taylor here is going to be my hands for the day."

Appearing surprised but not uncooperative, Taylor joins him in front of everyone. Ethan offers Taylor an appreciative smile before instructing the first ten participants—mostly children between the ages of eight and thirteen—to line up across from the targets.

"Sorry to keep needing you like this," Ethan whispers to his impromptu assistant.

"Don't worry about it. I like being needed." A pink flush swishes over Taylor's cheeks, which he hides well by picking up one of the bows. Ethan wants to color-match that pink and paint his bedroom walls with it. "Shall we start?"

Ethan resurfaces from his fantasy and explains how the class is structured, trying to make it sound as engaging as possible. Next, he breaks down the rules.

"Boo!" one kid shouts while shifting from foot to foot. If Ethan's remembering correctly from check-in, this kid's name is Gus, and he had a similarly antsy vibe when they arrived.

Gus's mom tries to shush him from the sidelines, but Ethan steps in because he's personally experienced this exact feeling before from grown-ups in his own life who didn't know how not to shame him for his brain's natural impulses. "I know. Rules can be frustrating, but they're here to keep us safe. I promise once we power through them, we'll get to pick out our own bows and quivers. How's that sound?"

Gus's energy shines in his eyes. "Good." He shoots Ethan a thumbs-up.

Ethan rattles off the basics—always inspect your bow and arrow before loading, make sure your path is clear, shoot only when instructed to do so and only at the target. He may have said these things a million times before, but he always imbues them with the importance they deserve. Sure, the parents signed waivers, but in this day and age, you can never be too careful.

After explaining dominant eyes to the group, Ethan has Taylor take up the position in the center of the field about five yards from the target. Normally, Ethan adopts a do-as-I-do attitude. However, today, he's going to need to get hands-on in a very different way. Or *hand*-on given his injury.

"Isn't he too close?" Gus asks out of turn, breaking the flow as Taylor slides on the arm guard. Some kids shoot Gus weird glances. Others are completely uninterested, but their parents are perky and taking plenty of pictures to post on social media later, which is good business for Ethan.

"That's a good question, Gus," Ethan says. The praise and use of his name seems to engage him further. "Beginners should always shoot close to the target. It's more about form and practice than it is about distance."

Taylor comically takes another step closer, clearly making a show out of not wanting to embarrass himself in front of an audience. "My aim's not so great," he admits.

"We'll work on it," Ethan says to him and him only. It's alarming how, with Taylor, he can already focus like there's nobody and nothing else around. "Now, as I said before, my friend here's name is Taylor. Who can tell me what letter the name Taylor begins with?"

Every kid in the line raises their hand except for two—the youngest girl of the bunch, Lara, and of course Gus. "*T!*" Lara and Gus shout in near unison.

"Hey, that's not fair! I knew that, too," says Paul, a kid wearing glasses and a gray coat.

Ethan doesn't call attention to it. While he empathizes with Paul, reprimanding Gus or Lara isn't the way to go. "That's on me. I didn't say anybody needed to raise their hands. From now on, we'll wait for our turn to be called on before answering, okay?"

Back on track, Ethan explains how their bodies should mirror the *T* shape when drawing back the arrow. "That means we gotta push our front arm out and keep our back elbows up. Can everybody show me their letter *T* poses?"

Taylor's the only one with a bow, so after inspecting the lineup, he offers Taylor an arrow.

"Already?" Taylor asks.

"Practice makes perfect," Ethan says.

"Feels a bit like trial by fire."

"Which is something you know how to make now." Ethan lifts his eyebrows, awestruck by how they've known each other for four days and he's already comfortable making jokes with him. That can't be good...

Taylor places the bow and tries to assume the position. Ethan makes suggestions, but can already tell that the strong tension of the bow being pulled back is causing Taylor some trouble. "May I?" Ethan asks, holding up his left hand.

"Please," Taylor says in a strangely breathy whisper that stirs inside Ethan.

Ethan approaches, aware that he hasn't touched Taylor since Taylor bandaged his hand at the kitchen table. There was an intimacy to that moment, unmatched and still blazing somewhere in Ethan's sternum. He squelches that thought for the sake of the class, until his hand wraps around Taylor's at the front of the bow.

Taylor's slightly smaller hand, soft to the touch aside from where his rings rest, fits so well inside Ethan's larger, calloused, powerful one as he instructs him how to nock the arrow.

"What now?" Taylor asks, words compressed as Ethan circles around behind him. He can't help but feel like a predator out in the wild stalking his prey. The primal quality of his unwelcome attraction to Taylor shreds at his already tattered resolve.

"When you draw back, you want to anchor. Touch your face. Consistency is key in getting the hang of the sport." Taylor does as he's told, and Ethan yearns desperately to be the bow gently grazing Taylor's smooth cheek.

"Like this?" Taylor asks.

"Almost." Ethan steps close, maybe too close, mirroring Taylor's stance from behind. He adjusts the lower limb and Taylor's elbow. From afar, it probably looks like they're preparing to begin a ballroom dance routine. Momentarily, he wonders if Taylor has rhythm in those hips of his. "Before you let go, remember to keep your stance, your eye on the target, and to follow through. That means keep the elbow up and back. Gentle release."

Christ. What Ethan would give to experience gentle release with the likes of Taylor Frost.

Whiz. The arrow slices through the air and hits the target with a slap.

"Pretty good for a first try," says Ethan, stepping away and waving his hands. Almost as if he's clearing the air free of feelings and ridiculous fantasies. "The first arrow is always the scariest."

Taylor lowers the grip and turns to face Ethan. His eyes have expanded, and his smile is the size of a billboard. "It's like I'm Katniss Everdeen."

"It's a cool feeling, right?" Ethan asks. It's an overriding high that's never left Ethan since he was eleven and was gifted his first archery kit from his father. From the moment he drew back on that tense bowstring, exalting in the gooey contraction of his back muscles, he was hooked. The riveting sensation has only ever been matched by one other activity in his life. The one synonymous with "gentle release."

"Way cool," Taylor says, locked in place with his jaw half slung down. His gaze rests still upon the target. Is he still processing the *thwack* of the arrow's impact? Is he craving his next go?

Ethan suddenly remembers the line of antsy tweens behind him, eager for their own turns. He clears his throat and throws his professional mask back on. "Who's next?" he asks as every hand flies up.

An hour and some change later, as they put away the archery supplies and the class disperses, Taylor asks, "How did you get so good at archery?"

"Practice," Ethan says matter-of-factly. Then goes hot in the neck. "What a nonanswer."

Taylor chuckles. "No, it's okay. I didn't ask the right question. How did you get into it?"

The drug-like high that fuels him after a well-attended archery lesson swirls down the drain at this question. "My dad."

They're inside the cobweb-crusted shed. The wood walls are dark, and the canopy of trees above blocks the sunlight from leaking into the corner where they set the target amid various other pieces of sports clutter. The shadowiness of the space without the overhead bulb pulled on makes Taylor's expression inscrutable, yet Ethan can feel his curiosity. Taylor's palpable interest prompts him to share the more painful aspect of his lifelong hobby.

"He was—my father, I mean—a champion archer. He almost went all the way to the Olympics one year. Great man. Great dad. He taught all three of us boys to shoot. I'm the only one who stuck with it," he says, voice drowning in a sepia-toned memory of his father. Broad-shouldered. Tall-standing. More at home sitting in the dirt of a campground than in an armchair in the family room.

"That must mean a lot to him," Taylor says, audibly catching his breath.

"More now that he's in a wheelchair." Every time this fact crosses his mind, his nervous system zips into overdrive as if cowering in fear over what might be. "He was diagnosed with MS when he turned thirty-eight."

A single beam of light cuts through the nearby pane of glass. Taylor steps into it, his face a mask of sympathy that charges the air with importance. "I'm really sorry to hear that. That must be tough."

"He is the strongest person I know." Emotions tower up inside Ethan's throat, but he swallows them back like a cup of cough syrup. Easier down than out. "He takes everything in stride."

"Does he live close by?" Taylor asks.

"Only a few towns away with my mom. I stop by a couple times a week to bring them groceries and make dinner," he says. They are the most important trips of his week and not even his ADHD could knock them out of his mind.

"I'm sure they appreciate that."

"Not as much as I do, I think." He laughs to himself. "The

older I get, the more I visit, and the more my mom says, 'Ethan, we love you, but we're managing fine. We don't need more organic carrots. We're going to get carotenemia.'"

"What's carotenemia?" Taylor asks.

"Sounds fake, doesn't it? She read somewhere that eating carrots too much can cause discoloration of the skin." Don't even get him started on the number of e-mails he got from her on the topic after she brought it up. Links to WebMD. Reddit threads. The works. Despite their silliness, he reads them. Every single one. And responds in kind. His mom cares. Maybe too much. But that's not such a bad trait, is it? "I think when your partner gets sick the way my dad is, you become hypervigilant about everything else. The littlest change in the body becomes an alarm bell."

"I can't even imagine."

"I've asked her a dozen times if she wants to see my therapist, just to have someone to talk to about the anxiety she's feeling, but that's a moot point," he says, shaking his head to himself.

"I'm sure it's a generational thing."

That statement shocks Ethan into another age-based realization. He and Taylor are of two entirely separate generations, yet here he is confiding information that he rarely brings up with anyone, even Gabriel, his closest friend. He won't even touch the fact that his closest friend is also his employee which runs red tape around a lot of what he already shares about his personal life. He sighs. "We should finish cleaning up."

They go back out to the now-empty field and collect the bows and arrows and discarded finger protectors. When everything is properly stored, Taylor asks, "Would you be interested in joining me for dinner tonight in The Thirsty Goat? My treat. I've been eyeing the fish and chips on the menu since I arrived."

Ethan's mouth waters at the thought of devouring a plate full of fried cod with tartar sauce made by Antonio, the best cook the resort has ever had. But it's one thing to eat together in the privacy of his house. It's another to be seen together by the guests in the restaurant. That's not the kind of talk he wants circulating. "I try not to dine in here often except for special occasions. It's not the best look for management."

"Oh, right. Sure. That makes sense. How about I grab us takeout like—" He stops short, but Ethan infers he meant to add *last night*. Last night when Amy's call disrupted another bout of oversharing. A ringtone hauled Ethan right out of that sweet, domestic simulation he was too happily partaking in.

If they'd finished the meal, he imagines they'd have done the dishes together. Hot, soapy water filling up the sink basin and splashing onto Taylor's shirt. Taylor peeling it up and over his head unself-consciously...

Ethan pops that fantasy with a pin before it bubbles out of control.

Just because he and Taylor are sharing a house doesn't mean they should be *playing house* as well. What if he becomes too accustomed to Taylor's presence, conversational skills, and openly handsome face?

If Ethan were to spread his arms right now, he's certain the tips of his middle fingers would grace the worn wood on either side of this shed. And if Ethan were a bolder man with less propriety, he might take advantage of their close proximity. Unclench his fists and offer them up for Taylor to take.

Because, well, that look on Taylor's face when the arrow met the target was so attractively unguarded that it might appear on the insides of Ethan's eyelids when he tries to fall asleep tonight. The memory of that expression is only surpassed by the pleasing anticipation traced in the upward curve of Taylor's eyebrows now, which is enough to make Ethan lose his breath, but not his control.

"I forgot I have plans tonight. I won't be around for dinner. Please help yourself to whatever is in the fridge or pantry. Pans are under the drawer with the utensils. There's a spice rack by the mugs and..." He rambles on, unable to stop himself from basically detailing every corner of his kitchen. Despite wanting distance, he can't avoid the need for Taylor to be as comfortable as possible. As Gabriel reminded him, it's been so long since he's hosted someone in his home.

Taylor rocks back on his heels. "All good. Thanks. I should probably start putting together the welcome baskets for Samara's guests. I originally only came to observe for a minute or two. I didn't expect to be in the middle of the archery action."

"Thanks again for doing that. I would've normally asked Kerry—one of my managers—to assist, but she's out for a few days," he says, then freezes. "Which reminds me, she usually does Tuesday night dessert story time for the kids. She's our best reader. I guess I'll have to fill in for her, even though I'm terrible at it."

"What if I did it?" Taylor asks, voice brightening.

"I couldn't ask you to do that. You've helped me out enough as it is."

"Please, it would be no trouble at all. I used to read stories to my siblings all the time. I liked it. I'm even good at the voices," he says, followed by various impressions ranging from Mickey Mouse to Kermit the Frog.

Ethan bites his lip to temper the full range of the smile the voices elicit. "Those are pretty good. Are you certain?"

"Absolutely. Is there a story already?"

"No, it would be yours for the choosing."

"Excellent," Taylor says before dipping his chin to his chest and wiggling his fingers together. In a voice reminiscent of an evil queen, he repeats, "Eeeeeeeeeexcellent."

Eleven

TAYLOR

Samara's dusty, pink bookshelf is stuffed full of glittering, golden spines. Every title is a thin, cardboard movie tie-in that has Disney dust sprinkled all over it.

Taylor rolls off his knees and plops onto his butt, defeated. He was hoping if he moved some of these out of the way he might find a fairy tale picture book with a little more grounding, a little less polish. No luck.

He lies supine on the plush, tan carpet. Stares up at the ceiling, which has its own mural. He hadn't noticed this on his first night while snooping, but the second night he spent there, he accidentally fell asleep with the lights on. When he woke up, somewhere around 2:00 a.m., he was faced with this detailed starry sky overhead.

It's just as mesmerizing now in the afternoon daylight that yawns through the gauzy pink curtains in streaky waves.

Squinting one eye and lifting his arm, he uses his finger to play connect the dots. He's attempting to summon some of his childish wonder to help him recall which stories lit him up most as a kid.

The obvious answer trots into his head as he's repeatedly outlining what he believes to be Cassiopeia.

Well, he needs to go into Calico anyway.

First stop, a mom-and-pop craft store in a standalone red-brick building with a hand-painted sign swaying over its door called DIWhy Not? It's a cute name, and the store itself is even cuter. The place smells of potpourri. At the checkout counter, a white woman with a dark pixie cut wearing big glasses and a shockingly green smock works on a fake flower arrangement in a painted mason jar. "Let me know if I can help you find anything."

"Could you point me in the direction of beads?" Taylor asks.

He doesn't have to go far before he's in front of an entire wall of beads. They stock every size and color of the rainbow. Overwhelmed with choice, he makes his best guesses. Nothing too frilly or girly. Samara hates that. She prefers the deep purples of Olivia Rodrigo's album covers and the electric greens of Billie Eilish's early career hair. She's got an edge to her, and she and Taylor have bonded over that angsty-lite music.

Out of the corner of his eye, Taylor spots a set of beads for the different astrological star signs. The most prominent one in the bag is for Sagittarius, the archer. His body responds in kind. He's reminded of the competence porn that is Ethan Golding instructing him how to shoot an arrow. After one lesson, Taylor understood completely why someone would practice this sport long-term. It's like standing by the bass speaker at a high-octane concert; that full-body reverberation could become addictive.

He tugs the set of beads down off its hook, adds it to his basket and brings his treasures to the register where Pixie Cut has completed a beautiful arrangement worthy of Instagram. "That's stunning. Do you sell those?" Taylor asks as she scans the stretch cord, then the washi tape.

"Not really," she says with a shrug. "I took a class on floral arrangements and started making them for my sister's baby shower a few years back. Now I mostly do it for fun. When we're not busy, it's a good distraction and always brightens up my day."

"My boss's daughter's sweet sixteen is next weekend and we never landed on table centerpieces. If I sent you the color scheme, would you be able to make six or seven of these as decorations? I would pay you, of course."

Pixie Cut whose name tag reads Lola fiddles with her arrangement. "Wow, um, yeah, sure, why not? Sounds fun."

Taylor swipes Amy's business credit card for the cost of both the bracelet supplies and the new arrangements he'll pick up in a few days.

Instead of going right back to the car, he retraces his steps from the other day until he stands in front of Word Play, the town's independent bookstore. The window displays are awash with primary colors and oversize blocks. When he enters, he realizes it's a children-centric store fully stocked with a wide array of genres. Perfection.

Inside, he easily finds an illustrated edition of *Grimm's*

Fairy Tales that includes the exact story he wants to read for tonight's Sugar Cookies and Story Time.

Knights and Knaves, the recreation room in the back of The Castle, has a story time nook in the far corner. A round, dark purple rug leaves ample space for little ones to sit and snack on the sugary confections made by the local bakers. Crumbs dribble down their chinny-chin-chins. Taylor recognizes a few faces in the group from the archery lesson earlier today. Parents hover on the periphery to listen, holding steaming cups of tea or decaf coffee, which give the air notes of berry and a hint of richness.

Ethan stands by the foosball table and gives Taylor a thumbs-up when they're ready to begin.

"Hey, kids. Welcome to Sugar Cookies and Story Time. My name is Taylor," he says, relishing all the attention on him for a change. He's so used to standing beside or behind someone else and blending in. It's nice to have center stage to himself for a moment.

"I remember you!" Gus from the archery lesson shouts from the back. He's double-fisting sugar cookies.

"I remember you, too," Taylor says, taking a page from Ethan's book from earlier. "Our friend Gus back there reminds me to tell you that stories are shared experiences. It's okay to laugh or to cover your eyes or shout out with our inside voices. Feel free to react in any way that feels natural to you. Deal?"

"Deal," the listeners chime in unison.

Taylor cracks open the book, a nervousness weaseling through his stomach. How long has it been since he's done this? He rolls out his shoulders and clears the discomfort from his throat.

As he starts reading *Snow White*, the shadowy, erudite illustrations paired with the simplistic, eerie language remind him how truly grim the Grimm brothers were with their tales. Bloody red speckles the charcoal landscapes, giving credence to a new swelling unease.

The light mood presiding over the room progressively grows heavy and cloudy, and the children grow quieter and quieter.

When Taylor turns the page to reveal a new picture, a child in the front row's face sours—from the story or from finishing his cookie? Taylor's stomach is thrust into a state of free fall as he recalls his younger brother Finn hiding under a blanket during one of their thunderstorm sleepovers. During *this* specific story.

Too late to veer off course now, though. Maybe these kids are particularly mature? Hope is a fleeting feeling as the thought of disappointing Ethan enters the mix.

When he reaches the end of the story, he reads the line about how the Evil Queen wears the enchanted shoes, and they make her dance until she...*dies*? He gulps loudly. That can't be right.

A choir of wails rings out almost instantly. A frenzy of sticky hands stretch skyward. Kids beg to be held and consoled over the frightening story Taylor chose to share. He slams the book shut, keeps his eyes downcast. If he could disappear into this corner, he would.

So much for wanting the spotlight. Now he's practically burning under the illumination.

Ethan claps his hands to gather everyone's attention, says things Taylor only half hears over the *buh-bum-buh-bum* driving away in his eardrums. The din of the room calms, but only slightly. Taylor doesn't need to glance up to feel the heat of detesting glares slashed in his direction. He's properly whipped by his misjudgment.

Once the room is cleared and cleaned, to Ethan, Taylor offers a mousy, "I'm sorry."

Ethan remains silent.

Taylor supposes he deserves that.

On the walk back to Ethan's place, Taylor mentally flogs himself for not having read the story again in advance. If he had, he would've remembered and picked out one of those Little Golden Books instead. Offered up the fairy tales this generation is used to. Ones with "I Want" songs and lessons learned and smiles all around.

Taylor's father's voice rings with surprising clarity through his brain: "These ones are more authentic. These ones will prepare you kids for the real world."

From his pocket, Taylor retrieves his phone. In town today, he saw that small boutique inn. Hopefully, they have a vacancy until Amy and Samara arrive and the roof on the Snow White (*Jesus, he can't escape it!*) cottage is fixed. He obviously can't stay at Ethan's after the chaos he caused.

Sheepishly, he follows Ethan into the house, hangs up his coat and takes off his shoes. He shuffles straight for the hallway to begin packing before he's stopped by laughter that starts small but grows gradually louder. At its crescendo, Ethan is practically guffawing. His booming laughter infects his entire body, doubling him over. The resonant sound bounces off the walls and zips back to Taylor.

"What's so funny?" Taylor asks. Had he missed something?

Ethan collects himself enough to say, "That. Back there. That was funny."

Taylor's computation skills have gone offline. How did that horrendous situation turn this brick house of a man into a bouncy castle? His shoulders and belly and legs go up and down, up and down with the erratic cadence of his laugh. "I'm... Huh? Aren't you mad at me?"

"Mad? Why would I be mad? I told you that you had free rein to pick whatever story you chose." His laughter fades marginally.

Taylor loosens the fists he has buried in his pockets. "But what about the kids?"

"What about them? Nobody was hurt."

"Physically not, but mentally? I'm not so sure. Scarred, at least!" Taylor's jaw tightens. His brain is saying, *Shut up already! Don't test his forgiveness.*

Ethan splays a palm on one of the living room walls while the other plants itself on his hip. He must need the support otherwise another laughing fit might knock him entirely off his feet. "Look, was it ideal? Not in the slightest. Was it refreshing? Absolutely." His misty blue eyes produce a faint outline of tears that sparkles in the lamplight.

For a second, Taylor is so taken by the beauty of those eyes—so pale near the pupils that they're almost gray—that he forgets what they were even discussing. "I can't tell if I should apologize again or not."

"Taylor, kids are far more resilient than you think. Most

of them have probably already forgotten about it," Ethan says in a surefire vote of reassurance.

"I'm sure the parents haven't." Messing up always makes Taylor feel sick. Nobody was ever around to help him fix things if he did, so he learned early on to double- and triple-check himself, to prioritize perfection. Maybe that's why Amy likes him so much. Maybe that's why he's so afraid to put his wants and needs first for a change.

"Fuck the parents!" Ethan yells through a laugh, then snaps up to attention. Posture becoming statuesque. "Excuse my language." A blush paints itself above his beard line.

"No excusing necessary." Taylor's heart flings itself against his rib cage.

Hearing a curse word in Ethan's low register—nearly a rumble—is a next-level auditory experience. Not to mention one lock of Ethan's dirty blond hair has fallen from its perch. It swoops down across his forehead in an exasperatingly attractive way. Taylor's hands emerge from the caves of his pockets as if ready to reach out and brush it back into place.

"Those Grimm's stories are fucked up," Ethan says before his riotous laughter returns. The sound makes Taylor feel like a pulsating jellyfish—all blobby and floaty.

Taylor bites his lip before saying softly, "I think they're darkly beautiful if you listen close enough."

Sure, he probably shouldn't have read that version of *Snow White* to six- and seven-year-olds, but he's glad he bought the book. There are so many tales in there that he wants to revisit now. Maybe he'll do so tonight before bed. He'll need something to distract him from thinking about what Ethan is doing just on the other side of the thin wall.

"Would you read me some?" Ethan asks, stroking at his throat to the left of his Adam's apple. Born of his laughter comes a sudden boldness, peppered thick in the air.

Taylor's stomach flutters at the unexpected request. "Only if we can trade off," he says after a beat.

"Aw, I'm no good at the voices." The laugh that follows is strangled. Not at all like the ones earlier. Apprehension appears in his eyes.

"Fair is fair," says Taylor, unwilling to take no for an answer. Pushing the boundaries of what might be.

Probably sensing that Taylor's resolution is strong, Ethan doesn't argue.

They go to their respective rooms and then reconvene in the moonlight-swathed living room twenty minutes later. Taylor has changed into his thin sleep shorts and T-shirt, left behind his socks and perhaps his inhibitions, too. On the coffee table, Ethan set out two wineglasses and another bottle of the same red wine from that first night beside the fire pit.

"Is this your favorite?" Taylor asks while Ethan plates more mint Milanos for them. Once Taylor goes back to California, he won't be able to see these cookies in the grocery store without thinking of Ethan. He'll forever associate the taste of bitter dark chocolate and a shock of spearmint with this ruggedly handsome man.

"You could say that. I only drink socially and rarely wine, but this was gifted to me several years ago by a man I was dating at the time and I loved it, so I went out and bought a whole case of it to entertain with. It's been languishing in the garage ever since," he says.

Taylor's attentive listening snags on the word *man*. From Amy, he'd gleaned that Ethan was bisexual.

"How long have you been out?" The shiny foil on top of the wine bottle is a struggle to skin, so Taylor sits picking, happy for the excuse to be looking down and not at Ethan.

"Ouh who womb ehaly?" There's already a Milano—like a plump, unlit cigar—nestled between Ethan's perfect teeth as he sets the plate down on the coffee table.

"Oh, just in general," Taylor says, easily decoding Ethan's speech.

The couch is an old maroon, blue and tan corduroy that's seen better days, yet despite its gaunt appearance, it's comfy. So comfy, in fact, that the cushions have distinct imbalances from the places where people have sat watching movies or reading books or drinking tea over the years. Because of this, it dips noticeably toward the middle, so when Ethan sits six inches away, it's as if the cushions conspire to throw the two of them closer together. Their shoulders knock as Taylor pours the wine. Neither of them acknowledges it. If Taylor did, he'd have to confront the freshly lit sparkler that's taken the place of his arm.

"I came out to Amy before we got engaged. To my family after the divorce. The people that needed to know knew *when* they needed to know," he says. "With Amy, I wanted to be as honest as possible before we made any big life commitment. She knew me better than anyone, and once I figured out that piece of myself, it only felt right to share it. With my brothers and parents, we all live relatively close by. I didn't want me out and about with a man at some point to pass around like some whispered scandal. I got ahead of it as best I knew how. How about you?"

"Practically my whole life," Taylor says. "You can't really keep secrets with a family as big as mine in a house as small as the one we grew up in. Everyone was chill about it."

"That must've been nice, not having to hide," he says.

"In a way. I was so consumed by school, work and my siblings that I never really had time to explore what it meant. I knew I liked guys, but I had no time to date them."

Ethan nods contemplatively as silence wraps the room.

"Where should we begin?" Taylor asks, unable to bear the stillness any longer. He drapes the fuzzy cream-colored blanket from the back of the couch over his lap. Angling his body, he sets his back against the armrest, figuring that if the closest body part to Ethan is his feet, he's in the clear of any further accidental brushes that might break down his walls.

"Which one is your favorite?" Ethan asks. "That seems like a good place to start."

Taylor runs a finger down the table of contents, trying hard not to imagine what it might be like to trace this very finger along the furry bit of chest peeking out over the loose collar of Ethan's T-shirt. He settles on *The Frog-King* and begins to read aloud, though attraction cakes the inside of his throat.

The crunch of cookies mingles with the too-appropriate ribbits of outdoor frogs and the clinking of glasses set on coasters. Back and forth the book is passed, over and over. For an hour, maybe more. The couch becomes sinkier and lovelier beneath them.

"I like these," Ethan says. "At least, unlike the Disney ones, they don't all end in a massive marriage, as if that's the only way to be happy."

Taylor drains the last of his wine and asks a question he probably shouldn't ask. "Would you ever marry again?" He passes the book to Ethan for him to pick the next story.

"Naw."

It's a weird answer. Nearly noncommittal. Taylor feigns a glance in his direction. His face is a mask of mismatched emotions. Eyes bright. Mouth tipped down. Eyebrows going off in their own directions. "Why's that?" He has to wrestle the question out around a mysterious rock that's lodged in his throat.

"I'm just not sure it's the magic formula the stories suggest it is. Rings and paperwork don't necessitate promises kept and steadfast happiness," he says forlornly. Taylor's heart goes out to him. He's been broken up with, but divorce seems like a much messier affair.

Taylor's at a loss for what to say to that, so he allows Ethan to read on.

Ethan tests out a falsetto to play Rapunzel. There's not a note of self-consciousness in his portrayal. He wonders why Amy ever referred to Ethan as too dreamy or too romantic. Taylor doesn't know how too much of either of those qualities could ever be bad.

Two glasses of wine deep, Taylor swears he's only resting his weary eyes as Ethan goes on with the tale. He won't go to sleep yet. He's listening, envisioning. The illustrations from the book come alive on the insides of his eyelids until the projector of his mind blinks off and everything is black and quiet and peaceful.

Color doesn't come back until he's jostled. A newfound weightlessness overtakes his body.

Is this a dream where he's soaring above the clouds?

No. He goes from limp to rigid. His body is alert, but his mind is...somewhere else. Another dimension, maybe.

When his eyes finally adjust, he's met with a tired-looking Ethan glancing down at him from above. Oh, he's being carried? That makes no sense. This is definitely a dream.

"Where are we going?" Taylor asks in a scraping whisper. His throat and mouth are dry from the wine. His head is a Weeble Wobble.

"Oh." Ethan's cheeks redden. So do the tips of his ears. "I was just going to get you to bed. That couch—it's unforgiving. Trust me. I wouldn't wish that kind of sleep on my worst enemy. Sorry. I can put you down."

Taylor, relishing the cozy nearness and downright chivalry, shakes his head. "No, we're almost there." He nuzzles his head farther into Ethan's broad, sexy chest. His pecs have a pleasing squish to them, and his big arms are like a gently swinging hammock that Taylor never wants to roll out of.

By dream logic, Ethan should be taking Taylor straight to the master bedroom and having his way with him, but they end up in the guest room. Jeez. Even Taylor's subconscious is trying to do the right thing here. *Boring.*

Ethan sets dream-Taylor down in the guest bed and pulls the covers up around him so that they're snug against his body. This kind of attentive care was unheard of in the Frost household. New kids came quickly, so if one was old enough to walk, one was old enough to put themselves to bed. There was no babying, no coddling. There was care, yes, but it was doled out in increments, in waves. Who needed it most and at which minute?

All muscle tension leaks out of Taylor and gets absorbed by the mattress. The air thuds with tenderness and warmth and fervid attraction. Taylor, sensing this dream scenario about to come to an end, slides up onto one elbow and brushes that one unruly, curled strand of blond, silken hair out of Ethan's face. "Good night," he says.

Then, because it's a dream and in dreams the rules of society don't matter, he pitches forward and kisses Ethan on the mouth. The scratch of his beard is a welcome sensation, and his lips are as soft as velvet.

The last thing Taylor sees are Ethan's widened, blue-gray eyes before the scene in his mind vignettes at the edges, culminating in a curtain of black.

Twelve

ETHAN

The flavor of cabernet sauvignon had only ever been just okay until Ethan tasted it on Taylor Frost's lips.

It was a quick kiss. A chaste kiss. A kiss that could mean nothing or everything.

A kiss—Ethan's first in some time—that is occupying so much of his brain space that he likely will get nothing productive done today.

"Why do you look like that?" Gabriel asks, rattling by the reception desk with his toolbox in one hand and a coffee from How Do You Brew in the other.

"Look like what?" Ethan asks, hackles up.

"I'm not sure. Like you took an edible and put on a Bruce Springsteen record."

Ethan squawks, "Is that what you think I do in my spare time?"

"I have *seen* you do that in your spare time," he says with oomph. "That time you asked me to come over and help you with the hot water heater. I was late. I think you thought I wouldn't show."

"In fairness, you're not always the most reliable when it comes to timetables," he says, coming out from behind his desk to reorganize the brochures in the stand near the entrance. Barely anybody takes them these days what with Google and Yelp, but this wood unit has been there since they opened, and he can't bring himself to part with it.

"Says the guy who arrived fifteen minutes late this morning, and I had to check in the first guests." The sides of Gabriel's mouth draw up as if by fishing hooks. "Oh, *meu amigo*. You got laid last night, didn't you?"

Ethan's stomach hardens. "No."

"Hey, your secret's safe with me." Gabriel clicks his tongue.

"First off, I know that's not true. You tell Giselle everything."

"I'm not supposed to tell my wife about my friend's escapades?" he asks, eyebrow quirked and hands spread. "Your secret's safe with *us*."

Ethan deadpans, "There's no secret to tell. We had some wine, we read some stories, he fell asleep on the couch and I carried him to bed."

"Whose bed?" His eyebrow quirks up even higher.

"*His* bed. The guest bed. The bed in Samara's room."

"You *carried* him?"

His fists clench even though he's holding brochures for the Calico art gallery. The glossy paper crunches into a ball in his palm. He'll have to go into town and replace these. "You know firsthand how awful that couch is to sleep on. Remember years and years ago when you and Giselle were fighting?"

"I learned my lesson. I don't critique her pasteles de nata anymore. But it seems like you don't learn your lesson *ever*. The lesson about how I inevitably get everything out of you eventually, so tell me now or tell me later, but you'll slip up and I'm going to—"

"He kissed me! Okay, happy?" Ethan slaps his hands against his thighs.

Gabriel sports a shit-eating smirk. "You dirty dog."

"I am not—"

"Help! Please, I need some help." A woman rushes into the lobby. Her hair is a mess, her sunglasses are half falling off and her body language is frantic. He places her as Gus's mom from the archery lesson and the story time yesterday.

"Ma'am, what's happened?" Ethan asks.

"My son— He's—" she attempts to catch her breath "—wandered off. He does this sometimes. We checked all the usual spots and with the pond and the woods and the road, I'm… I need to find him."

Ethan snaps the walkie-talkie off his belt buckle and immediately radios the entire staff to start looking. "Don't worry," he reassures her. "We'll find him. He can't have gone far."

Adrenaline pumps through his bloodstream as the search ensues. Gabriel branches off in a different direction so they cover more ground. Birds chirp happily from the treetops, but their calls have an eerie ring to them. Birds push their babies from their nests as early as twelve days after they're born. A human parent could never. The urge to protect, to keep near, is too strong. God, he misses Samara more than anything, which zeroes in his focus until a familiar tie-dyed hoodie steps into his path.

"What's wrong? You looked panicked," says Taylor.

His heart palpitates inside his chest, and his lungs feel incapable of gulping in enough oxygen. Somehow, he manages to spit out, "There's a child missing. We're all looking for him." He doesn't stop to converse. Instead, he continues around Taylor on the path. If his panic over Gus missing met the panic over Taylor's good-night kiss, he'd be too dizzy to go on. His knees would cease to function.

A second set of footsteps crunch on the path behind him. "It's okay. We're handling it." The words come out gruff, and they burn a little in his throat.

"Have you checked the pool house?" Taylor asks, suddenly in lockstep beside him, undeterred by Ethan's remark.

"No. It's closed. The pool is closed."

"When has a Closed sign ever stopped a curious kid before?"

Ethan doubles back without giving Taylor any credit for the good idea. They're picking up speed as they pass the picnic area. The wooden door is locked and sealed, but he locates the right key on his bulbous key ring anyhow and pushes inside. The bathrooms and curtained changing stations are disquietingly empty. Like the moment in an '80s slasher movie before the masked killer jumps from his hiding spot.

Ethan still hastily knocks on every stall door just to be safe.

Already back outside, Taylor scouts the perimeter of the pool area. The mist-sheened cover is on, so there's no chance Gus tried to go for a swim, thankfully. Ethan furiously rakes his hands through his hair, nearly clawing out the pomade he sometimes uses on mornings when his hair won't cooperate.

Taylor appears focused but calm. "We're going to find him. Like you said last night, kids are surprisingly resilient."

"It's not Gus that I'm worried most about. It's his mom," Ethan admits over the noxious pounding in his ears. "I would not wish this feeling on any parent. It's the worst." He clutches his chest.

"Samara doesn't seem like the type to run away," says Taylor as they inspect along the tree line at the perimeter of the property. What are they even looking for? Footprints? Hansel-esque bread crumbs?

"When she was eight, we'd driven over an hour and some change to the Palisades mall to buy Amy a birthday gift. Samara had watched some teen movie that had a mall in it, and we don't have one local, so I figured, what the heck? The novelty will be fun. We'll shop in person instead of online for a change," he recounts as they venture into the trees. "I regretted it immediately. I forgot how crowded and loud malls are. I was in a bad mood. I left her at a table in the food court while I went to order her chicken nuggets and, when I came back, she'd disappeared. I frantically started asking everyone around if they'd seen my daughter. This was before she had her own cell phone. I felt like the world's worst dad. I was scared out of my mind."

"I bet," Taylor says.

"I remembered she'd thrown a fit in Sephora over a lip gloss I wouldn't buy for her. She was too young. We were there to get her mom makeup wipes, not some Jenner-approved nonsense. I found her at the register, talking to the salesperson, asking if she could pay for the lip gloss with two quarters and a punch card for Froyo. The saleswoman was a parent and knew immediately what I was going through from the frenzied look in my eyes."

"Did you buy Samara the lip gloss?" Taylor asks.

Ethan sighs loudly. "I…did. Not because I'm a pushover but because the saleswoman was going to give it to us for free, and I figured if I couldn't hit home the lesson about listening to your parents, I could at least show her that you should only accept gifts if you're in need."

"Not sure I agree with that."

"It was a seven-dollar lip gloss, and I got the woman's employee discount anyway. She'd done enough."

"You're a good dad, Ethan," Taylor says.

Ethan wants to balk at this. How can one be a good dad from hundreds and hundreds of miles away? But the force behind Taylor's words makes them sink in. He is fiercely protective of his daughter. He imagines this is more than Taylor can say about either of his own parents. "Thanks," Ethan says, smiling down at Taylor. "I wonder where Gus's dad is in all this…?"

Taylor's features brighten. "Wait, the kid that's missing is Gus? The one from the archery class?"

"Yeah, why?"

"Because at the end of the lesson, he was begging his parents to go over and play with Nana. Does Nana have a doghouse anywhere?" Taylor asks.

Their brains meld. They sprint off in the direction of Ethan's cottage. For a few minutes, there's nothing but the sounds of their panting and the soles of their shoes slamming the ground beneath.

In the distance, Gus kneels down beside Nana, whose head pops out from the inlet of her teal-colored doghouse. Her wagging tail thumps against the inside walls, sounding like a drumbeat. She perks up at the boom of Ethan's voice.

Gus stands up and steps back with a posture that screams *I've been caught.*

"What are you doing out here?" Ethan asks Gus as they jog up to the house.

He shrugs innocently, lips zipped. Shame zaps off him.

"It's okay. You're not in trouble," Taylor says, though Ethan's not so sure from the way Gus's mom was looking when he left the lobby. A harsh grounding might be in the child's future.

Gus's wide eyes tilt up. "My mom wouldn't let me pet the dog yesterday. I just wanted to say hi. And today she's been reading her stupid book all day, and I got bored, so I went looking and I got lost, but then I found this cottage and saw the doghouse and I'm sorry. I shouldn't have. I know."

How many times had Ethan wandered into a different aisle in the grocery store as a kid, giving his mom a heart attack? Boredom is a beast for those with ADHD. Not that Ethan should be diagnosing a child he barely knows. He just sees bits of his own neurodivergence in the kid's behaviors. That's all. A kindred spirit that he hopes grows up with more support than he had.

So instead of reprimanding him or scolding him, Ethan leashes up Nana and together all four of them return to the main resort.

"A lost boy with Nana. So Peter-Pan-coded," says Taylor to lighten the mood.

Ethan can breathe again now that the boy is in sight, so he lets out a hearty laugh and leads the charge to reunite the family.

Thirteen

TAYLOR

Earlier this morning, when Taylor looked in the bathroom mirror before brushing his teeth, he knew instantly that that kiss wasn't a dream. He'd done it.

Oh, he'd really *done it*.

There was a light redness above his upper lip. He has intensely sensitive skin—barely a hint of facial stubble ever—so what appeared there in the mirror was unmistakably the pesky scratch of another person's beard. Even one as fresh-smelling and soft as Ethan's.

I'd suffer for that scratch again. That sentence races through his mind as he sits cross-legged on the floor in front of the coffee table. There's a wicker basket in front of him filled with the faux grass that comes out at Easter and all the luxuries and necessities Samara's friends will need for a full weekend of birthday fun.

Three finished baskets sit to his left and the thirteen yet to be touched sit on his right. An unlucky number. Let's hope it's not an omen.

Because as much as he would like to kiss Ethan again, he can't. He loves his job. Kissing Ethan again would be a swift, certain kick to the end of the unemployment line if Amy caught wind of it.

The front door lumbers open. Ethan tumbles inside as Nana skirts around him, already off her leash and jetting toward Taylor. Taylor greets her with open arms and gentle pets, though he could do without the lolling, dripping tongue that is ruining some of the sparkly tissue paper.

"Nana, heel, girl." She dutifully follows Ethan's instructions. "Sorry about that."

"All good," Taylor says as Ethan slips off his coat and hangs it on a hook by the door. "No more mishaps today?"

"Managing a resort is almost all mishaps," Ethan says. "But no more major ones. Thank you for your help with Gus earlier."

Taylor waves that away. Too many other irksome thought-flies are buzzing around him at the moment. He stands and brushes his joggers clean of glitter. He's going to need to run the vacuum several times tomorrow, but that's not the current priority. "In the chaos earlier, I didn't get to apologize for what happened last night."

"No need," Ethan says, already bounding across the room to fill Nana's bowl. As if this conversation were a gas station bathroom he needs to exit as quickly as possible for fear of contracting some sort of disease.

"*I* need, though," Taylor says, cringing at the plaintive way it comes out. Still, it does the trick. The clang of kibble land-ing in a plastic bowl stops and Ethan stands to face him head-on. "To clear the air, I mean. I'm sorry I kissed you last night."

"Hmm."

Is that a grumble of acceptance? Dissent? Taylor rambles on without any further hints to go off. "It's no excuse, really, but I was half-asleep. Part of me thought I was dreaming. We can forget about it. Simple as that." It's a feeble offer when Taylor's brain has already committed every millisecond of that kiss to permanent memory.

A gulf-like silence stretches between them. Then, Ethan says contemplatively, "Is it really that simple?"

The question is a powder keg plopped between them. Taylor's unable to form words.

Ethan goes on, "I don't kiss people often, so when I do kiss someone, I don't easily forget. I'd be happy to move past it if that's what you were suggesting, but only if you answer a question first."

"Okay," Taylor manages to say.

Ethan's voice is as steady as a metronome at rest when he asks, "Did you feel anything?"

This has to be a trick question. All kinds of caution tape have been torn down by four seemingly harmless words flung carelessly into the air. Taylor has zero seconds to catch those words because he's too busy building a courtroom-worthy defense. If even a fraction of truth flies out, his massive, inappropriate crush is sure to surface next. "It was late. I'm honestly not sure. I wasn't fully awake to consider it."

Okay, so he's no Erin Brockovich.

"Are you awake now?" Ethan asks.

Another four words. Another powder keg. Another reason for Taylor's heart to combust from overwork.

Without thinking too hard about it, he nods. The only possible answer to the question when his throat is this tight. When his wants are staging a mutiny against his rationality. When was the last time he allowed himself to have something he really wanted all to himself?

"I could kiss you this time to get us to a proper answer," Ethan says.

Taylor doesn't process Ethan crossing the room. All he's aware of is the blue-gray of Ethan's round eyes, which remind him of the ocean at Moonlight State Beach at sunrise.

There Ethan is. In kissing distance. Looking handsome and rugged and needful. Want is a fearsome wave Taylor intends to surf to shore.

"Kiss me," Taylor recklessly whispers.

The hazy memory of last night is overwritten by this. A full-body press. Pillowy lips that don't quit. A tongue that sneaks out of its cave for seconds of tantalizing exploration.

Taylor gasps at the rush. Finds himself clasping Ethan's forearms for support, so he doesn't faint from the sharp spike in blood pressure. It's like his cardiovascular system doesn't know where to send the blood; his nervous system doesn't know how to compute any of these sensations. His body is at delicious war with itself.

And he likes it. No, he more than likes it. He could live inside this sensation forever and a day and never grow tired of it. Because he likes Ethan's business acumen and his buttery laugh and his neurodiverse mind. This kiss is all the evidence he needs of that.

"I feel something," Taylor admits when Ethan breaks off the kiss. You can't cross a line that's already been erased, right? The truth can't topple any carefully preserved restraint at this point.

"Me, too," Ethan growls. *Really* growls. "It's against my leg."

Embarrassment knocks Taylor backward until he stumbles into the couch. His overexcitement is *showing*. This is one hazard of going commando all the time.

"Please don't be embarrassed," Ethan says. Less of a growl, more of a groan. "I'm showing my feelings, too." He bows his head, which Taylor takes as permission to look. The front of Ethan's jeans is spectacularly full and growing more so by the second. The millisecond, even. There's a nearly imperceptible twitch that makes Taylor gasp.

"Must be hard to take care of your *feelings* with your hand still busted up," Taylor says. The words are coming faster than his brain filter has any fighting chance of keeping back.

Ethan honest to God chortles. "Yeah, you can say that again."

Again. A tantalizing idea drapes cozily across Taylor's shoulders. "I've been your right hand before…" The grilling. The archery. Third time's the charm?

"Are you suggesting…?"

Some tucked-away confidence slinks out of its hiding spot. "Yeah."

Two steps and ten million heartbeats later, Ethan's lips land on Taylor's again. Taylor sags against the back of the couch, scooting up to sit on it. It wobbles slightly, so he grabs tight to the thick, scratchy flannel of Ethan's shirt. Ethan doesn't even flinch.

Ethan's immovability only heightens his attractiveness. Firm chest, soft belly, strong arms. Stable. So fucking solid.

If Ethan Golding wanted a rag doll tonight, Taylor would comply.

But Ethan's persistent kisses say otherwise. They say, *Slow*. They say, *Sweet*. They say, *I may look unbreakable but I'm not*. His still-bandaged but healing hand is proof of that.

Taylor strokes Ethan's beard to signal that he's up for the game no matter how Ethan wants to play it. The rules are completely theirs to make.

"Let's get more comfortable," Ethan scrapes out.

Taylor starts toward the hallway, but Ethan tugs him back. "Stay here."

Taylor can't complain about the discomfort of couch sex when Ethan is unbuttoning his shirt with his unharmed left hand, exposing his thick neck inch by inch, which triangles down to broad shoulders. On one, there's a tattooed compass. On the other, a bow and arrow. Between those trunk-like arms is a hair-covered torso. Two perfectly pink nipples stand out against the dark, brushed fur that Taylor itches to run his fingers through.

"Your turn," Ethan says, nodding down at Taylor's hoodie. It slips off so fast it's as if he were never wearing it. He flings it across the room, uncaring of the baskets and supplies he knocks over. He's afraid if he loses eye contact with Ethan that they'll both put a stop to this.

For now, sense has been banished outside to the cold

Catskills night; its breath fogs up the glass of the nearby window as it disapprovingly watches this heady moment unfold.

The room grows hotter as Ethan struggles to undo his jeans. "Let me," Taylor offers. He slides across the couch cushions, ignoring the slight static shock against the bottom of his joggers, and pops that troublesome button out of the way. The sound of Ethan's zipper parting sends shockwaves through Taylor's body. Instinctually, he reaches out to plunge his hand into the depths of the plaid cotton boxer shorts that do nothing to contain Ethan's cock, but Ethan's calloused hand comes down over Taylor's to halt him.

Gently, Ethan's right knee finds purchase on the couch between Taylor's spread legs. With a searing kiss, he tips Taylor onto his back until they're both horizontal and parallel, their bare torsos grazing each other. Desire sinks its vampiric teeth into Taylor's neck.

"You don't need to be gentle with me." Taylor swings his legs around Ethan's waist, uses his calves to tug Ethan closer. Flush. A grunt escapes Ethan's mouth as Taylor nibbles on Ethan's bottom lip.

Something about that thrust. That nibble. Those eager actions in quick succession break the spell.

Ethan's eyes snap open, and Taylor is helpless, lying there as Ethan retreats to the other side of the couch. His unbandaged hand swipes down his face.

Taylor's stomach drops. "I'm sorry."

"It's okay. I—I liked it."

"Then why are you all the way over there?" Taylor suddenly feels like he should stand and grab his hoodie from the floor. Cover up. What if Ethan can see how fast his heart is beating through his chest?

"Because I need you to be gentle with *me*." This is a voice Taylor hasn't heard before. It reminds him of a guitar string plucked and then distorted by a too-loud amplifier. "If you want to continue, I mean."

"Yes. Absolutely. Whatever you need. I had a moment. It won't happen again." Taylor's chest grows tight as he says this. He hates how his selfishness can lead to impulsiveness and impulsiveness can lead to this, the hottest man he's ever had the pleasure of kissing feeling the need to withdraw from him. He wants to pour cement into the fault line he's accidentally created between them through unabashed neediness.

"Because I haven't done this in a while." Ethan's confident posture closes in.

"I understand."

"And it was a lot at once."

"I totally get it."

"And you're *so* sexy."

Taylor's overtaken by a full-body blush that makes his dick pulse. "Thank you. So are you."

"Appreciate it." A side smirk weasels up onto his face. "It's just been me and my—" he holds up his bandaged hand "—well, claw right now...for some time, so I need a bit of rev time to settle into the pulling and the biting and the roughness."

Taylor sits up, levitated by an idea. "We could start there. You could show me what you do when you're alone, when your hand isn't a claw."

Ethan lets loose a nervous laugh. "Would you...like that?"

Taylor's nod is almost involuntary. "So much."

Ethan freezes for a moment. A thousand thoughts whiz through his eyes before he leaves and comes back with a towel and a bottle of water-based lube. He throws Taylor a glance that reads, *Are you sure about this?*

Taylor nods encouragingly, hiking up his joggers and crossing to the corner where there's an armchair angled for the best view. Ethan shucks his jeans and socks. His wide, bare feet are kicked up on the coffee table. Unlike the palms of his hands, the soles of his feet are smooth, inviting. Taylor's cock responds in kind, standing at attention, ready for one hell of a show...

Fourteen

ETHAN

Taylor's eyes rake over his naked torso from across the room as Ethan strokes his cock with his nondominant hand beneath the thin fabric of his boxers. It is not the aphrodisiac he hoped it would be.

From time to time, Ethan turns on a cam model to get off to. His dick answers to the spontaneity, the banter with the live chat. But he never felt a desire to be an exhibitionist himself.

Now, in the limelight, under Taylor's smize, he can't keep his hard-on. Nervousness invades every touch of his hand. Every tug. Every tweak. The loudest sounds in the room are the wall clock ticking, and his own ragged, annoyed breaths.

His mind insists on wandering. Is he doing this well? Is Taylor turned on? He seems to be, but he's twenty-seven. When Ethan was twenty-seven, a phallic-shaped monument could give him an erection. The slightest breeze against his cock could cause it to stir.

Jesus. This isn't going to work.

Taylor, in a calm voice, asks, "Is this how you usually do it? In silence?"

He shakes his head. "I usually put on, uh…"

"You can say porn."

Heat rises to his cheeks. "I was getting there."

"What kind of porn do you put on?" Taylor asks as his hand moves from the armrest to his crotch where he starts groping himself through his sweatpants. Ethan's dick jumps at that, making words nearly impossible. "You can tell me. It won't scandalize me or anything. I'm intimately familiar with almost every Pornhub category."

"Every one?" he asks, eyebrow raised. "Even 'virtual reality?'"

"I was exaggerating," Taylor admits.

"I know. I was stalling." The back of his neck becomes sweaty. So do his palms. Good for slickness, bad for his composure in this highly new situation.

"Put it on," Taylor says. "If you want. You don't need to tell me. I'll hear it. It's not for me. It's for you. Make like I'm not here."

That's downright impossible. The sexiest twink—*twunk? Doesn't matter*—he's ever seen is sitting in his living room with a rock-hard dick. Ignoring him would be like ignoring a giraffe in the middle of the highway.

However, he's here and he's horny so he tries. He grabs the remote, turns on the Smart TV, and queues up one of his favorite MMF scenes. It's a sensual one with none of that cheesy acting in the beginning. No story, just sex. That's how he likes his porn. Light on the talking, heavy on the penetration.

As the scene plays out, despite having watched it a couple dozen times, his cock still gets hard and begs for his hand back. Opening the fly of his boxers, he hauls out his dick and coats it in a layer of lube. The coldness startles him at first, but a few enjoyable strokes warm it up and help him relax into his pleasure.

For a moment, he closes his eyes, channels his breathing. The skin right beneath the underside of his circumcised cock head has always been deliriously sensitive. He teases that spot with the pads of his pointer and middle finger. An unself-conscious moan gets away from him before he remembers he has an audience and has every reason to be self-conscious.

Only, when his gaze pings to Taylor, Taylor's joggers are around his ankles. And his long, left-curving, uncut cock is on full display. The dick-print he'd seen that first day Taylor arrived had been accurate. Taylor's got quite the impressive pipe.

Ethan's dick grows unimaginably harder at the erotic sight gracing his living room. Thinking entirely with his dick, he asks, "Would you like to come watch with me?"

"I've got a perfect view already," Taylor says, then bites his lip.

"You could get a closer one." His own brazenness surprises him. Need is a cobra in his chest ready to strike.

Taylor stands, steps out of his joggers, and strides toward the couch—completely at home in his nakedness—before sitting where he sat last night. Too far away for Ethan's liking. "Closer," Ethan growls.

Where is that coming from? This low, grumbly, resonant

sound. It's definitely not the teddy-bear-with-a-head-cold voice people in his life mock him for. It's more keyed in. Deeper, somehow.

Taylor acts swiftly, stealing the space between them so he's right on the next cushion, ass planted on the towel Ethan laid down. Wonderment swirls through Ethan's chest. Which lucky star should he thank for this wildest-dream scenario?

He's so entranced in the heat of the moment that he barely registers when Taylor asks for the lube. "May I?" Ethan asks.

After Taylor nods, he squeezes the bottle over the tip of Taylor's large cock. A shiny, slick coating of lube drizzles down the sides. Taylor's eyebrows egg him on further, but it's the words he says next that make him quiver. "You can touch it. Rub it in."

Even though Ethan's hand is shaking, he grips Taylor's shaft. The first firm touch is enough for a moan to flee from Taylor's mouth.

"Too much?" Ethan asks.

"Not at all."

Ethan stops what he's doing to himself and focuses on Taylor. The up and the down. The torment and retreat. It's an art form he's perfected with his own cock. But cocks are like snowflakes, yeah? No two are the same. That means no two explode with the same tried-and-true tricks. And Taylor's uncut, unlike Ethan, which poses its own enticing challenges.

"Tell me what you like," Ethan says firmly, needing some coaching to ensure he's doing his best work.

"That," Taylor says in response to his medium-tight slow stroke. "I like that."

After several moments of Taylor lounging back, arms loose

at his sides in ecstasy, he perks up. Perhaps too close to the inevitable. "Can I have a turn?"

Ethan swallows hard, yet nods. He can't recall the last time another man touched his cock, which only reifies how badly he needs this.

Surprisingly, Taylor slips off the couch and onto his knees, maneuvering himself between Ethan's legs and the coffee table. Ethan might just bust hands-free from this drool-inducing sight. This beautiful, floppy-haired stud is peering up at him with these lustful brown eyes that contain hidden worlds.

Taylor's talented. There's no question about it. The moment he locks his grip around Ethan's shaft, Ethan is gone for him. His own left hand could never compete with the expert pull of Taylor's satiny fist. The corded muscles braided up Taylor's forearm bulge with the work of it, but the expression on Taylor's face makes it seem like he's made for this job.

For a minute, Taylor breaks the intense eye contact. His gaze wanders south to Ethan's cock, "It's so pretty," Taylor whispers, sounding mesmerized. *Dickmatized.*

Taylor pulls his hand away so they can both look, really look. It's maybe six and a half inches (he hasn't broken out the measuring tape since college) and above average in thickness. That second part became apparent after a few spoiled hookups over the stretch being too much for his receptive partner. Whatever its misgivings, his cock has always provided him pleasure, and for that he's been grateful. But, pretty? That seems extreme.

Yet the glimmer in Taylor's eyes makes his cock tremor, makes him appreciate his member anew. He even appreciates

Taylor more as his head rears closer to Ethan's crotch. Creating scale. "Can I taste it?"

Ethan's chest hiccups at the request. "There's lube all over it. I'm not sure you'll want—"

"I don't care," Taylor says. The directness and ineffable hunger are what push him to agree.

Kissing Taylor's mouth was enchanting. Now to have those same supple lips suctioned around his dick is like being transported to a fantasy realm. His fingers, laced together, find lodging on the top of his head where he almost expects a crown because Taylor's making him feel like a fucking king.

Taylor picks up the pace as he scratches his trimmed nails down the insides of Ethan's sensitive thighs. The tickle is nothing compared to the pressure building inside his cock, the tightness he feels in his heavy balls. There's a slapping just out of sight. Taylor must be stroking himself in sync.

Not once do Ethan's eyes jump from Taylor—brushing his bangs out of his eyes as his mouth continues to move—to the screen where the porn is still looping. He may never watch porn again. He could get off on the memory of this moment for a million and one years if he had to.

He feels wanted. He feels cared for. He feels…so close to unloading.

"I'm right there," he says in the growl he's growing to like.

"Come for me," Taylor says, removing his mouth but not his hand, which takes over the same exact rhythm, pressure…

Sounds Ethan has never heard or made before rip out of his mouth as his whole body shudders. A shower of cum rains up his torso at a distance and power he hasn't experienced in a long time. He doesn't live inside this too long, though, because whimpers break out beneath him. Fuck if he's going to miss Taylor reaching orgasm.

He resurfaces quickly enough to lean forward, place an encouraging hand on Taylor's shoulder, and growl out, "Let it out, Taylor. Let it go."

And he does. It's a similarly impressive shot that nearly clears his right shoulder. Taylor's face softens from ecstasy. A lazy, easy smile takes the place of an openmouthed pant.

Ethan pauses the porn, laying a blanket of silence across the room. He doesn't even possess enough energy to shimmy the towel out from under him to clean up.

"I could fall asleep right here," Ethan says on the most luxurious exhale.

"I thought you said that couch was unforgiving," Taylor says playfully. "Or was that just a convenient excuse?"

Ethan's heart beats out a new message: *I want more of this.*

Fifteen

ETHAN

"The roofer is here," Gabriel radios to Ethan, who still hasn't gotten out the door this morning.

He overslept, which was to be expected after being up so late.

No, not with Taylor. That ripped-right-from-a-movie fantasy ended after they cleaned up, shared a chaste cheek kiss in the hallway, and then retreated to their separate bedrooms.

It's not like he could invite Taylor in to share his bed, right? Taylor had shut the door to the guest room by the time he was even hovering close to an answer.

Which meant he awoke sometime around 2:00 a.m., drenched in sweat, hard as an obelisk, and jerked himself off to the memory of Taylor's eyes lingering over his naked body. And again, earlier today in the shower, when the hot spray carved up memories of the inviting wet warmth of Taylor's mouth. It dug out questions of: *Will I ever experience that again?*

The last time he had a sex drive like this, he was still living in his parents' house. It feels like a scientist has done an experiment on his brain chemistry, and now he's incongruously sex-starved.

He rushes out the door to meet Lee, the best roofer in town, to see what can be done about the Snow White cottage.

Lee is a tall man with big arms and tattoos that climb down the sides of his neck and unmask themselves when he splays out his hands. His coworker—a preppy guy, Lee's perfect antithesis—describes to Gabriel what needs to be done. They've driven their truck up and into the first enclave of cottages. Usually this wouldn't be allowed in the middle of a busy day during spring break, but it's gotta get done.

"How's it looking?" Ethan asks Lee, getting down to business. Bypassing any apology for his tardiness. He's worked with Lee long enough to trust him implicitly. Whatever he thinks needs to be done will be done, and he won't be charged a cent over what's fair. Gabriel, on the other hand, would take an apology as a reason to yoke him over what he's been up to.

"Nothing a half day's work can't fix," says Lee, meeting Ethan for a firm handshake.

Ethan avoids Gabriel's eyes. Even though he senses them dissecting his every microexpression. He will not display even an ounce of his disappointment over this extremely expeditious timeline. One, because his business comes first and the cottage needs fixing for Samara's party, which is mere days away. Two, because Gabriel can't know about the fiery sex he had last night.

Gabriel is, for all intents and purposes, Ethan's closest friend. That is complicated by their working relationship.

That is further complicated by the fact that his wife is Amy's friend. Still. Even after she moved away five years ago, they keep in constant contact.

The kiss he let slip. That can always be forgiven. But this is being kept sealed, locked and heavily guarded. Too bad, too, because he really could use someone to talk about this with. This is the price he has to pay to avoid the fallout of Amy's judgment and retribution. While she's not vindictive, she has been known to overreact and then use Samara as a chess piece she guards with her petty pawns.

"We should be out of your hair right after lunchtime," Lee says.

"There's no rush, Lee." Sure, he schooled his expression, but his words have a way of slipping out. Like last night when he said he couldn't just forget about that sleepy good night kiss. "I only mean, take the time you need. The cottage isn't needed until Samara's friends arrive."

He'd face-palm if he could. That's the last thing he should've said.

"Half day was overselling it," Lee says. "Three hours, tops. Seriously, your tarp work saved you from any further damage."

Fantastic, his oversight brought Taylor closer and now his foresight is ripping him away right when things are about to get good.

Not that they should get good, or better, rather. His head is so jumbled with desire and guilt and lust and shame, but what's overriding all of that is a tiny voice. At first, it sounded like his conscience. Now it sounds more like Amy, reprimanding him for making poor choices.

"How could you?" she'd say bitterly.

But the only response his mind supplies is, *How could I not?* For real, from the moment Taylor stepped foot in the lobby, Ethan felt a seismic shift. As if an earthquake were about to roll in and wreck the resort he's loved since it was only a plot of land and a dream. But now four dinners, two bottles of wine, one bag of mint Milanos and two exceptional orgasms later, he wonders if that rumbling he felt was isolated to his tiny square of floor. If the universe was only signaling that Ethan's carefully walled life was about to crumble, not his livelihood.

Storybook Endings is only a place; general manager is only a job. Maybe Taylor Frost's youthful optimism is cracking Ethan open, giving him the energy to imagine a new beginning for himself. Onward and upward.

"We'll leave you to it, then," Ethan says, clapping his long-time contractor on the back and walking off without Gabriel.

Gabriel, however, doesn't get the memo that Ethan wants to be left alone. "The cottage isn't needed? What's going on in that house of yours?"

"Nothing. I'm just not going to make Taylor move again. He's got his supplies for the welcome baskets everywhere. His clothes are unpacked. His groceries are in my fridge. It would be rude to ask him to go," Ethan says gruffly.

"Sounds like he's made himself at home." Ethan doesn't need to glance over to know Gabriel's eyebrows are going up and down at a mile a minute.

"He's my guest. He has every right to."

"Oh, he's *your* guest? I thought he was Amy's guest."

"I don't have time to get into the semantics. There's a wedding tonight. I've got to check in with our event staff. Please make sure Lee has everything he needs and treat them to complimentary lunch from The Thirsty Goat. Whatever they want. On the house," Ethan says, stalking off and in the direction of the barn.

If everything's going right with the roof repair, everything's going wrong with the impending wedding.

"Our officiant's flight got canceled," cries one of the brides into her mom's shoulder. "The next flight out won't get her here in time. What are we going to do?" Her auburn hair is already falling out of the strategically pinned updo somebody no doubt spent at least an hour perfecting.

The barn is bedecked for a queer wedding ceremony. Rainbow-colored tulle swans between rows of white folding chairs. There's an arch of purple flowers at the end of a long, rectangular carpet. Employees dance around the perimeter, obviously attempting to eavesdrop on the unfolding situation. Nobody is quite sure what to do.

"I could do it," one of the bridesmaids says. She's a dark-skinned woman with a short fade and a nose ring. "It can't take that long to get ordained online."

"I think there's paperwork we wouldn't get in time," says the mother.

The second bride steps into the picture. She's got milky white skin and platinum blond hair down to her butt. She's paired a sparkly tiara with her tuxedo. "What if we do the ceremony tonight as planned and then do the courthouse thing later? Tonight will be for everyone and that part will be for us."

The room is so silent you could hear a pin drop, and they

literally do when the first bride shakes her head. Several more golden pins fall to the floor. "It's all ruined."

This is a severe overreaction, but Ethan recalls being in a state himself on his wedding day, pacing and carrying on and playing darts with his groomsmen just to let the jitters out. He may not believe in happily-ever-after or marriage as an institution any longer, but he runs a wedding destination for God's sake. He's intimately aware of how these types of rituals and ceremonies and dances and dinners can become integral to the fabric of a person's life. The last thing he wants is for these two seemingly lovely women to leave here with a gray cloud hanging over their relationship.

"Excuse me," Ethan interjects, stopping another brainstorm happening among five to six people in the wedding party. "My name is Ethan Golding. I'm the general manager here. I know I don't know either of you personally, but I happen to be ordained and would be overjoyed to officiate your ceremony if you'll allow me."

He's perhaps overselling his excitement with the word *overjoyed* paired with a cheesy, customer service smile. His gut roils. He tends to give every wedding on the property a wide berth whenever possible. The white dresses, the spilled mimosas, the flower petals. It's all a lot for him to process.

Bride Number Two says, "That's nice of you but—"

Bride Number One jumps in, "We accept! Thank you! Thank you! Thank you!"

"But it doesn't matter what I say because she's happy, so I'm happy," says Bride Number Two, squeezing Number One into her side. Her tone drips with truth. That's love for you, and love is something Ethan will never stop believing in.

He loves Samara, he loves Nana, he loves Gabriel and Giselle and he loves Storybook Endings Resort for all its faults. He's even open to the possibility of falling in and being in love again one day. Someday.

In his mind's eye, he conjures Taylor from last night in the hallway, cleaned up and back in his pajamas. Equally as beautiful as he was when he was buck naked and panting for him.

"Good night, Ethan," he'd said, a flattering pink flush still stuck to the tops of his cheeks.

"Good night, Taylor." Unsure what was appropriate, Ethan leaned in and, with his hand on Taylor's right elbow, he kissed that warm pink flush.

But there is no use considering an impossible future. Feelings are as fleeting as the weather. Today, a downpour. Tomorrow, a drought. That's the usual score, so he won't succumb to improbabilities.

For the next several hours, he talks with the brides—Sloane and Kimmie—so he can get a sense of their personalities. He's even able to coordinate with one of the mothers to get an e-mailed copy of the original officiant's script, so he can play mouthpiece instead of the all-knowing voice. Of course, he'll make plenty of tweaks so it comes out authentic.

Later, he finishes a few odds and ends at reception, then returns to the cottage in search of his best suit. It's been ages since he's worn it, which accounts for why he tears apart his already chaotic closet, but not for why it doesn't show up in the piles.

"Looking for something?"

Ethan jumps at the sound of Taylor's voice. He hadn't heard

the door or the footsteps, too frustrated by his fruitless hunt. "My suit."

"What's it look like?" Taylor's eyes scan the room. It's only then that Ethan realizes what an untenable mess he's made. That happens sometimes. He gets so lost in the haze of a task that he makes a million new tasks for himself in the process. Taylor appears entirely unfazed, his face showing zero judgment.

"Uh, it looks like…a suit?" Ethan rubs his sweaty palms on the front of his jeans, in patches where the denim is already worn and likely near tearing. Taylor yips out a laugh. "It won't come as much of a surprise that I don't dress up often. Not many reasons to, as of late."

"What reason do you have now?" Taylor asks, leaning in the door frame.

"The wedding tonight lost its officiant. I offered to stand in since I'm ordained."

"You are?" Taylor asks.

"Why do you sound so surprised?"

"I don't know. I guess I just thought…"

Ethan's eyes fall to the floor. "It was before the divorce. Started as a joke and became a thing among our friends."

"I see. Well, if I find the suit for you, do I get to witness this officiating?" Taylor asks, eyebrows up in apparent challenge.

Ethan folds his arms across his chest. "Why would you want to attend the wedding of two people you don't know?"

"I like weddings…" he says jovially. "I'm also curious what you look like in a suit."

Flattery gets you everywhere. "Fine. It's a deal."

Less than two minutes later, Taylor's back with the suit

hanging inside a dry cleaning bag. It crinkles loudly as Taylor hands it to him. "Here you are."

"I never stood a chance, did I?" Ethan asks.

Taylor shrugs, smiles shamelessly. "I remembered seeing it in the hall closet when I was on a hunt for a robe the night of the storm." He slowly backs out of the room, hands in his pockets, eyelashes fluttering. Too bad last night proved that this innocence is an act. "I'll leave you to get ready. What time should I be there?"

Sixteen

TAYLOR

It's amazing that a man who doesn't believe in marriage could bring an entire wedding venue to tears. Taylor reaches for the tissue he stuffed into the inside pocket of his blazer, sniffling at Ethan's words.

Ethan stands under the flower arch between the two brides. Taylor sits in the very last row of the barn, which is beautifully decorated with rustic touches. The acoustics are also top notch. Taylor feels the notes from the electric organ in his bones, causing goose bumps to dash up and down his arms.

Nothing causes more goose bumps, though, than Ethan Golding's impassioned musings on love and connection. He spins a speech as well as he can wear a suit. The tailored, charcoal number Taylor fished from the hall closet near the washing machine is lucky to be worn by such a man.

Ethan addresses the room. "We are not here to witness

Once Upon a Time… Kimmie and Sloane's love story began six years ago during a particularly memorable sorority rush." This garners laughter. "Today's ceremony marks a beautiful transition. A formal turning of the page to a new chapter— from partners to wives. Before this gorgeous crowd of family and friends, they publicly commit themselves to a long-lasting union of respect and honor."

Taylor's heart is a fritzing elevator, riding up into his throat and down into his stomach. Last night spilled the water glass all over the control panel. Now there's no telling what might happen as he listens with rapt attention.

"Love is an infinite resource. It constantly renews and replenishes," Ethan says, looking up from his note cards with a bashful smile. "Today, the romantic love between Kimmie and Sloane joins with all the love in this room and reforms stronger for the future. For that, we can rejoice."

Nobody in the room seems like the religious type but a few "hallelujahs" and "amens" get shouted out. Taylor folds his hands in his lap and tries not to read too much into Ethan's words. If he thinks about his own love life as a story, he's not sure he's ever truly picked up the pen to author it. But the man at the front of the room is providing ample inspiration to start, even if Ethan can't—or won't—play the second hero in it.

At the end of the sweet, sentimental ceremony, guests are ushered outside into a heated tent where appetizers and specialty cocktails are served under a canopy of twinkling lights. The happy couple goes off with the photographer to take pictures while the event staff turns over the barn for the full-scale reception and dance party.

Taylor holds ground beside the propped-open doors for

Ethan. The night air feels good on his warm cheeks where tear tracks are surely still visible. "Look what you did to me," he says jokingly, holding up a crumpled tissue in his fist.

"I take my duties seriously," Ethan says with a rumbling laugh. "Shall we head home?"

Ethan Golding should not be allowed to look like that and ask questions like that at the same time. He deserves jail for such a lethal combination. Of course Ethan means *his* home, but Taylor's brain brews up a steaming fantasy where it's *their* home, which he gulps down with fervor regardless of the scalding, permanent burn it may cause.

In stride, they start up the path. Ethan's hand brushes suspiciously close to Taylor's. He yearns for the lightest touch, to know whether last night meant something equally as salient to Ethan as it did to him.

Heart skittering, he's just about mustered the nerve to reach out for the hold and test the waters when they're intercepted by Sloane and Kimmie. "Where do you two think you're going?"

"Home," Ethan says. There it is. That word again. Taylor wants to live inside that word. Snuggle up inside the O with Ethan and never leave.

"Congratulations," Taylor says, sensing his fantasy usurp his critical thinking skills.

"You can't skip out now. The party's just getting started," says Sloane.

"We wouldn't want to overstay our welcome," Ethan says.

"Your welcome? You run the place and you saved our wedding. Get a kebab, grab a drink and come dance with us," Kimmie says.

"Please," Sloane begs, vowels stretched like Silly Putty.

Unable to resist, they U-turn back toward the tent, grab drinks—a draft beer for Ethan and a cosmo for Taylor—and they find an unoccupied table near the back corner to stand in.

The alcohol loosens Taylor's lips, so much so that he muses aloud, "I hope my wedding is like this someday."

"I assume based on—" Ethan clears his throat "—last night that you're not seeing anyone."

"You would assume correctly. I haven't seen anyone in a long while." This cosmo might as well have a truth serum mixed in it.

"Slim pickings in California?" Ethan asks, elbows resting on the table. He's looking out into the crowd of well-dressed, talkative people.

"No, but I do have a specific type," says Taylor. Ethan's eyes shift sideways, loaded with intrigue. "That, and I don't have the time to meet people. My life is Amy Lu."

"I know what that's like." Ethan tips his glass so it taps Taylor's. His brain supplies the *clink* that never comes because the glasses are plastic.

"What was Amy like?" Beat. "Back then?"

"Oh, she was… I guess I would say she was like…" It's difficult to witness Ethan struggle for words when he was so eloquent during the ceremony. Taylor can sense this is a common experience for Ethan—thoughts chugging along faster than he can feasibly get them out.

"Like someone *you* could fall in love with?" Taylor asks. The question churns thick in the air. He shouldn't have asked it. Especially not here. This way. Words ringing back, it sounds dismissive. It wasn't meant to be… It's just…

Ethan wears a slack-jawed expression, eyes two pools of wonder. "I'm not sure what to say because I couldn't have said it better myself."

Taylor's seen it play out with his siblings. There are those like Finn and Sasha, who throw themselves so completely into their careers and mold their lives and personalities and social circles around it. Then, there are those like Sam and Todd who work to live. Jobs are a means to an end to pursue hobbies and passions and lives.

Ethan is most definitely the second kind of person, unchanging in his values or objectives simply because of the industry he finds himself in. No wonder it didn't work out with Amy. She goes where the work takes her. Ethan takes the work where he's at. Could Taylor be like that, too?

Taylor closely inspects how he's changed himself around Amy Lu. That's how he knows Ethan's stronger than him. Without having known him for long, he understands Ethan's strength goes much deeper than the physical brawn. And he sees why Ethan had to step away from his family unit to maintain his peace.

"I think when you meet in your twenties like we did, you're still inventing yourself. In your late twenties, you solidify. You say to the world, 'This is the kind of adult I am.' But then your thirties hit, and you start wondering if you ever truly knew yourself at all. If you were too hasty in your projections. Who we were in our twenties were compatible. Who we became in our thirties just weren't," he says. "Which I think is why weddings are hard for me now because if people aren't static— right?—if we're constantly growing, how can you be sure that this person you've grown with won't start to grow in the opposite direction?"

"You don't," Taylor says. "I guess that's why you have to choose to live in the now."

Ethan steps closer. The outside edges of their shoes touch, and their upper arms brush. "Like last night, I was completely in the now."

Taylor's breath catches. He wasn't sure they would discuss the topic. It could've been a fiery fever dream, destined to cool and fizzle away. "Me, too."

"I have to tell you something." Ethan's hand rakes down his beard. "The Snow White cottage is back in commission. It's yours again, if you want it."

"What is it that you want?" Taylor asks, voice breathy.

Their eyes lock. "Now? Frankly, I want another night like last night."

Every word Taylor's ever learned leaks from his brain and out through his ear. Heat blossoms across his covered chest.

Ethan smirks. "At thirty-nine, I never would've been able to admit that."

"Then I'm glad you're forty," Taylor says.

"Is that your type?" Ethan asks, stretching out his smirk.

"Doesn't matter," Taylor says, pivoting to face Ethan. Because it truly doesn't. This is for the night, not forever. There's not even a possibility of forever. Not with someone who doesn't believe in it. Not with someone who lives on the opposite coast. And most importantly, not with someone who was formerly married to his well-connected boss.

So, he can do sex tonight.

He can even do sex in the morning, followed by a nooner, ending in one final tryst before sleep on Saturday.

On Sunday morning, he'll move his things back to the Snow White cottage, drive the nearly three hours to pick up Amy and Samara at the airport and put this whole escapade behind him.

That sounds far better than giving this up earlier than necessary.

It's what Ethan wants, and Taylor gives people what they want.

It's a nice bonus here that it's what he wants, too.

"Let's get out of here," Ethan says, glugging back the last of his drink and slamming it down on the table. Taylor's in no mood to argue with that firm sign of assurance. They leave the crowded, stuffy tent behind in a hurry.

The minute they're through the front door of the house, Ethan hauls Taylor off his feet as they kiss. Injured hand be damned. There's that delightful weightlessness again from the night of the bedtime stories. This go-around, he doubts he's being taken to the guest room for a good night's sleep. Tonight, he's going to get fucked like a king on the queen-sized bed he saw in Ethan's bedroom.

Except Ethan hesitates at the bedroom door. Sets Taylor back on his feet. Or tries to. Taylor's knees have grown weak, so he tips forward into Ethan's chest, clutching the man for balance. His breath shortens. "Everything okay?"

Ethan presses the inside of his forearm to the top of the door frame, rests his head there, closes his eyes and exhales loudly through his nostrils. "This is going to sound silly. I haven't slept with anyone in there since Amy."

Taylor fumbles for a good response while he processes this and clicks together why last night they had to stay in the living room. The guest room isn't a good option, either.

"Now I've gone and killed the mood," Ethan says, voice emulating a tire with a nail in it.

"No," Taylor says, shaking his head for emphasis. "No, I'm...thinking about what we can do. You said the Snow White cottage is—"

"I can't go and get the key now. It'll look too—"

"The couch?"

"It's old. I'm afraid it won't support that kind of...activity." Ethan bites his bottom lip.

Taylor slumps back against the wood of the door. "I understand."

Only then does the timid man from the couch last night vanish. Ethan's blue eyes go dark gray and wolfish with need as he places one strong hand on Taylor's waist and uses the other to push open the bedroom door. "Fuck it."

Ethan's holding him so tightly that he could almost forget to breathe. Not that he really needs to. The high of being this close to Ethan Golding after he just said *fuck it* is giving him all the life he needs.

Ethan lifts him again and lays him across the duvet. Ethan's blazer is a blur of fabric shot clear across the room, and his purple tie—which was already crooked after the ceremony—gets ripped from his neck in one frantic tug. Needfully, Taylor takes Ethan's face in his hands and guides him in close. Lips brush.

It doesn't matter how Ethan is acting or what sexual confidence he's radiating right now. Taylor won't forget what he said last night. *I need you to be gentle with me.* Heaps of vulnerability were needed to admit that, so Taylor keeps his touches light and his kisses inbounds. It's not until Ethan undoes his belt and hauls out his solid, thick cock between the fly of his trousers that Taylor's ardent hunger takes over.

Holding back is impossible when faced with that mouthwatering dick. He swings around onto his stomach, head near the edge of the bed, mouth open. Ethan works himself between Taylor's lips. He's overwhelmed with the taste of musk and saltiness and the sage and bergamot bar soap, which Taylor's been secretly borrowing in the shower every morning.

Precum tickles the back of his throat as his nose buries itself in the neat hairs at the end of his length. Ethan's groan is a gunshot; Taylor is the racehorse leading the pack out of the gate. It's a symbiotic thrust and gulp, sink and bob. His right hand reaches up to play with Ethan's large balls, which are surprisingly heavy despite his spectacular load last night.

"You're wearing far too many clothes for my liking," Ethan says, combing his fingers through Taylor's hair and rearing himself back. "Allow me."

Ethan starts with Taylor's dress shoes, which he unlaces and carefully sets at the foot of the bed. He's much more considerate with Taylor's clothes than he was with his own, but Taylor really wishes he wouldn't be. He craves nakedness. Now. Yet…

His mind is a whirlpool of comfort. Luxuriating in this tender moment reminds him of being young—only one kid of two. Of falling asleep on a long car ride home from whoeven-remembers-where and his dad carrying him up to bed, tugging him out of his street clothes, and tucking him under the blankets in the bottom bunk of the bed he shared with Owen. This was before the baby boom, the chaos, the fend-for-yourself of it all. And here Ethan is, resurrecting a memory, a sensation of care he thought he'd never experience again.

The next kiss is a thank-you, though Ethan can't know that. Can he?

When Ethan finishes the job of stripping Taylor down to nothing, he smiles in a knowing way that makes Taylor wonder some more if Ethan's secretly a mind reader. Wonder morphs into awe when Ethan lunges toward him and takes his entire dick in his mouth. *Holy mother of—*

"Christ, you're a delicious mouthful," says Ethan, coming up for air, but only momentarily.

Taylor falls right off the perch of his elbows, head bouncing on the mattress from the rapturous impact. Ecstasy swings slow through his body as his erection grows harder and longer, impaling the back of Ethan's throat. The pressure and the warmth are enough to make him blow.

"Ease off," Taylor says.

When Ethan retreats, he looks like he's posing for an X-rated Bear of the Month calendar. He's naked from the waist down. Up top, his white shirt is unbuttoned and flung open, tie like an ornament around his neck. Tall, sheer socks slip up and around his large, firm calves. If this image were preserved on a calendar, say, hung above Taylor's desk in his bedroom, he'd never get any work done. He'd be too busy staring, salivating, groping the front of his pants all day.

"Not good?" Ethan asks, appearing almost bashful for nearly sucking the soul straight out of his dick.

Taylor can't help but laugh heartily. "*Too* good."

Ethan's toothy smile has a dastardly glint to it. "I've been without practice. Good to know I've still got it."

Taylor rises to his knees so he's eye to eye with Ethan, who's standing beside the bed. Leisurely, he drapes his arms over Ethan's hair-dusted shoulders and kisses him slowly on the mouth. Their cock heads kiss, too, causing a fizzy jolt to shoot through Taylor's pelvis. He rocks into it until the rock becomes a steady grind and their kisses include more tongue.

It's sloppy, maybe, and dazedly filthy, but it makes Taylor's heart sprint like never before.

"Am I being gentle enough?" Taylor asks, remembering himself suddenly. "I can keep my tongue to myself."

"That sounds like a fucking punishment," Ethan says through a gravelly throat. "I want your tongue. I want it everywhere."

So he starts with the shell of Ethan's ear. It's inferno-hot, and there's a slight coating of sweat along the side of his neck that Taylor happily laps at. That saltiness is quenching in a strange way. Before long, his tongue is winding circles around Ethan's nipples, hidden in the dense forest of his perfect, fluffy chest hair. It finds rest at the tip of Ethan's swollen dick that leaks like a faucet. He takes one, long dreg from the tap before turning around so his ass is lined up with Ethan's sharpshooter.

At first, Ethan's cock just rests there along the cleft. The heat and pulse are enough to drive Taylor mad. Just knowing that thick cock is primed right there at his hole is a great tease. The slow slip of that spit-covered cock gliding between his cheeks sends waves of pleasure up his spine.

There's Ethan's tongue—flat and wet and explorative.

Then, there's Ethan's fingers—thick and nimble. Last, there's… nothing?

Taylor's eyes had closed as he sank deep into the digital stimulation. He expected the natural chain of events to go forth without intervention. Now he finds Ethan standing behind him, cock solid, condom in hand, eyes closed.

"Do you not want to fuck me?" Taylor asks.

"I do," Ethan says, not opening his eyes. He lets loose an audible exhale. "I'm sad to say that I just don't think this is going to last very long." Embarrassment ebbs out between his words.

Taylor spins around and grabs Ethan's chin, which prompts his eyes to flutter open. "It doesn't matter if you last twelve seconds. I just want to feel you inside me." Taylor's chest hiccups. His statement feels more naked than his body does. Expressing his personal wants has never been his forte.

But the heat rushing through every corner of his body makes him bold, and Ethan's dick stretching him open makes him gasp, and his own hand between his legs makes him come harder than he ever has before.

Seventeen

TAYLOR

"Hey, you've reached Sasha Frost. I'm out doing something awesome…or sleeping. Take your best guess! Leave me a message or shoot me a text. Have a great one!"

Sasha's bubbly voicemail message fades out right before a grating beep.

Taylor pauses, momentarily tongue-tied. Should he blurt out that he had two rounds of intimate, soul-searing sex with his boss's ex-husband last night? The house is empty. Even Nana went with Ethan to the resort this morning, so it's not like anyone will overhear him.

He would text it all out to her, but he's afraid of keeping a written record of it anywhere but the logs in his mind. Besides, he needs both hands free to finally finish these baskets. Only two more to go and then he's done.

"Hey, it's me," he says way after the beep has ended. "I hope your voicemail box is empty because this is a real whopper." From there, the PG-13 version of events bolts from his mouth.

He's fluffing up some tissue paper as he concludes, "I don't even feel guilty about this. Am I broken? Am I a bad person? A good person would regret it, I think. A non-selfish person would realize he's made an irrevocably fucked-up choice, but I...want to do it again?" He palms his own face. He's certain the slap was recorded for posterity. "I know you don't want to hear this, but the sex was *sooooooo good*. So good."

Breathless, he seals up the wrapping on the penultimate basket with a ribbon and sets it aside. "Tomorrow, Amy and Samara arrive, and I know it's going to be awkward, but I sort of don't care. I should! I know I should! I love my job. I love Storybook Endings. Why did I do this to myself? No, actually, I know why I did this to myself, I—"

The voicemail cuts out with another unsettling beep.

Fine. At least now he doesn't have to admit aloud that he did it because Ethan said he wanted it. Multiple times! Again, it boded well that their wants overlapped in such an alluring way, but Taylor's programmed to appease the wants of those around him. Those he *cares about*.

Yeah, it's time he faced it. He cares about Ethan. Six nights under the man's roof, and he's chiseled out a room for him inside his somewhat stony heart.

It's easy to care for Ethan. Not only because he's got soulful blue eyes and hands that could move mountains, but because he's been vulnerable and open. Because the people Taylor sees most in the world—Amy Lu and Samara Golding—are undoubtedly linked to Ethan and are products of being around him for so many years. He admires both those women immensely for their strong wills and their penchants for beauty.

After finishing the last basket and cleaning up, he returns to the living room to find Ethan inspecting his work.

"What are you doing back?" Taylor asks, surprised.

"I'm taking the rest of the day off."

Taylor warms at this, even though he's certain he shouldn't. "Does that mean we get to spend the day together?"

"That depends. Are you up for a trip into town?" he asks, sheepishness cutting through his question. "I've earned the world's worst dad award. I forgot to get Samara a birthday gift."

"Don't be so hard on yourself. My dad once got me an ice cream cake with my brother's name on it," he says. "In the pantheon of dad bluffs, yours doesn't even come close. Let me grab my coat."

ETHAN

Seeing the Catskills—or as Samara calls it, "the Cat's Hills"—through Taylor's eyes is refreshing. The magic and the mystery are replenished with the bonus of another's excitement.

"New England is really different from California. There's a lot of architectural history here. The buildings are interesting," Taylor spouts, pointing toward the firehouse-turned-pub. The scene of Ethan's bad date with Kurt before Taylor arrived. Funny how he almost swore off dating right before Taylor appeared in his lobby.

Not that they're dating, but this—strolling the main strip toward the antique shop on the penultimate day of March, talking life and buildings and birthdays—sort of feels like a date. Perhaps he should scrap that thought before it runs away from him.

"Taylor! Taylor!" comes a voice from behind them after they pass DIWhy Not? The bespectacled woman, no more than twenty-five, who works the register stands in the middle of the sidewalk without a jacket, holding a painted glass jar with silk flowers in it. "What do you think?"

Taylor gasps with delight. "It's perfect!" He grabs for the arrangement excitedly.

"Ethan," he says, extending a hand by way of introduction.

"Lola," she says, her pixie cut swishing around as she nods energetically.

"What is this for?" Ethan asks Taylor.

"Centerpieces for Samara's party," he says quickly. "She loves flowers, but she's allergic, so I figured this was a nice compromise."

Ethan's chest melts at Taylor's thoughtfulness. He clearly cares a lot about Samara. Maybe that's where Ethan's mind should be, too. On the daughter he rarely sees who is hitting a milestone birthday soon.

"I'll pick these up tomorrow morning?" Taylor asks.

"If you'll be in town for a bit, I can have them ready before close tonight," Lola says with a smile.

Taylor looks to Ethan. "How long will we be here?"

"As long as you'd like," he says, that warmth in his chest sneaking onto his face.

With a whole day stretched out ahead of them, Ethan leads the way to Refurbished for Me, the town's nicest antique and thrift shop. Every time he comes in here, it always looks different. The owner, Baxter—an eccentric with hickster (his term, a combination of *hick* and *hipster*) tastes—is constantly rearranging the sections and window displays as new items come in so you never have the same shopping experience twice.

Today, they're greeted by a gold, velvet sofa with an art deco vibe that has a cross-stitched cat pillow laid out in its center. Behind it is a handcrafted coatrack where each hanger hoists up a different costume hat. One with feathers, another with a veil.

"Why here?" Taylor asks with genuine curiosity as they venture in farther.

"It's tradition. One of my hobbies in the spring is fly-fishing, so when Amy was working the resort or away and my parents couldn't watch Samara, I'd wake her early and make her tag along. She didn't hate it, per se, but I'm sure nine-year-old girls have more interesting ideas about how they'd like to spend their Saturday mornings," he says. "Nevertheless, for being a trooper, we'd stop here on the way home and I'd buy her something—a piece of costume jewelry or an old VHS tape. She said to me once that she preferred things that were preowned because they were more interesting."

"Yes! She and I share that. Backstory makes everything more beautiful in my mind," Taylor says. Ethan wonders if all the sharing he's done has made him more beautiful in Taylor's mind as well. "I wish my siblings had felt that way. Everything in my house growing up was a hand-me-down, but out of necessity, not desire."

Taylor wanders away. Ethan enjoys Taylor perusing. His amble has no logic. Some folks, like Ethan, start at the perimeter and make their way in. Others go straight for the shiny section that catches their eye. Not Taylor. He seems content to zigzag and double back and touch everything like a kid in a petting zoo.

Once he stops staring after Taylor, the first item to draw Ethan's attention is a music box. A lovely, lilting piano melody trundles out when opened. Samara could put all of those old pieces of costume jewelry in here—the purple ring and the chain and the brooch with the bumblebee on it.

Sold. That didn't take long at all.

Ethan spins to flag down Taylor and show him. He towers over all the displays so he'd spot Taylor's bright orange coat easily if he were anywhere to be found.

Music box in hand, he wanders into the clothing area. It's a hodgepodge of gowns and trench coats and cowboy boots with a standing, gilded, full-body mirror in the corner. In the reflection, he fixes that one pesky strand of hair that always falls across his forehead. The curtain to the changing room behind him slides open with a screech.

Taylor steps out wearing a psychedelic button-down shirt. It's got wavy, fuzzy purple and white stripes. It reminds Ethan of a lava lamp he had in his college dorm room. Amy always made fun of him for it. Called it tacky. Secretly, it calmed his mind, watching those blobs dance at random.

"What do you think?" Taylor asks, stepping around Ethan and toward the mirror.

"I *think* we were supposed to be looking for a gift for Samara," Ethan says with a flirtatious air.

"No, *you* were looking for a gift for Samara. *I* already got her something," he says, still turned to the mirror. "I'm just here for moral support."

"What did you get her?" Ethan asks.

"This rare Record Store Day vinyl she was dying for. It's a super limited printing. She even begged Amy to let her go with her friends to camp outside the store at four a.m. the night before. There was no way that was happening, so I went. My sister Sasha really likes the artist, too, and the shop lets you buy two copies of each title, so I gave one to my sister and saved one for Samara's birthday."

Taylor's thoughtfulness quota flies off the scale. "I didn't even know Samara had a record player," Ethan grumbles.

"It's a recent thing for her. Maybe a year or two ago. One of her friends, Lily—you'll meet her—is really into them. Trends come and go. You know how teen girls are."

In truth, he doesn't. Not really. He grew up with two brothers. He had Samara solely under his roof until she was ten. They talk all the time, and they see each other for holidays, but it does often feel like Samara is editing herself during those visits. Ethan, too, if he's honest. They're bringing their best selves to those occasions. Ethan doesn't get to muddle through those teenage tantrums over record store lines or whatever. Is that a blessing or is he missing out?

"Anyway, thoughts?" Taylor asks. "I'd want to wear it to Samara's party. It matches the decorations." The top two buttons of the shirt are undone, exposing some of Taylor's chest, and that's when they both notice the shirt isn't the only thing that matches the party's color scheme. A fresh, amorphous purple hickey is displayed on the right side of his collarbone.

Taylor's eyes bulge as he shakes his head.

"Sorry about that," Ethan whispers.

Taylor demurely catches his gaze in the reflection of the mirror. "Don't be," he whispers back, fingering the spot.

Ethan's pulse quickens, thinking about how wonderful it had been to give Taylor that love bite.

When was the last time Ethan had given another person a hickey? College, probably. Amy, most likely. But she hated them with a vengeance. Anytime his mouth neared her neck she shirked away. That's her right. But the way Taylor seductively smiles on his way back to the dressing room makes him think he could turn Taylor's collarbones into a detailed map of the Galápagos Islands and he wouldn't care one bit.

He's tempted to follow Taylor into the dressing room and do just that behind the shelter of the curtain, but he knows the owner, and this place is small. Word travels like wildfire in this town.

Dizzy with the thrilling fantasy, he sits down on the plush, round bench outside the changing room. "Whatcha got there?" Taylor asks when he returns with the shirt back on its hanger.

"Check it out."

Taylor's mouth quirks to one side when Ethan demonstrates the music box.

"What? You don't think she'll like it?" Ethan asks, self-conscious suddenly. "You got her a record. She loves music, and she can put her jewelry in here."

"It's just…" Taylor's fingers waggle like he can summon a word from the dust particles suspended in the air. "Doesn't it feel a little young? Don't get me wrong—it's beautiful. Anyone would be lucky to have this, but it's not really Samara. She wears the same earrings and choker almost every day. I don't know what she'd put in there."

"I see." Ethan hurriedly takes the box back. Guilt's nearest cousin, shame, takes a front row seat inside Ethan's stomach.

The weight of the emotion causes him to slump back down onto the bench.

"Sorry. I didn't mean to overstep." Taylor sits beside him. "You wanted my help. Not my criticism."

Immediately, he sets his closest hand on top of Taylor's in reassurance. "Taylor, no. It's nice that someone like you cares about and knows so much about my daughter. Weird, in a way, but nice. Thank you."

"She's easy to care about. She's like family to me. She's a great person," says Taylor, making no effort to move his hand away.

"I wish she were around more so I could see that greatness for myself." The words are heavy, but they bring about a lightness now that he's finally shared them aloud.

"It must be hard being away from her most of the year."

It's impossible for him to explain in the middle of this antique store that Samara not being near is like trying to live with only half a heart. The blood still pumps, the feelings still come, but not as strong nor as steady as he wishes they would. "Yeah" is all he manages to get out at first. "It's silly, but I'm still hoping she picks an east coast college so I can be the obnoxious guy at parents' weekend wearing a Proud Dad of an XYZ Student T-shirt without having to dump my savings on the airfare."

Taylor's face breaks out into a large smile. "Hey, I can drop some hints for you. She listens to me. I think she's leaning toward studying photography anyway, and there are some great art and design schools out here."

Ethan palms his forehead. "She's always been a shutterbug. How didn't I think about that before? There are tons of antique cameras here. Do you think she'd like one of those?"

"I think she'd *love* one of those."

Eighteen

TAYLOR

Taylor hadn't meant to spend the night in Ethan's bed. It just sorta happened.

They were making out, stroking each other's hard-ons under the covers as they talked about their best sexual experiences (each other notwithstanding) and at some point, they both dozed off. In each other's arms.

Taylor wakes up absolutely roasting. Ethan's body hair is like a third blanket against his skin. It physically pains him to extricate himself from the warmest bed he's ever slept in, but it's already eight-thirty, he has to leave for the airport by one and he conveniently remembers that he never did the walk-through he promised Amy he'd do.

Oh, and he needs to move everything he brought with him back to the Snow White cottage, stat. That includes the ample articles of clothing that are carelessly strewn across Ethan's bedroom floor. For what it's worth, he'd love to leave them there, slip on a robe and come back to this bed tonight. But he's got a career he's not keen to torch and a boss he's terrified of upsetting, so he throws open the hunter green curtains across the way and allows sunshine to tiptoe across the carpet.

"Good morning," Taylor says when Ethan groggily rolls onto his back and blinks awake. "I hate to wake you because you looked so peaceful, but we never got around to the walkthrough, and I need you to, uh, walk through with me."

"Right," he says sleepily. "Right. Give me twenty?"

"I'll go make coffee." Taylor's feet protest any effort to leave the crackling embrace of this room. Morning Ethan is rumpled, languid and handsome beyond reason. That curl of hair that always falls across his forehead at random times has made friends with others that hang limply, giving him the appearance of ill-advised bangs on a middle school girl. But Taylor is charmed by them. *Utterly* charmed.

Ethan sits up and stretches on a yawn. The sight of Ethan's masculine armpits, his impressive wingspan and the roundness of his belly hanging over the hem of the comforter are almost enough to send Taylor soaring back into bed. It takes all of his resolve to turn on his internal fans and see himself to the kitchen.

Nana follows him and nudges at her food bowl with her paw as the coffee brews. Taylor grabs her kibble and doesn't have to ask how many scoops to give her. He's carved out a space for himself in this cottage, garnered a familiarity. Is he really ready to give all this up?

Thirty minutes later, they're walking side by side along the path, holding to-go thermoses of coffee with oat milk creamer and laughing about the way Nana pouted when they left without her. "She's the best girl, but she's got an attitude. There's no doubt about it."

First, they come upon the picnic area. Taylor pulls his work tablet from his bag, the smart pen out of its holder, and starts his inspection. Of course, he's only half paying attention to his work because Ethan has a story for every stop they make, and Ethan's stories are more riveting and interesting than any responsibilities.

At The Thirsty Goat, Ethan talks about a wild thirty-third birthday party where he got so drunk he danced on one of the tables and it broke underneath him. He had to pay five hundred dollars for a replacement table and Gabriel twenty bucks to delete the resulting video and *not* send it in to one of those funny home movie shows.

Over by the pond, at the boathouse, Ethan skips stones across the surface as Taylor jots down notes. Aloud, Ethan reminisces upon when Samara befriended one of the ducks that made a home in the lake during springtime. She named him Donny Ducko. She was far too young to have seen the movie she was referencing, but it's one of Amy's favorites so she'd heard the name a hundred times before. They'd come out daily to say hello and feed him and his duck buddies oats and rice.

Ethan's winding trips down memory lane raise the tide of Taylor's feelings until he's deep in over his head. The more he learns about Ethan, the more he wants to scribe a biography of him on his heart, not fill out this silly inspection sheet that means little in the grand scheme of things.

Their stroll brushes up to lunchtime and the two of them

return to the cottage for a quick meal of sandwiches and fresh fruit before Taylor has to drive to the airport.

"Got everything you need?" Ethan asks, offering Taylor the crusts on his sandwich. Taylor gobbles them up, then is hit with a pang of sadness. Is he really growing wistful over four strips of bread? It's not like he'll never talk with Ethan again after this.

"I think so," he says once he's swallowed. The report is not his best work, but the place is in good shape. At least, he thinks it is. He might've borrowed Ethan's rose-colored glasses a time or two, but for the most part he was objective.

"Except, shit. I forgot about moving my stuff." The clock on the microwave reads 12:45 p.m. He needs to get on the road. Amy hates to be kept waiting.

Ethan waves off his worry. "I can handle that."

"Are you sure?" Taylor asks. "Because that would be really helpful."

"I'm all over it. Don't worry," Ethan says.

If only he knew that Taylor's stomach was a bottomless pit of worry. What happens now? What are they to each other? Twelve hours ago, it was simple to declare they'd wash their hands of one another once Amy and Samara arrived. Now Taylor feels like that glitter he spilled on the carpet while making the baskets: embedded in this cottage forever.

He attempts to swallow the golf-ball-sized lump in his throat. "Guess this is it, then."

Ethan solemnly nods.

"And of course, we'll see each other throughout the week."

"Of course."

Standing there with the rental car keys in hand, Taylor

exhales out as much resentment over the situation as he can. As much as he wishes he could stop the inevitable arrival— a delayed flight caused by a freak snowstorm would be a godsend—he has no power to contort the universe or its weather patterns. "I better head out."

"You'd better," Ethan says, glancing down at his watch. Ethan's gaze was the only thing keeping Taylor here, stilled like stone. Every second those eyes aren't on him, Taylor dies a little inside, but the marble casing around his body crumbles, reminding him what his limbs are meant for.

Taylor waits for Ethan to glance back up. One second. Two. But that large head stays tilted down toward the floor, eyes obscured by fallen hairs, and perhaps that's for the best. It makes Taylor's exit easier at least.

Taylor's just about through the door when Ethan surprisingly tugs him back in by the wrist, slams the door shut with a huge hand and kisses Taylor firmly on the mouth. "One more for the road," he says softly. Sweetly.

Taylor could drop to pieces bracketed in by this man. This gorgeous, strong, caring man. But he's already running late. "Thank you," he says. At first, it's for the kiss, but then he says it again and it's for everything. Everything up until this point. The food and the conversation and the sex—oh, God, the sex.

As he walks away from the cottage and Ethan, he can't help but go misty-eyed. He's got to let it out now because tonight, it'll be too late. There will be no time for tears or longing. No space to reflect. Too many responsibilities and eyes on him to fall apart.

He marches toward the parking lot with his feelings hanging heavy around his neck, knowing he's got three full hours of driving ahead of him, a new playlist from Samara in his text messages and a lot—*a lot*—of processing to do.

Grrrrr-pfft. Grrr-pfft.

"Nononononononono," Taylor shouts, sitting in the driver's seat of the rented Honda as he pushes the start button repeatedly. The engine won't turn over. Glancing up, Taylor's displeased to note the pull-down mirror above him is cracked open enough that the lights would've stayed on. "Shit."

The last time he'd driven, he'd checked his hair, checked his teeth and pinched his cheeks to bring some color to them—all in the name of looking presentable when he walked through the door of Ethan's cottage. He preened. He shared. He fell. Deeply. How had he let that happen?

Similarly, how had he let *this* happen?

He's already running late, and now he's running at full tilt all the way back to the cottage to see what can be done to salvage this. Amy refuses to ride with unknown drivers. She's sensitive to radio volumes and smells.

Speaking of smells, Taylor stops short in the entryway to Ethan's bedroom. Ethan must not have heard him come in, nor heard Nana's tag clanging as she trotted behind him. Because Ethan's standing in the center of the room holding Taylor's tie-dyed sweatshirt up to his nose. Taking a long hit of Taylor's scent. Eyes closed. Bliss crossing his round features.

Does he feel the way I do?

"Eherm," Taylor clears his throat. Ethan drops the sweatshirt like he's been caught shoplifting. "Sorry I—"

"No, I'm the one who's sorry. I—"

Their conversation ping-pongs like that for seconds. They're too busy trying to be polite. As if Taylor's heart isn't prancing a mile a minute. Nobody's ever missed him so much that they'd sniff his clothes before. He's only been gone for minutes.

The dead battery situation presses down on him once more, and he's yammering the way he did the night of the storm.

Ethan's as calm as the surface of the pond they circumvented earlier. He grabs jumper cables from the garage and loads them into his cherry-red Toyota Land Cruiser.

"Vintage, huh? Are you into cars?" Taylor asks to combat the anxiety-induced rumbling in his stomach. Amy's going to spend the whole ride to the resort with a pinched expression on her face, unspeaking. As if the ride weren't already going to be painful for Taylor.

"Just this car," Ethan clarifies. "It was my dad's. I couldn't let him sell it to some collector. This car is my childhood." He reaches in front of Taylor and pulls down the visor. Tucked inside is a photo of three boys and an older man, all wearing shorts, high socks with red stripes and sneakers. They stand in front of a camping tent. Taylor doesn't need to ask to figure out which one is Ethan. He towers above his brothers. On closer inspection, Ethan appears to be about fourteen. Already, Taylor spots stubble growing in along his prominent jawline.

"Must come with a lot of upkeep," Taylor says as they turn into the parking lot where the rental car is. Ethan skillfully shifts manual gears.

"I run a resort. My whole life is upkeep. What's one more thing to add to the list?" Taylor has been around the cottage enough to know that this isn't just a turn of phrase for Ethan. He keeps lists. Tons of them. There are lime-green sticky notes with them all over. Stuck to the fridge. On the coffee table. Taped inside the medicine cabinet.

Taylor gets out and pops the hood on the Honda. Ethan capably hooks it all up. As they wait the standard fifteen minutes—fifteen of the longest minutes of Taylor's life—they fall into distracting, companionable conversation about their respective histories with camping trips.

"All my outdoorsy gifts I got from my dad," Ethan says, a shadow falling over his expression. Despite not idolizing his own father, Taylor's sensitive enough to understand how hard it must be to look up to someone and then watch them physically deteriorate.

Taylor gives a small smile. "Your father must be really proud of you for carrying the torch for him."

"Perhaps," he says sullenly. "What about you? Did your family camp at all outside Boy Scouts?"

"Sometimes. We owned a powder-blue VW van. It was the one car that could fit the entire brood. My parents loved to travel, so anywhere we could go in that clunker, they took us. State parks, campgrounds, beaches. We'd pitch tents and pack our sleeping bags or get a nearby motel. We'd fit five people into two rooms and four beds. It was always chaos, but we had some good times," he recollects. "My parents weren't very reliable. Flitting off for new jobs, new places. But on those trips, they were present. They'd watch the younger ones while I went down to the surf shack to rent a board and flirt my way into a lesson."

"Flirt your way, huh?" Ethan asks with a chuckle.

"Yeah, the first guy I ever hooked up with was an instructor at one of the surf clubs I wandered to on a beach trip in

San Diego. He was this broad, burly-chested, suntanned guy with long blond hair. I mean, this guy filled out a wet suit like you wouldn't believe," Taylor says, calling to mind the overwhelming sight of this man. *M-A-N. Man.* That's what he was. The kind of sturdy, rugged guy Taylor wanted attention from most of all. "I'd seen guys out in the surf all weekend. The proximal adrenaline rush was out of this world. I wanted to get out there, so I got cash out of the ATM, but only had enough for the board rental. Not much you can do with a board and no skills, so this guy who was just getting off his shift overheard and agreed to take me out."

"In more ways than one," Ethan says, shifting so he's leaning against his truck, one boot crossed over the other. He exudes an unmatched confidence that Taylor never wants to miss.

"After a few hours in the waves, he did take me behind the lifeguard tower and teach me a few other things," he says, heat cresting across his cheeks. "It was only kissing. I was seventeen. He was in his midtwenties. He was a perfect gentleman in that regard."

"In *that* regard? Guess you've always had a thing for sleeping with older guys, then." Shock skulks across Ethan's expression after the words leave his mouth.

Had a thing for... Taylor's attractions aren't fetishes. A major ick crawls under his skin. He bristles; the hum of the car beside him infects his chest. "Are you insinuating something?"

"Oh, no..." Ethan stammers for a second.

"Because it sounded like you were."

"I wasn't suggesting—"

"Because if that's the only reason you were into me..." Taylor's been down this road before with men Ethan's age. They think being with Taylor is like drinking from the fountain of youth; they'll stay young by proximity. Lord some sort of authority over him by virtue of having spent more years on earth. That's bullshit. Taylor likes what he likes: secure men, stable men, men with maturity. Something Ethan is severely lacking in this present moment.

Ethan goes rigid. "It's—"

A click from the car startles them both. Taylor stomps back to the driver's side and tries the ignition. Still nothing. Instead of cursing, he slams his hands on the wheel in frustration. Everything is going sideways suddenly.

"Take mine," Ethan says, shoving his key ring through the open window.

"I can't just—"

"I won't need it," Ethan ensures.

"It's not that. I don't know how to drive stick." Admitting that feels like proving Ethan right in some way. That he's just a silly kid who wants protecting, to be taken care of. Adults want that shit, too!

Ethan's voice drops. "It's automatic. I just prefer the manual mode. I filled up the tank yesterday. If you leave now, you'll still make good time."

At a loss for better options, Taylor accepts the offer with muddled thanks. As he backs out of the spot and drives toward the exit, he's tempted to look back at Ethan through the rearview mirror. But he doesn't. Bad enough Ethan's bergamot scent lingers in the air here. He's going to be smelling that man all the way to the airport.

After that conversation, maybe it's for the best their connection ends now. If Ethan was only using him to feel young, then you can't build a relationship on that.

Relationship! Ha!

As if he could ever have a relationship with his boss's ex-husband. Especially when his boss's ex-husband is a man he's been told is so stuck in his ways.

Taylor's been entertaining a fool's vacation this whole time. Running off on a whim that could never last. This break is exactly what they both need to cool off whatever chemistry they explored. No more dalliances. No more distractions.

With that, he pulls over quickly at a gas station to queue up Samara's playlist, which he knows will be full of emo bangers to get Ethan off his mind, only to realize Ethan's car doesn't have an aux cord or Bluetooth hookup.

"Radio it is then," he mumbles to himself, speeding off and away.

Nineteen

ETHAN

Pulling Taylor's suitcase out from underneath Samara's old bed feels like saying goodbye all over again.

Why had he kissed him before he left the cottage and then said that boneheaded thing by the cars?

Because he's a stickler for self-flagellation, that's why.

This past week, he indulged too much on the sweetness of Taylor Frost, and now his stomach is upset as he folds Taylor's clothes and grabs Taylor's toothbrush and toothpaste from the bathroom they've been sharing. Even now, gone only for a few hours, the house is abysmally quiet save for the sound of Nana's paws pattering on the wood floor. It's going to take ages to reset to the stillness he'd made friends with.

No. Not friends.

You can't be friends with something you learned to tolerate.

That's what he'd done. As he steps back into his own bedroom, last night's acts still floating in the air, he notes the creak of a floorboard and dissects how different it is from the sound he heard when Taylor got up in the middle of the night to use the bathroom. A dull ache roils in Ethan's chest as if Taylor's brief absence were a virus taking root.

There are no antibiotics for being lovesick.

Only known cure: time, space and, with any luck, forgetfulness.

He hadn't meant to offend Taylor by his "older guys" comment. In fact, he had blurted it out because of his own insecurities.

Guess this is it, then.

That was the sentence that had gotten his hackles up since it sounded like Taylor was going to be able to walk away from this easily. Nothing in Ethan's life, when it comes to his emotions, has ever been easy. ADHD has made sure of that.

Ethan carefully folds Taylor's tie-dyed hoodie that he dropped on the floor earlier and rakes over how he'd fallen out of love with Amy, but still couldn't regulate his emotions when it came to the dissolution of his marriage, his family. His head knew the relationship had run its course. His heart knew the love was no longer there. But his emotions kept bouncing around, causing confusion.

His therapist called it Rejection Sensitive Dysphoria—overwhelming dysregulation. A feeling Ethan likens to Godzilla rampaging the city within his sternum.

In the kitchen, he takes the rest of the box of green tea Taylor likes from the cupboard and, from the pantry, he takes the untouched bag of mint Milanos he bought on his last trip to the grocery store. Both get dropped into a tote bag and left by the door.

Nana, clearly confused by this, yowls a bit at the disruption. She's a smart girl. She knows what suitcases usually mean. "Don't worry. I'm not the one leaving." Ethan's heart grows heavier.

Before he exits the cottage, he removes the extra towels from the bathroom and the sheets from the bed. Without care, he throws both in the wash together on a warm cycle. The wet splat of fabrics of differing weights tumbling around makes his stomach contract. Needing to get away, he leashes up Nana, pulls up the handle on the suitcase and beelines for the Snow White cottage. Hoping he doesn't leave mushy memories like bread crumbs along the way.

Be to the resort in twenty! Samara's text reads.

The twinkling chime of his phone beneath the counter stirs Ethan from his stupor. He doesn't know exactly how long he's been standing comatose behind the reception desk, staring out the window onto the front lawn where he can slightly make out the AND THEY LIVED... sign, but *far too long* comes to mind.

Can't wait to see you, 😊 he types back.

The next time the front door opens, he expects it to be Amy, Samara, and Taylor. Instead, Gabriel's wife, Giselle, swans inside wearing a shawl and sunglasses. When she's not at the law practice, she dresses like the coolest mom at Coachella, all flower patterns and flowy fabrics. How many colors is too many to wear at one time? Giselle doesn't care. "Hello, hello," she says, blowing Ethan a kiss.

"What brings you in tonight?" Ethan asks, trying to sound jovial. It's good practice for when he has to play the welcome brigade.

"Dinner, of course," she says.

"With Gabriel?" Ethan asks, not seeing him around.

"With the whole gang. Amy didn't tell you?" she asks with an air of disconcert.

Ethan stifles a groan. "Who exactly does the gang include?"

Gabriel comes up behind him, clapping him on the shoulder, which startles him. "Me, the missus, Amy, Samara and Taylor."

"Who's Taylor again?" Giselle asks after kissing her husband and leaving behind a plum-colored lipstick stain on his tan cheek.

Gabriel locks eyes with Ethan. "The assistant."

Almost as soon as he says it, the missing party members squeeze through the front door all at once. "Is anybody going to help with our bags?" Amy asks as if she's carrying any herself. Taylor comes up the rear, looking like a pack mule with a backpack, two duffel bags and a ginormous, metallic rolling suitcase clunking behind him.

"Amy!" Giselle coos, wrapping her up in a hug.

"Plug your nose. I smell like airplane," Amy says sardonically, mid-embrace.

When the group parts, Samara stands near the door, AirPods still stuffed into her pierced ears, looking around. Muscles in Ethan's body that he had no idea were clenched loosen. "Hi there, Birthday Girl," he says, his heart working better than usual.

"Sixteen. *Meu Deus!* Where does the time go?" He intercepts the hug Ethan has been craving since he last saw his daughter two months ago. Or was it three now? Christmas, for sure.

"Hi, Uncle Gabriel." Samara's gaze finds Ethan's over Gabriel's shoulder. She rolls her blue eyes, which match Ethan's own, and flashes a sarcastic smile before letting go and coming to him.

"Welcome home," Ethan says. He pointedly ignores the light chuff that Amy gives as he squeezes his daughter tight. My, she's gotten tall. And she's wearing the choker Taylor says is practically a uniform at this point.

"Bet Cat Town hasn't been the same without me," she jokes. Her makeup skills have sharpened significantly since the holidays. Not even a single smudge of eyeliner after being cooped up in transit all day.

"It misses you," he says, refraining from adding the painfully obvious *I miss you, too.*

When they break off from the hug, Amy does an overblown chill—always the performer. "I hope the table by the fireplace is open in the pub. I'm downright freezing. Ethan, the heat in your car doesn't work. Be sure to get that fixed."

Even in his personal life, Amy seems to think she calls the shots. Didn't she sign that privilege away in the divorce? Should he have ever given it to her to begin with? Maybe that's what's holding him back most from Taylor Frost. But he can't think of that now.

"I'm starving!" Samara cries, leading the way toward The Thirsty Goat. Ethan doesn't think he could eat a bite with the way his stomach is behaving right now.

"Why was she in your car?" Gabriel asks.

"Long story," Ethan grumbles quietly. "Let me grab the bags and store them until we're finished."

"I'll help," Taylor says, still encumbered by half the load.

The last thing Ethan wants is to be in tight quarters with Taylor right now. The luggage room behind the reception desk is a little larger than a walk-in closet. They can't accommodate that many guests, and most leave promptly after checkout. Today, however, the room is a minefield of tripping hazards. He makes a mental note to talk to his staff about their organization skills.

"Place them anywhere you can find room," Ethan says, not looking at Taylor. He shoves his way inside.

"I tried to get out of it," Taylor says, voice lower than Ethan has heard it before. He grunts as he sets down the loaded bags.

"Out of what?" Ethan asks.

"Dinner. I told Amy I was tired from the drive. I didn't want you to think I was crashing your family reunion," he says. There's sourness in the air like someone spilled expired cleaning agents all over the luggage. He wants back the luscious magic of the cottage again, feeling at home in Taylor's presence.

"Nonsense. You're not cra—"

Knock. Knock. Gabriel pops his head in. "Amy told me to come and find you two so she can order."

They've been gone, what, two minutes. Ethan hopes there are pounds of vacuum-sealed patience hidden somewhere inside one of these suitcases that he can borrow, because his limited reserve is not going to last him the next several days.

The Thirsty Goat is bustling and loud. The bar is full, as are most of the tables. Amy and Giselle have pushed together two four-tops right in front of the fireplace. He'd done away with the long table they had there for the longest time. People always complained it got too hot sitting right there. Amy runs cold, though, so he's not surprised to find her bundled in Giselle's shawl, holding court already.

The only two open seats are on the nearer side, beside Samara. Ethan takes the one next to her with Taylor on his right. As soon as he settles, he's split down the middle. His attention is unable to land on anything concrete because he's overjoyed that his daughter is here and yet too acutely aware of his recent lover's presence.

When Vanessa, the costumed "barmaid" for the evening, comes by to take their order—two plates of nachos to start, a round of non-alcoholic ciders and fish and chips for all— Ethan says a silent prayer that this will all go smoothly. He's about to ask his daughter about the ride, but she's already speaking over him.

"Did you get to listen to the new playlist I started? Indie Rock Realness?" Samara asks Taylor.

He shakes his head. "Your dad's car doesn't have an aux hookup. Oh, that reminds me." Taylor fishes Ethan's keys from his pocket. It's impossible for their hands not to touch in the pass-off. Shivers race through Ethan's body at the contact. His eyes dart around, worried the others at the table are closely observing him, reading too much into this exchange.

"Don't you think it's time for a new car, Dad?" Samara asks. "That clunker felt like it was going to fall apart every time we hit a pothole."

"I hit *one* pothole!" Taylor protests, and they both laugh like it's the easiest thing in the world. Ethan can't recall the last time he laughed with Samara that freely. Exchanges become stilted when an entire country rests between you for most of the year. He yearns for the days when he'd return to the cottage after work and join Samara in front of the TV, laughing at some cartoon.

"You should get a hybrid crossover," Amy says, adding her two cents into a conversation she wasn't initially a part of. "I've been thinking of maybe investing in company car decals. I'll give a little bonus to any employees willing to brand their rides as marketing."

"I like my car," Ethan says defensively, defiantly ignoring her ridiculous business idea. Their employees are locals. Who in the immediate area doesn't already know they are there? Though, he zips his lips. He gave up his right to overarching business decisions when he gave up the title of husband. Why was he willing to play his new role, but Amy insisted on maintaining their old dynamic?

"I like it, too," Taylor says, gaze fixed firmly on the frosted mug of cider that's been set in front of him. He murmurs a thanks to Vanessa as she passes by.

Taylor's defense, however muted, reminds Ethan how much history that car has. Amy would throw out the antique bath with the bathwater if she had the chance. He hopes Samara doesn't inherit that ideal, especially since he sank a lot of money into that vintage camera for her. What if she turns up her nose at it? That would kill him.

God, his heart feels like it's on a silver tray slapped down in the center of the table ready to be carved up and served.

"For Christmas, I'm getting you one of those cassette plug-ins," Samara says.

"Surprised you even know what a cassette is," says Giselle with a high laugh.

Samara rolls her eyes. "I know things! They're popular again! It plugs into the radio so you can still hook up your phone."

The conversation turns back to music. Samara and Taylor are volleying comments back and forth over a new song by someone named Phoebe Bridgers and a group (perhaps?) called boygenius. His head spins with all the references. Amy and Giselle are discussing some outdoor concert she went to with some man whose name Ethan doesn't catch. Gabriel is swiping all the best loaded nachos from the large plate while he thinks no one is looking.

Ethan is...overwhelmed. The back of his neck grows hot at all the stimuli. The proximity to the fire doesn't help. Neither does Taylor's nearness. In seconds, he's soupy.

It's times like these he wishes he carried around his noise-canceling headphones like his therapist suggested. It would filter out some of the background sounds so he could focus. Instead, he picks a fixed spot to give his attention to. Surely, he should find a better spot than the corner of Taylor's pale, pink mouth as it moves a mile a minute, spouting off song lyrics he has memorized, but it's too late. He's locked in on the place where there may just be the vaguest hint of a freckle Ethan hasn't noticed before.

And he's glad. Glad that Taylor and Samara get along so well. Taylor, despite his awkward departure earlier, is a stand-up person and a good role model for Samara. Someone responsible and friendly who takes Samara and her interests seriously.

Amy leans across the table with a napkin she wet in her

water glass. "You've got cheese all over your face," she says to Samara, blotting at her.

Samara recoils. "Stop it!"

"No, you stop it!" Amy responds harshly.

Samara stops fighting and lets it happen to avoid any more eyes cast in the direction of their table.

He supposes even if he had Samara under his roof, he'd still have this idea of her as a young girl who needed his constant attention and care. It's the way parents are. But Amy's behavior still grates on him.

Because there's control and then there's controll*ing*. He's lived under Amy Lu's thumb. For a time, it was comforting. Someone else could write the to-do lists, allocate the tasks, tell him where to be and when to be there. It skewered his executive dysfunction, but it also stopped him from developing skills himself. Her absence left him reeling with indecision and stagnation.

At this table, it dawns on him that as his wife, she was parenting him. He was letting her. And he doesn't want Samara to develop that sort of calcified resentment.

After the scene ends and the conversation restarts, he catches a sneaky glance shared between Samara and Taylor that says, *Can you believe her?*

A smile floats up onto Ethan's face as the fish and chips arrive. At least she's got an ally.

Ethan takes this opportunity to engage Samara about her photography, which lights her up almost as much as the conversation about music did. She's eagerly showing him shots on her phone of different pieces in her newly-minted portfolio that she's proud of.

"Portfolio?" he asks. Even to him, from his mouth, the word sounds way too grown-up.

"Yeah, all real photographers have them. My teacher has been telling me for ages. I'm thinking of starting a website. Taylor is going to help me," she says.

Taylor nods and smiles. For the first time tonight, Taylor really meets Ethan's eyes and there's something about their unlikely trio on this side of the table that feels right. Like the rest of their dinner companions have flown away and it's just the three of them, chatting excitedly about shutter speeds and lens lengths and how much Samara missed the fish and chips here.

Ethan doesn't need an X-ray to know that his heart is whole again for the first time in many, many weeks.

Twenty

TAYLOR

It's after 10:00 p.m. and Taylor stares out the new back window of the Snow White cottage where he will be sleeping alone tonight.

To think that without that shattered window and clipped roof, the last week would've been drastically different. He never would've known what Ethan was like behind closed doors—what he dreamed about, what he tasted like, what he sounded like in the mornings.

Perhaps it would've been better that way because now there's a pit of want in his stomach that he'll never be able to fill.

Unzipping his suitcase, he unpacks his clothes, including the new shirt he bought at the vintage store. Slowly, he puts everything back in the drawers of the chest where it was before his trip took a surprising detour. When he's finished, he wanders over to the kitchenette, to the kettle, remembering then that he used the last of his tea the night of the storm.

In the corner, there's a Storybook Endings tote bag that he's certain isn't his. Inside, there's an unopened bag of mint Milanos and the last of the green tea he bought. His heart mirrors the electric kettle, bubbling and spewing out warmth.

Ethan's thoughtfulness supersedes whatever weirdness he felt in the parking lot during the dead battery disaster. Jumping to conclusions is one of Taylor's special skills. Anticipating needs is part of his job description. But he can see how sometimes that might backfire.

From meals to archery to sex, Ethan never treated him like some young thing that he used for fun to later be discarded like a loaded condom. Every glass of wine poured to every utensil set out, every touch to every kiss, respect sparkled in the air. Appreciation, too.

The click of the kettle underlines Taylor's hasty assumption. An overwhelming urge to apologize for getting snappy circles him. But it's not like he can sneak out—

Knock.

The sound is so soft he mistakes it for the wind.

Knock. Knock.

It's his imagination. He's almost certain. Like that old Poe tale. The one about the raven. Now that really would've scarred the children at story time.

Knock. Knock. Knock. Knock. Kno—

Finally, he opens the door expecting Amy. Earlier, she was complaining about her cell service up here. She switched carriers back in California—with Taylor's patient help—and there seems to be fewer towers out here getting her the 5G she's used to.

In the doorway, there's a person, much larger than Amy, wearing a black sweatshirt with the hood up. Even though his face is obscured, his size and age and bergamot scent give him away. Without pausing for an invitation, Ethan comes inside, shutting the door and the curtains behind him.

For a second, Taylor contemplates whether he conjured Ethan at his doorstep with his wish to apologize. Does this fairy tale resort have witch's magic running through its grounds?

"Sorry to barge in on you like this," Ethan says, revealing himself fully. Ethan's hood whacks that one long curl loose and it hangs pleasingly across his forehead. "I came to apologize for earlier. What I said was unthinking and unkind, and I am sorry."

Taylor hadn't been expecting that. Amy had always gone on about how Ethan wasn't one to apologize. Now he fears he's been holding too tightly to some of the things Amy said about her ex-husband. At no point has Ethan proven himself to be the stubborn, inflexible man she's always painted him to be. Maybe he never apologized to her because she was in the wrong. "Thank you," Taylor chokes out finally. "And I'm sorry, again, for intruding on dinner."

Ethan's eyes crinkle at the corners. "I was happy you were there."

"You were? I feel like I stepped all over your conversation with Samara," he says, toying with the tea bag in his mug. Which is probably overly steeped at this point, but Ethan's blocking the trash can. Taylor's worried that if he makes any sudden movements, Ethan will prove to be a wishful apparition, a fabrication about to whisk away in a sudden burst of light.

"Not at all. You get her. In a way I never could," he says. It rings like a compliment. Yet— "Are you saying I have the mentality of a teenage girl?" Taylor asks.

Ethan's eyes widen. "Not at all! I—"

"I'm only teasing you," Taylor cuts in quickly. Maybe some of that defensiveness from earlier still needs to burn off. He isn't interested in riling Ethan up like that. If anything, Ethan deserves peace, ease. He wishes he could massage every tense muscle of Ethan's.

Ethan runs a hand across his beard, which does nothing to cloak his growing smile. "What I meant was that Amy still treats Samara like a little girl. Probably because she isn't the best at listening. She probably thinks Samara's interest in music and photography are whims or silly hobbies. You treat them like they're passions."

"Because they are," Taylor says. He wrinkles his brow, trying to get to the bottom of why Ethan thinks somebody wouldn't do that. The simplest thing in the world is taking someone else's hopes and dreams seriously. If you don't accept and believe in someone, you can't expect them to shine.

"That's just it. I see her—what?—four to five times a year in a good year. All I get are snapshots of her life, her world. I can already tell the world of an almost-sixteen-year-old girl is far more complex than all those Netflix movies make it seem." He wanders over to the new window, looking out. "She's not a snapshot. She's a whole gallery. I see that you *see* that. I have the excuse of distance, but what's Amy's?"

Taylor is still rendered confused. "I don't know what you want me to say to that."

"I don't want you to say anything. I just want to thank you for being there for my daughter when I can't be. When her mother won't be. You are...you are a really caring, good man," he says. When he turns back to face Taylor, there's a shiny line of tears waiting to fall from his eyes. "I see you as a man, Taylor. I'm sorry if my rude comment earlier led you to believe otherwise. You are more mature and put-together than half the people I know and associate with. Maybe even more mature than me."

"I wouldn't go that far," Taylor says, worried if he lets those words snuggle too close to his heart that his guard will fall. He's still got his job to consider—Amy's certain ire if she caught the two of them alone like this.

"I would. I would go further. But I'll spare you the whole monologue," Ethan says with this tinkling note of chivalry. That's the foremost word Taylor would use to describe Ethan if pressed: chivalrous. Also noble. And insightful. Taylor's crushed with the urge to hug him, but shows restraint, despite the difficulty.

"What if I want the whole monologue?" Taylor asks, venturing into treacherous waters without a paddle.

Ethan's blushing now. "I'll give you the abridged version. Last week meant a lot to me. I couldn't put into words how much if I tried. I know this has to be over now that Amy is here. I'm not going to put myself between you and your work because like Samara's passion, I see yours in the career you've chosen. Amy will most certainly open the right doors for you. You're where you're meant to be."

The sacrifice of what Ethan's saying sways between them like a sharp pendulum slowly descending, evilly set on severing. Before the slice, Taylor has to say this: "Last week meant a lot to me, too. I haven't connected with someone like this in a while, and I hate that we have to pretend now like none of it happened."

"I wish there was a better way," Ethan says with a gallant air, like he'd cross land and sea with only a tattered parchment map if he could find the treasure chest of more tomorrows together. "I really wish there was."

Ethan starts toward the door, and Taylor suddenly concludes that the pendulum was only ever in his head. Yes, he wants to be treated as an adult, seen as Ethan's equal and respected as Amy's colleague and heralded as Samara's role model, but he's also twenty-seven. He is young. He is spry. He is willing to sneak around and keep a secret and play the dangerous game if it means Ethan Golding stays in his presence for a few more nights.

"Please don't go," Taylor says. "Not yet. I'm not tired. I was going to have some tea. There's a Scrabble board in the top of the closet. We'll keep the curtains closed. We can be friends, can't we? There's nothing wrong with us being friends."

He's grasping at turtle-saving paper straws, and he sees Ethan register that. Contesting thoughts wiggle across Ethan's expression. *I would love that*, and *Won't that make the parting harder?* Ultimately, Ethan says, "Watch out. I'm a killer at Scrabble."

Over green tea, mint Milanos, and seven letter tiles per turn, the two of them keep company at the drop-down table by the fireplace with the curtains closed and the heat turned up. They pretend, at least for the time, that nothing has changed except their location.

Amy is not across the resort going through her twelve-step skincare routine before plopping on her satin sleep mask and getting her regimented eight hours. Samara is not in a cabin across the way, luxuriating in a rare moment of privacy before all her friends arrive tomorrow morning. If he focuses, Taylor can almost paste in the sound of Nana's adorable snores under his feet even though she's surely back at the cottage and dreaming of squirrels to chase.

Conversation ebbs and flows between long bouts of thought. There's an adorable crinkle of competitiveness in the set of Ethan's brow. Taylor is tempted to bend across the table and kiss it. But the only place his lips land are the edge of his mug with his second cup of tea.

"How much should we tell Amy? Just so we have our stories straight," Taylor says, certain they should've hashed this out last night before he picked them up from the airport instead of going ahead for that third round, which was slow and sensual and lasted well past 3:00 a.m. Every time he has sex from here on out, he's going to compare it against that. Against the connectedness and the blissed out stretch of Ethan Golding.

He's literally and figuratively fucked.

But at least he has this. Now. Ethan sitting across from him, mug paused partway to his open lips, lost in thought. Taylor wants to dive inside that neurodiverse brain of his and swim laps in his beautiful thoughts.

"As little as we can get away with," he says finally. His swallow of tea is like cannon fire in the mostly silent room.

"Which is...?" He plays the easiest word he can think of: *LAMB* on top of Ethan's previous *BOATS*. Ethan records Taylor's points on the Storybook Ending's notepad from the drawer by the bed. Ethan is leading, but not by much. "Gabriel already brought up the issue with the roof and the window at dinner."

"He didn't say which cottage, though," Ethan is quick to note.

"So I never stayed with you?" Taylor asks, worried that if

they begin lying, the truth will become a watercolor painting hung in direct sunlight: apt to fade into unrecognition.

Ethan cringes as if he's got cramps. "I don't see a way she won't read into it. If we had told her when it happened, it would've been easier, but now…"

His sentence falls off the cliff of understanding. It's the truth. Why hadn't either of them said anything to Amy and Samara? After a moment, Taylor comes to a single conclusion: he was hoping this would happen.

Not this, playing Scrabble over cups of tea, but everything before—with the cuddling and sex and stories. From the first time he laid eyes on Ethan Golding in that hospitality magazine, his whole body stirred to sharp attention. Then, when he began working for Amy, images of Ethan were constantly floating across his laptop screen. The attraction was undeniable, despite Amy's condemnations of Ethan's stalwart ways. Only when Taylor arrived here did he realize he'd be attracted to Ethan's heart and mind as much as his body.

"We never stayed together," Taylor says it as matter-of-factly as he can muster. Ignores the way his stomach churns over it.

"You still did story time," Ethan says with a playful smirk that lightens the mood.

"If we're lying, can we at least say I was a success at it?"

"Where would be the fun in that?" It's so flirtatious that Taylor could kiss him. Damn, someone needs to hog-tie his hands to this chair, duct-tape his lips shut. Trouble is not only in the air between them; it's manipulating the tiles.

Ethan plays *LOVE* off *LAMB*, and Taylor's chest nearly snaps open like a piñata.

"I know you were excited to see Samara after a long time away, but what was it like seeing Amy?" Taylor asks. Because there's nothing less flirtatious than asking your hot former bedfellow about his acrimonious ex-wife.

"The same way it's been for the last five years—like taking an ice bath after an injury. Awful at first, but once you adjust to the temperature, it feels good. I know maintaining that relationship, no matter how much strain, is in my best interest. It's healthy."

"An Amy a day..." Taylor jokes.

Ethan laughs from somewhere in the back of his throat. "If I had to see her every day, I don't know that I'd be so generous. Don't mistake me. She's not the villain of my story. I don't think she's a bad person for falling out of love with me."

Taylor probably shouldn't ask, but since they've agreed they can be friends and friends share vulnerable truths, he says, "Do you still love her?"

"Oh, of course. I always will," he says certainly. "But I stopped being *in love* with her some years ago. Even before the divorce, if I inspected the evidence closely enough. There's a lot you don't see when you're living with undiagnosed ADHD. Your mind gets pulled in so many different directions that you sometimes fail to see what's occurring right in front of you. Right inside of you even."

"It's amazing that you've learned this about yourself, and that you've claimed peace with the way things turned out," Taylor says. The game is now forgotten. Sitting between them on the table like the remnants of an appetizer nobody really wanted.

"Peace? Not quite. A piece of peace, maybe."

"A piece of peace?"

"Sure. To me, peace isn't a mural. It's a mosaic. Things have to break before they can be rebuilt into something beautiful and serene again."

Taylor's heart tumbles down a never-ending rabbit hole of emotion. The depth of that statement warms his bones yet sends feverish chills down his spine. The world contained behind Ethan's blue eyes is remarkable. "And your mosaic isn't complete?" The question is little more than a choked-up rasp.

"Far from it," Ethan says.

The intensity of their eye contact makes Taylor wish he could snap off a piece of himself and add it to Ethan's mosaic. Desperately, he wants to be part of what makes Ethan's life colorful, beautiful, serene. *Fuck.* These next few days without being able to touch Ethan and say lovely things to him are going to suck.

"It's late," Ethan notes, shattering the time lock they were in. "I should be getting back."

At the door, before he shrugs his hood back onto his head— a poor disguise but a good look for him—he tips his head down and his lips land on Taylor's cheek. If the rest of his days were lived inside this single sensation, Taylor would be forever happy.

"Good night," Ethan says before stalking off into the night.

Back in California, Amy only ever talked of the stubborn beast that was her ex-husband. Now more than ever, Taylor sees the prince beneath the fur and the shuttered windows and the snarl. Taylor so clearly sees *Ethan* and, sadly, a blissful future that can never come to pass.

Twenty-One

ETHAN

Around 11:00 a.m. on April 1, fifteen teenage girls pull up in a limo outside The Castle with backpacks and suitcases and perky, high-pitched laughter.

Ethan's medicating a tension headache from lack of sleep with the strongest morning blend they've got at How Do You Brew. He usually takes it black, but this morning, he went a little wild with the sugar. Lord knows he'll need it to keep his energy up with this bunch who've already shot off confetti poppers on his freshly mowed lawn.

From here on in, not only does he need to supervise and assist his daughter and her friends, but he has to pretend that he and Taylor are passing acquaintances. Today, he is Eve in the garden and Taylor is the apple. Does that make Gabriel the serpent for nudging him to take a bite? And if so, does that make Amy God because…?

"You good, Dad?" Samara asks, waving her hand in front of his face.

"Yeah. Great!" It's an overcompensation for sure. He leads the charge inside to get the girls all set up with their cottage assignments and keys. Suddenly, he's a school trip coordinator, too. But, really, anything for Samara is worth it. The smile already stamped on her face as she talks with her best friend, Lily, about the songs she plans to use for her candle lighting ceremony does more for Ethan's headache than the coffee ever could.

The festivities begin with a tour of the grounds. Each girl wears a pair of trainers and lululemon leggings. "Was there some kind of dress code?" Ethan asks Taylor when they're on the march back to The Castle for bracelet-making.

"It's the style."

Taylor placed boards over the foosball table and took the net down on the ping-pong table in the Knights and Knaves game room. Each girl has her own chair marked by a sparkly nameplate and her own DIY friendship bracelet kit. Music pumps out at a low volume from the speaker system in the room—no doubt a song by an artist Taylor and Samara were discussing last night at dinner. Ethan resolves that forty is the year he expands his musical knowledge. Whatever this is, he can't help from bopping his head along.

In the front corner is a small table from How Do You Brew with dozens of different bead styles. Ethan doesn't know when Taylor had the time to do this, but he's impressed all the same.

Unlike story time, which took a bad turn, Taylor commands the workshop with ease and skill, knowing when to step in and when to let the girls fail on their own. Like when

Lily forgets to tape her string and the beads go clattering to the floor, rolling off in eight different directions.

Thankfully, nobody laughs. Jeez, kids must've gotten nicer since his childhood days.

Bracelet-making is not rocket science, yet when Ethan tries his hand at the craft just to get out of further small talk with Amy, the only other adult in the room, he finds his thick fingers aren't made for this kind of work. Samara's already on her third, and he's busy grinding his teeth together with frustration.

Ethan abandons his string, instead choosing to watch as Taylor makes one at the front of the room. The beads are purple and gold—the colors of Ethan's favorite flannel. That's certainly not why Taylor chose them, but Ethan can fantasize. For a moment at least.

"The new signage looks superb," Amy says. It was only a matter of time before their conversations turned to business— the only topic they have between them besides Samara these days.

"They're shiny, that's for sure."

"Taylor gave me the inspection report and it seems as if everything is shipshape. Thank you," she says. He's certain she doesn't mean for this to come out like he's her underling, yet it rubs him the wrong way all the same. They whispered sweet nothings to each other once. He doesn't want *that* back, but surely there's a better middle ground.

"Of course. I love this place. I wouldn't let it fall into disar-ray." He regrets it the minute he says it. There are too many ways to misinterpret his words. And he really shouldn't be throwing around the *L* word in particular. After playing it in

Scrabble last night in Taylor's cottage, it seems to be popping up everywhere. Even one of the girls nearby is making a friendship bracelet in all pinks and reds that says it. Is it a warning sign?

She nods, eyes flicking over him in appraisal. "What happened to your hand?"

"Accident with some glass," he says, hand burying itself into the pocket of his jeans on instinct. She always knows how to strike a chord, even if she doesn't intend to.

The reverberation of that plucked nerve, however, lasts until he's out at the field, once again realizing he can't teach an archery lesson with a healing cut on his palm.

Thankfully, Taylor is present and ready to step in like last time. Ethan would have asked the birthday girl herself, but as most teenagers do, she possesses strong warring affinities for attention and self-consciousness. As he lays out the markers, he witnesses his daughter shrink, not wanting to be the only one in the group with any sort of skill at this. As if she won't be the only one in a lavish ball gown and a tiara tomorrow evening. Or whatever her equivalent of the look entails. Did she ever send him a picture like he asked her to? Whatever. He'll be surprised on the day.

Ethan schools himself into appropriateness as he goes back through the motions with Taylor, ignoring the thrumming just underneath his skin.

Getting into his *T* shape, Taylor turns his head, and Ethan gets a strong whiff of his shampoo. It's not the ocean-scent he keeps stocked in his own shower any longer. It's the neutral, floral scent stocked in the canisters of every shower on property. Noticing this makes his heart pinch and his words stutter, though the girls seem none the wiser.

Ethan's about to let Taylor shoot, but his hands are burning balls of desire. Even though Taylor doesn't need the adjustment, Ethan sidles up behind Taylor, mirrors the pose, and adjusts his front hand. Gliding his finger pads along Taylor's smooth knuckles is enough to satiate the shouting devil on his shoulder that wants him to take this sharp, capable man back to his cabin and keep him there forevermore.

Zip. Taylor's arrow slices across the field and hits the mark right at the bull's-eye.

The cheers from the girls take up in Ethan's chest. That target might as well be Ethan's heart, and the arrow directly from Cupid's bow.

Later, Taylor's off with the decorators and other staff members getting the barn set for tomorrow night's party. Dinner was thin crust pizza with custom toppings, and Ethan is stuffed to the gills. Everyone sits around the fire pits on the outdoor patio with blankets over their laps and pillows at their backs, making s'mores and chatting about guys from school.

Ethan is awed by how easily these girls express their feelings without guise. Has he ever had someone to do that with before? He sips from his beer bottle and considers it. Amy comes up beside him, snickering at the turns of the conversation.

"I don't think I was ever that young and that romantic," Amy says, bordering on judgmental.

Ethan bristles. "I beg to differ." He remembers moonlit boat rides and candlelit dinners and chocolate covered strawberries fed to each other naked on Valentine's night. "We had our share of romance."

"Because of you," she says, some of the edge to her voice wearing down. "You were the romantic. I was the realist."

"I suppose opposites attract," he says, tipping his beer up to his lips as fortification. What number beer might she be on that she's talking this openly with him?

"I don't know. I think Silvan is a realist as well, and I quite like him," she says.

He tries to place the name, but comes up empty. "Who is Silvan?"

She huffs, folding her arms. "Did you not hear me talk all about him at dinner last night?" The cadence of her question is unsettlingly familiar. He's whisked back to nights where he got lectured for forgetting to take the chicken out of the freezer to defrost in time for dinner, or the time he nearly got them into a car accident when he glanced up and saw a green light, only to realize as he slammed on the break that it was the left turn only arrow.

At present, he can understand both of those symptoms as ADHD. He's even shared this diagnosis with Amy, not as some sort of excuse for his past actions but as important information needed to coparent with.

"What does that matter?" she'd asked. "It's not like you're in school and taking tests and need extra time."

She couldn't understand. Or didn't want to understand. That's her right.

Still, the difference between Amy's reaction and Taylor's is stark and blazes through his mind.

"He's the photographer for the California location. We connected last week," she says.

"Should you be mixing business with pleasure like that?"

he asks, despite knowing better. There's a dark string between his brain and his mouth that grew strong toward the end of his relationship with Amy. He learned to give the provoking comments as good as he got them from her. Over time, he worked hard to find the sharp scissors needed to snip that string, extricate that impulse, but here it is, weak yet still present.

"Oh, please. You're one to talk," she says, elbowing him in the arm. Four beers down, at least. There's no way she'd elbow him otherwise. And that elbow sends a worry spiraling through his core. Does she know something? Did she infer something he fought hard to conceal during the archery lesson?

He asks around a huge wad of spit in his throat, "What does that mean?"

Her right eyebrow quirks like she thinks he's brainless. "You and I. Storybook Endings." She gestures around at the expanse with her free hand.

A relieved sigh slips out of him. "Right. Well. Look how that turned out."

Something in his sentiment moves Amy. Her shoulders—always thrown back, poised—rise and inch forward. Her mouth relaxes, from pursed to pleasant. There's a hint of the Amy he met in undergrad. "We had many good years, we launched a thriving business and we made a great daughter. In this day and age, I don't think marriages get more successful than that."

To that, he must concede. Some of the hurt he still harbors chips away, enough that he tips the neck of his beer bottle to hers.

Come to my cabin? I have something for you. Ethan's already halfway there with his hoodie pulled up when the text pings in. There is no way he's losing a single solitary moment alone with Taylor when he is leaving in two days. He crunches up to the cabin door and knocks.

"That was fast," Taylor says, gesturing him inside.

This time, Ethan takes off his shoes and hoodie and makes himself comfortable. He intends to stay for a while. Instead of saying anything, he produces a bottle of wine from his hiking backpack. Taylor, with a knowing smirk, goes and grabs some glasses.

"What is it you have for me?" Ethan asks, heart a slingshot against his rib cage. There's another question lying in wait behind his lips that he's nervous to let out.

After setting down a glass of wine in front of Ethan, Taylor fishes into the pocket of his joggers and produces a friendship bracelet. "For you," he says, gently setting it in Ethan's palm.

It's the same colors as his favorite, trusty flannel and in the center are his initials, separated by a bow and arrow symbol pressed onto a flat circular bead. String and plastic should not be able to hold this much raw emotion, yet pleasure fans out from the place where it sits in his palm. "Thank you," he mutters, struck still.

"Do you like it?" Taylor asks. The hesitation in his voice is endearing.

"I love it," he says, breaking the muzzle in his mind telling him not to utter that word. He slips the snug bracelet on his wrist, then holds it up, admiring the way the light gleams off the yellows.

"I had fun being your right-hand man again today." Taylor's eyes appear hooded over the rim of his glass. He's got his knees tucked up to his chest, his bare feet resting on the lip of the wooden chair across the table. Christ, Ethan could rip this table clean off the wall with the heavy-duty hormones coursing through him.

Ethan taps his fingers against the tabletop. "You're a natural instructor. You'd make an excellent activities coordinator at a Storybook Endings location."

The sides of Taylor's pretty mouth fall. "One day, maybe. That would be a dream. During my interview for the assistant position, I was drawn in by all the talk of career growth and hospitality opportunities, but nothing like that has materialized in the three years I've worked for Amy. Maybe I'm only meant to be an assistant." He stares into his wine.

"That's categorically untrue. Your initiative for Samara's party alone has shown you to be far more capable than coffee and scheduling—I'm sure of that," he says with all the conviction he has stored inside. Building Taylor up is the friendliest thing a friendly friend can do. Because they've agreed to be friends.

Yet…

Fuck.

That's the dominant *f* word that keeps rising to the top of Ethan's tall glass of thoughts.

"Thanks." Taylor's bashfulness entices Ethan to lean in.

"I'm only stating the truth," he says. The flourishing power of truth and his now-empty wineglass compel him to add, "You have no idea how badly I wanted to turn you around and kiss you today during our lesson."

Taylor gulps loudly. "I could tell by the way you adjusted my hand. I wish you could kiss me now." His brown eyes dip to Ethan's lips.

"Friends don't kiss their friends the way I want to kiss you,"

Ethan says. His internal filter dematerializes. "Friends don't fuck their friends the way I want you to fuck me."

A delicious shock sparks on Taylor's face. "I didn't know you had such a dirty mouth."

"I didn't until you showed up," he growls. It's nearly animalistic and reminds him of mating season in the nearby woods. Oh, the sounds that keep him awake at night as nature takes its course. "I had no desire to bottom before you showed up either, yet here we are."

"Have you ever...?"

Ethan shakes his head, warding off any embarrassment because Taylor won't judge him. He's not somehow less queer because he's never been on the receiving end of anal sex. "I've explored alone. I have a toy. But never with someone else. Nobody sees a six-foot-six, two-hundred-and-seventy-five-pound bear and thinks, 'He wants to take it.' They expect me to be in charge." If only he had the words to tell these men that it would be nice to take direction for a change. He may seem firm and resistant, but he's capable of submitting for the right reasons, for the right person. "It's hard to find someone you trust to try something new with."

"For sure," Taylor says. He's holding his glass around the rim, swirling it. Clearly, he's lost in thought. "Friends with benefits exist for a reason, right? Friends do help friends out every now and then."

Hearing his own rationale in Taylor's voice pumps up his pulse. "Could we be those sorts of friends?"

"Gladly."

They're horizontal on the bed in seconds, clawing at each other's clothing—a frustrating impediment.

As his long-sleeved T-shirt is peeled off, Ethan's shedding

his old skin, as well, like he's that tantalizing, devilish snake. It occurs to him then—all hard and exposed—that in his metaphorical Garden of Eden, he plays all the parts. He's Adam; he's Eve; he's the serpent and God. With heady breath traveling through his long limbs, he's the living tree that bears the divine fruit, and when Taylor's teeth bite the hair-covered, sensitive flesh on the inside of Ethan's right thigh, he's the apple, as well. Shiny, alluring, ready to be plucked. *Devoured.*

Taylor primes Ethan's hole with care. Ethan showered and cleansed and used his toy to ensure he was ready for this, so all Taylor needs to worry about is helping Ethan relax enough to accept the stretch. Glancing down between Taylor's legs, he's reminded of just how much of a stretch it's going to be. Does Taylor's back hurt from carrying that trunk around all day? Ethan takes a deep breath, committed to the challenge.

On his knees, facing the window, Ethan drops his broad, furry chest to the mattress as Taylor instructs. Suddenly, there's warm wetness at his hole. A lapping sensation that eclipses his mind. For once, those sprinting thoughts slow to a jog.

"Oh, yes," Ethan croons. Ethan's ass has always been large, and he savors the way Taylor makes a meal of it, running his mouth along the hair-dusted fleshiness. Taylor's hands aren't wide enough to fully grasp the globes of him, but Christ does he try. It's in the trying that Ethan begins to pant. "In my bag, uh-*fughhu*, you'll find lube…"

Taylor springs away to procure the spoils and snatch a towel from the bathroom. Turning onto his back, Ethan widens his hips by holding his legs up in the air behind the knees. Easily, Taylor slicks his pointer finger and glides it inside. It barely registers.

"Add more fingers," Ethan says, eyes closed. Then, he remembers himself. "Please."

"Sure thing. Only because you were so polite about it," Taylor says, sending a second finger to join the first. Ethan opens even more from hearing this dominant, assured voice roll out of the slender surfer he's been desperate for. Taylor's decadently slow in-and-out motion turns him feral. "How's that?"

"Still not enough," Ethan says, realizing that this may not be as much about submitting as it is about taking what he wants. About filling his desires and his hole.

"Somebody's hungry," Taylor teases.

That third one does the trick, causes that idyllic ache. It's the trifecta of fingers. The slow brush of their pads against his prostate makes Ethan's cock leak onto his furry stomach. He cries out Taylor's name as precum pools in his belly button.

"That's it. Say it. Say my name."

"Taylor."

Brush. "Again."

"Taylor."

Brush. Brush. "One more time."

"Taaaaaaaaaaaaylor."

The finger-fucking starts in earnest, and Taylor's other hand comes up to grip Ethan's cock. In perfect sync, he fucks and strokes. Ethan's body can barely process the sparring sensations that send him tumbling through the looking glass, to a world of rabbits and flowers and hearts and smoke and... "Fuck."

"Is that what you want?" Taylor asks, bringing Ethan back to earth. "You want me to fuck you?"

"Yes, please," Ethan begs.

"My, what manners you have," Taylor says with a smirk,

underscored by him breaking open the condom box. Magnums. Far from what Ethan usually buys.

"I'm a gentleman," Ethan says, sitting up.

Taylor lies on his back, head on the pillow. "We'll see how long that holds once you've got all of me inside you."

Terror pulls back a heavy curtain and steps into the room with them. Looking more fully now, his toy comes nowhere close to Taylor's length and girth. Far be it from Ethan to shy away from a trial, but even the strongest will sometimes isn't enough.

Taylor's hand reaches out and brushes that pesky strand of hair off Ethan's already damp forehead. "It's meant to feel good. If it hurts or you change your mind, say the word and we stop."

The trust he's built with Taylor in such a short span causes tears to spring up into his eyes. He glances away to blink them back. Bottoming is vulnerable enough without the waterworks. Once composed, he brackets Taylor's hips with his thighs. This shouldn't feel as death-defying as it does, like he's about to jump off a craggy cliff and into the raging sea below to escape a band of pirates, but it does. Just Taylor's lubed tip lying in wait between his ass cheeks is enough to turn his blood into pure adrenaline.

"Slow now," Taylor says once Ethan grips the shaft and shifts himself backward.

Christ, he wants to scream. Not because it hurts, even though the tender burn does border on that feeling. But rather because doing this for the first time with Taylor ignites his pleasure center in a way he's never experienced. A way he may never experience again.

Resolved, he's going to milk this for everything he can. Inch by inch, he takes Taylor inside him, gasping for breath, stopping every few seconds to adjust and then descend some more before rocking gently up and down.

"That feels amazing," Taylor says encouragingly, letting his hands rove over Ethan's ample, hairy torso. "You feel amazing." Taylor's palm brushes over Ethan's right nipple and then crests the curve of Ethan's belly.

"You feel—" Ethan's words get stuck in his throat when Taylor's cock hits a spot deep inside him that feels like a foot stomping on a car brake. "Oh, I—" He contorts his face, wiggles unnaturally.

"Hey," Taylor says softly.

Ethan ignores it, grinds away...

"Hey." The word is powerful now. Taylor's got Ethan by the chin, forcing him to take in those stern brown eyes. "Ease up. I don't feel good if you don't feel good."

Ethan nods, Taylor's fingers brushing against his beard hairs. "Okay." He crashes forward to claim Taylor with a kiss.

Sitting up a bit more, he finds his comfort spot again. Their tongues tangle while his hips circle. Taylor groans into his mouth, high praise that shoots straight to Ethan's dick. He reaches his right hand between his legs and strokes against Taylor's smooth, taut stomach.

His body temperature rises in time with his heart rate and, swiftly, he's feeling that illuminating awareness from underneath. The pressure cranks up to a thousand. He's not sure how many minutes it's been, but he knows within the next few he's going to—

"Come," is all he ekes out.

"Come for me, Ethan. Come on me."

Rope after rope, he paints Taylor's chest, never stopping the exquisite grind that got him there. The undulations of pleasure hit every one of his muscles from his toes to his forehead. He can practically feel the orgasm in his teeth, in his caps and fillings. It's everything.

He's loath to stop. He wants to bring Taylor to the place he's just been, but now that full, superb niggle in his hole has morphed into overload. The sparks fly sharper, so he slows to a standstill.

Perceptive beyond measure, Taylor places his hands on Ethan's ass and guides him gently up and off. "But—" Ethan chokes out.

"Shh," Taylor says.

Ethan lies spent beside Taylor on the bed and watches as Taylor removes the condom, ties it off and then uses Ethan's cum as lube to stroke himself. "Kiss me, Ethan."

Ethan does so without hesitation, sending one arm up and behind Taylor's head so it rests around his shoulders. He tugs Taylor to him as Taylor's pumps become more frantic. "I'm going to come," he pants into Ethan's mouth as heat spurts dramatically between them.

Twenty-Two

ETHAN

The first licks of morning light are like being bathed in Nana's rank slobber.

One glance at the digital clock is the only impetus Ethan needs to shoot up. He's overslept. *Woof.* His head spins, and his mouth is dry. Mixing beer and wine was a bad move. His clothes seem unimaginably far away.

Over his shoulder, Taylor sleeps on his stomach. The cleft of his ass peeks out from beneath the top sheet and the quilted comforter. His hair splays in tendrils across the cream-colored pillowcase. A light droplet of drool shines on the edge of his lips—the very same lips Ethan explored with vigor last night.

Last night, despite everything, did not feel like an ending.

A part of him thought bottoming for Taylor would seal off their connection, encase it in amber to be preserved, but never thawed for fear of the ramifications. Christ, he's seen *Jurassic Park* too many times.

But as the sunlight shifts through that new window to his left, maybe the damage has already been done. His heart, it's clear, won't ever be the same. But those are words he needs to keep to himself because today is Samara's birthday and to-morrow, Taylor leaves for good.

He needs to get himself dressed and get back to the cottage with enough time to screw his head back on straight, so he can be clear-minded and present for his daughter's big day.

Hoodie, keys, shoes. *Check, check, check.*

He's almost out the door without waking Taylor when a voice hits him from only paces away. "Ethan?" The question mark is there, sure, but the accusation behind it is what wallops Ethan most.

He shuts the door too hard behind him, and it bangs in its frame.

Ethan curses under his breath before letting his hood fall so he can look up.

In the early-morning light, he faces Amy.

She's wearing a white, long-sleeved button-down shirt, a tan vest, tan slacks and a light jacket. Her hair is up in a bun, but it's her shoes that draw his eye: bright red, the color of her blood—which he can practically hear boiling. "What were you doing in there?"

"I was, uh, checking on the roof issue," he says, finally meeting her eyes. They've gone black. In her hands, she holds a clipboard and wedged inside the clip is a pencil. The bold text on the top of the page reads: RESORT INSPECTION.

Why is she double-checking Taylor's work? And so esoterically at that?

She cocks an eyebrow. "The issue with the roof was with Taylor's cabin?" she asks, then doesn't wait for him to answer. "Why were you here so early? And why are you checking the issue in last night's clothes?"

This is what a wild bear must feel like right before the cage walls of a trap fall in around him. "Amy," Ethan starts. "Don't make me say it."

"Don't make you say it?" Amy asks. Her words are dart pins and he's a wall of water balloons. "Don't make you say that you're *sleeping with* my assistant?"

The creak of the door behind him only serves to make the situation worse. Taylor's heard the kerfuffle and come to see what's happened. The worst of it is that when Ethan turns to find him there, he's wearing Amy's old robe. Stupidly, Ethan must've packed it in Taylor's suitcase when he hastily cleaned out the guest room.

Amy's head looks like it's about to bobble right off her neck. "This is outrageous and unprofessional on every level."

"Amy, I—" Taylor steps out, holding the robe closed.

"You're fired," she says.

Ethan holds up a hand. "Let's not be hasty."

"You don't have a voice in this conversation," she says, shutting him down.

Taylor, red-faced and breathing audibly, steps farther onto the porch. "Amy, please, I'm sorry. You have every right to be upset with me—"

"Thank you for your permission to feel what I'm feeling," she says, stock-still and fuming.

Taylor jostles a bit. "I...only meant that I deserve to be fired." He chokes a bit. "But Samara's party is tonight. Her special day doesn't deserve to be ruined over this. I still have to—"

"You have done more than enough. Your services are no longer needed here," she says with icy venom. "Pack your things, but first bring me the iPad so I can book you the first flight out of here."

Whatever fight Taylor had in him evaporates like the morning dew. He hangs his head and slinks back inside the cottage, leaving the door half-open as if he doesn't even have the energy to shut it.

Hating the downtrodden expression on Taylor's face, Ethan's voice drops to a quiet, piercing place. "You're acting like a teenager."

"And you're sleeping with one."

"He is *twenty-seven years old*, Amy."

Her thumbs are punching at her phone. "Maybe he should act like it. What was he thinking? What were *you* thinking? Do you really dislike me that much? Is this some act to spite me for moving on with my life and the business?"

Ethan can't control the laughter that starts low in his gut and falls out in a surprising wave. She looks at him with pure disgust. Once the fit subsides, he says, "It might be hard for you to believe, but this—" he waves back toward the door of the cottage "—had nothing to do with you. This was about me and him. *Him.* He is a wonderful, empathetic and intelligent man who is passionate about your company and these resorts, and you are squandering him as your errand boy."

"You know nothing of what he does on the daily. He is not some latte-getter. He has responsibilities," Amy huffs without looking up. Whatever she's trying to do on her phone, she's struggling to accomplish it.

"Manning your schedule, booking your meetings, overseeing your travel, heck, he even oversees *our daughter*." That might strike below the belt, but fighting fair isn't exactly his top priority right now. "He wants to work in hospitality, not under your thumb. Heck, you give him one speck of responsibility and you're double-checking his work." He nods derisively down at the clipboard in her left hand. She has the gall to slide it behind her back as if placing it out of sight will make it disappear.

"The way I run my company and delegate tasks to my employees is none of your business because, guess what? You forfeited any say in the business when we finalized our divorce. You're lucky replacing you here would be a nightmare, otherwise I'd fire you," she says, finger waggling, but never fully committing to the point.

Is that what the divorce was to her? Her firing him from the position of husband?

His nostrils flare, but he holds his ground. "I am lucky, but not for that reason. I'm lucky because I was present when you sent Taylor out here all by himself to put together our daughter's sweet sixteen—something that, in my mind, shouldn't have been outsourced—but we were *both* lucky it was outsourced to someone like Taylor who cares deeply about the people he loves."

At the end of Ethan's speech, he's startled by Taylor clearing his throat behind them. Taylor's shed the robe and is wearing his normal clothes now. The sandals and tie-dyed hoodie. A uniform Ethan is going to sorely miss. There are tears rimming the edges of Taylor's eyes as he says, "Here." He passes the almighty tablet to Amy.

She grabs it from him without looking him in the eye. He retreats, but then she says in a gentler voice, "Taylor." His posture shifts when he pivots. "I can never remember which app it is for the airline points."

He slumps over. "It's this one." He taps the screen on her behalf.

Ethan stifles his snort of disapproval. This scene is spectacularly pathetic. They are three adults. They should be able to hash this out as such, but that seems impossible when the outside air is clouded with a thick smog of misunderstanding.

Taylor slips back into the cabin without another word, Amy stomps off in the direction of The Castle and Ethan is left standing there, alone, surrounded by the mucky fragments of his own heart.

TAYLOR

He can barely see through the tears as he packs his suitcase.

He doesn't know what's making him cry more: that he got fired or the sweet, loving words Ethan said about him.

Nobody—and he truly means nobody—has spoken about him that way before. Not even his siblings. His burden in childhood was an invisible one. From the time his older brother abandoned the family, Taylor took the extra responsibilities, strapped them to his back, and ignored the stress pains it caused him.

Because it's easier to accept his lot than waste energy wishing for a different one. Life doesn't miraculously start doling out kindnesses because you've suffered. The only way to excavate the good in the world is to dig through the bad.

"Please stop packing. Don't go," Ethan says, appearing in the doorway that, try as it might, can't contain the grandness of him. Not just the scope of his incredible body, but the hugeness of his heart. The one Taylor can almost see stitched to his sleeve right now.

Taylor's hands continue to move on autopilot. "You heard Amy. She doesn't want me here anymore. I'm not needed." His selfishness has charred his career to a crisp. So long to any chance of working in the hospitality industry ever again. He wouldn't be surprised if Amy had him blacklisted or something of the sort.

"That's not true. Samara needs you here. Her friends need you here. I need you here." His voice pitches upward as Taylor's heart tunnels down, down, down into the floorboards.

"Thank you for everything you said. It all means a lot to me," Taylor says, feeling a second swell of tears coming on.

"But not enough to stay? Even though I'm asking?" Taylor can't help but liken Ethan's pleading eyes to Nana's when she doesn't get any dinner scraps from the table. He reserves the impulse to reach out and smooth the hair behind Ethan's right ear.

"Ethan," Taylor says, followed by a sigh. "Family comes first. Samara only gets one sixteenth birthday. I won't be the reason there's tension or unhappiness on her big day. Let me go, okay?"

Ethan must understand this because he leans back and his head thunks against the door frame. "When this is over, I can call you, though, right? We can see each other again, can't we? Friends call each other and see each other."

"I think…" Taylor begins, but then gets choked up, emotions forming a lump in his throat. "I think this has shown me that I have some work to do on myself. A lot of work, actually. And I'm just not sure I have room enough in my life for a friend as important as you right now."

He's spent his whole life putting other people's needs first, and for one week he got drunk with the newfound pleasure of selfishness, a word he no longer finds repugnant. It has true merit in his life. He must find a balance without Ethan on standby. Otherwise, he'll be too tempted to stage-manage the fallout with Amy, temperature check Samara and ease Ethan into long-distance friendship. A clean break feels like the only kind way to reduce harm for all involved.

Ethan's hand swipes down his face. "Right. Of course. That makes sense. I'll leave you to finish up, then."

"Wait," Taylor says, hand finding a thin square inside his suitcase. "Can you make sure Samara gets this?"

Ethan takes the wrapped record from him. "There's no card or tag."

"It can be from you," Taylor says, on the brink of losing what little voice he has left. He's parched and aching to leave here before he causes any more destruction for the Lu-Golding family.

"Are you sure?" Ethan asks with a tone that conveys he's not only asking after the record.

Through a scratchy throat, he says, "I'm sure."

Shoulders rolled forward, Ethan walks out the door of the Snow White cottage and out of Taylor's life.

The last thing he did before leaving the Snow White cottage was trash the half-eaten bag of mint Milanos still sitting on the counter. Such a waste, but he couldn't bear to bring them as a car snack on the long drive back to the airport.

After dropping the Honda off in the designated rental car area, Taylor made his way through security, tail between his legs like he'd seen Nana do after she tracked mud in through the living room the day after the storm that launched a thousand kisses. Taylor elbows away memories of bathing her with Ethan in the bathtub and how silly she looked, all huge and sopping wet.

The unforgiving overhead lights, the glass-and-chrome structures and the harried travelers in the terminal serve to dizzy Taylor further as he steps onto the moving walkway toward his gate. The airport is crowded, but he locates a seat near an outlet far enough away from others and pops his headphones in. He's just about to press Play on the new playlist Samara had sent him when a phone call rings in.

"Sorry for not returning your call sooner!" Sasha's voice unspools some of his stress. "I've been prepping for this major exam and my phone has been acting up. I finally traded in that piece of crap and got a new one to reward myself for acing it."

"Hell yeah, congrats." Taylor says, though it's strenuous to gather up his excitement right now. "Which exam was this again?"

"It was for my pain management course, which you know has been a pain in my own ass."

"Surprised you didn't call me while you were studying, threatening to drop out," Taylor says jokingly. It's their special routine. He knows she only ever half means it, and he's obscenely proud of her despite how awful he feels.

"Growth! Even I'm capable of it," she says in her usual self-deprecating way.

He smiles as he watches a plane take off through the floor-to-ceiling glass window. "Congrats, Sash."

"Enough about me. What's the situation with hot-single-dad? Still having an ethical crisis?" she asks. Even though she's phrased it as a joke, her concern floats out through Taylor's phone and hugs him.

Taylor clears his throat, overcome once again. "Not exactly."

"Oh, thank God. I'm glad you're allowing yourself nice things for once," she says. "I've seen pictures of that man, and he is not just nice, he is fiiiiiiiine."

"It's not like that."

"What's it like, then?" she asks, concerned.

He blinks back inconvenient tears to no avail. "I'm waiting on an airplane to take me home."

"Wait, sorry. Color me confused. Aren't you supposed to be My-Super-Sweet-Sixteensing today for your boss's daughter, or do I have my days mixed up?"

His lip quivering makes it impossible to answer. In his head, images of the barn all set up for the shindig swipe through like a slide show. He won't be there for Samara's grand entrance in her short poufy dress or for the mousse cake or for the candle lighting ceremony. What Ethan said to Amy was true. He does care deeply about Samara, and he wanted to be there to celebrate. It was nice of Ethan to ask him to stay, but he refuses to be the barf in the middle of the dance floor—everyone swaying around the mess until it can be dealt with.

Taylor has made it his life's mission to not need to be dealt with. His parents, despite all their flaws, taught him to accept the consequences of his actions. Isn't that why they read him all those fairy tales? To drill in that lesson?

"Sash, I got fired," he says.

"Oh, shit. Your boss found out? I'm so sorry, Tay."

"It's fine. It's just—" He starts blubbering then. Good thing he's in the corner and facing away from the rest of the seats so he can't view anyone's reactions to his undoing.

"Aw, Tay. It's just what?" she asks, airdropping care to him clear across the country. He could use a real tight hug right now.

"It's just…" he says, but the sentence falls off again. Because what's he supposed to say? *IT'S JUST THAT I COULD SEE MYSELF FALLING IN LOVE WITH HIM.* There's no way he could admit that because it's ludicrous. Who falls in love with someone over little more than a week? That's the part of fairy tales his parents didn't promote.

Whatever he was feeling was probably just excitement or newness or the forbidden nature of it.

A boarding call sounds out through the gate area, and Taylor tries his best to pull himself together. "We're getting ready to get on. We can talk when I get back."

She sighs. He can tell she wishes she could teleport there to comfort him on the long flight home. A sappy rom-com with two hot straights on the in-flight TV will have to suffice. "Call me when you land, please?"

"Will do," he says, shoving a crumpled tissue into his jogger pocket.

"Love you lots," Sasha says.

Every time he pushes that word down it pops back out like a broken jack-in-the-box. "Love you, too, Sash. See you soon."

Twenty-Three

ETHAN

The barn looks lovely with its twinkle lights and fake flower arrangements, and his daughter looks lovelier in her deep purple cropped ball gown with sparkly Dr. Martens beneath it and a punk rock tiara pinned in her hair. She stands behind a board of tall candles. Despite being surrounded by all this loveliness, Ethan can't bring himself to *feel* lovely.

How can he when—judging by the time on his watch—Taylor is on a cross-country flight? Lovely is absent in his grab bag of emotions right now. His stomach and his head are warring for which hurts worse.

Samara continues the traditional ceremony. "My second candle goes to Ora and Smith. Photography club forever! Ora, thank you for always helping me find the perfect light. Smith, thanks for being the best assignment model a girl could ask for. You both are amazing friends. Please come up and light my second candle with me."

Ed Sheeran's "Photograph" blasts at an inhumane volume. Ethan hovers on the perimeter of the party, one hand holding a beer, the other stuffed into the pocket of the suit pants that he wore to officiate the wedding last week. His emotional life was much simpler then. He had to go and mess it all up by falling for the most off-limits person possible.

"My third candle goes out to someone who came into my life three years ago. Even though he had to leave suddenly for a family emergency, I still want to dedicate this candle to Taylor Frost. He may be my mom's personal assistant, but over the years he's become my friend—almost like a brother. Nobody is a better listener or has better taste in music." She winks at the phone one of her friends is holding up, presumably videoing this to send to Taylor later. He hates that Amy told her a lie about what happened with Taylor. Like the situation with the napkin at The Thirsty Goat, she's babying Samara. "Thanks for being the best chauffeur and sing-along partner a girl can ask for. Mom, since Taylor isn't here, would you come light this one with me?"

Amy stands beside Giselle on the other end of the room. Since their blowout in front of the Snow White cottage, Amy's given Ethan a wide berth. The only time they came within touching distance was when they walked Samara inside the barn to rapturous applause and phone flashes. She didn't even bother picking up her camera to take a picture of the father-daughter dance. It's remarkable how wedding-like these celebrations can be. Seems as if every life hallmark is just preparing young people for an inevitable exchange of rings.

Ethan and Amy are the only two in the room who can sense the black cloud of awkwardness. Samara, none the wiser, smiles brightly for the hired photographer who is snapping memento shots with a loud clicking shutter.

Ethan's retreated so far into his own mind over how much Taylor means to Samara that he nearly misses his own candle. Crossing in front of the crowd overwhelms him, but as soon as he hugs his daughter, he returns to his body. He relishes the contact.

"Cheer up, Dad," she says when he bends way down to kiss her cheek. "It's my birthday! It won't kill you to smile." She shows him what she means, flashing that massive, toothy smile she's had ever since she was a kid. He'd do anything for his daughter.

After the ceremony concludes and the cake is cut, out on the dance floor, his brothers, their wives, and his nieces and nephews dance happily around one another. Even his mother and father, on the outskirts of the main, rambunctious action, wiggle in their own way to whatever remix is shaking the floor, causing the table legs to jump.

His father, taking note of him isolating, wheels himself over. "What are you doing here all by your lonesome?"

Ethan looks down at his father, recalling a time when they were nose to nose. Ethan was probably eighteen or nineteen at the time before that last spurt of puberty shot him past his father's six-foot-two frame. Now his father's body may be unrecognizable from the man who taught him to fly-fish and shoot a bow and arrow, but his spirit is the same as ever. A phoenix, constantly on the rise. "I'm taking it all in."

"Good. You should. That daughter of yours has got spunk,"

he says, jutting his chin over to where Samara has set her phone up on one of the lavender ring lights Taylor had custom-made for the occasion. Samara and her friends are posing in double-time to the beat of the song as colorful lights dance and shimmer off their outfits.

"Ain't that the truth," Ethan says, letting an inkling of happiness infuse his mood. "Are you having a good time?"

His father toys with a quizzical look. His facial muscles, after bouts of drooping and spasming, don't have the same strength they used to, but Ethan's had a lot of practice in cataloguing his new range of emotions. "I think the better question is, are you?"

Ethan's eyes land on his father's wedding band. Did his parents hold the secret code to lasting love, or are they just of a different generation where staying together is expected? Granted, his mother is not the kind of woman to walk out on a man with an autoimmune disease that's eating at him from the inside. But still. He wonders...

"Is everything okay?" his father asks in a warm tone.

He nods uncertainly. "It will be."

"When you came to bring us our groceries last week, you told us you couldn't stay because there was a young man named Taylor waiting for you back home. I don't see him here today," he says.

In this moment only, he wishes his father's memory wasn't so sharp. "He had to leave unexpectedly."

"Does that have anything to do with the glum expression you've been wearing all evening?" he asks.

Ethan shifts at that. "That noticeable, huh?"

"By an old pro like me," he says. "This Taylor wouldn't happen to be the same one Samara mentioned in her speeches?"

"The very same," Ethan admits, burned out from hiding behind his fortress walls too long today. The only living being he told any of this to was Nana and while she's good for a listen and a cuddle, she's not a paragon of advice beyond the occasional *arf*.

"Sticky," his father says, referring to the situation.

"Very."

"Did I ever tell you the true story of how your mother and I got together?" he asks.

"Of course. You taught her archery. You've mentioned this many times." He slugs back a sip of beer.

"That wasn't exactly the whole truth…"

Ethan's jaw unclenches. It's hard to hear his father fully through the roar of the music so Ethan helps them relocate to a table in the back of the room, eager to know a family tidbit he's somehow missed all these years. "What is the whole truth?" Ethan asks.

"Your mother didn't actually attend the school. Your grandfather, Jeb, who you never met, owned the school. He wanted to teach the next generation of archers, but I think he was peeved he and his wife had three girls and no boys. He wouldn't let his girls near the sport. He said it was too dangerous and unladylike, but you know your mom," he says.

"I do, I do," Ethan says, eyes flicking over to where she's dancing with abandon. Always an explorer. The only reason she wasn't in any of their camping photos is because she was the only one who ever remembered to take any pictures on their trips.

"She didn't like that reasoning, so when I became an instructor at the school, she would corner me after classes. At first I thought she was flirting with me. I wasn't exactly a looker, but I was good at the sport, three years older, a big man around the school. Eventually, I realized she wanted me to teach her lessons without her father knowing," he said.

"And did you?" Ethan asked, childlike eagerness nesting in his voice.

"Of course I did. I wasn't going to pass up an opportunity to get close to a pretty, smart girl like her. A few months passed and our lessons grew more personal—some might even say romantic. There's something about the secret that heightened all the feelings. Our time together grew more date-like, and as our feelings grew so did our sloppiness, which is how we ended up getting caught," he recalls with a sense of humor only hindsight can provide. "Your grandfather was furious— threatening my job, threatening to ground her for life—but I looked him right in the eye and said, 'Let her shoot.' He didn't know what I meant at first, but I suggested that if she performed a perfect shot, she'd get to keep learning and I'd get to keep seeing her. He laughed, but ultimately relented."

"She got a perfect shot?" Ethan asks.

"No, not even close. But I was pretty persuasive back then and I asked him for a retest, one week later. If she couldn't shoot a perfect shot, I'd resign and leave their family alone," he says.

"And this time she shot a perfect shot?"

He chuckles. "No, she didn't, but she was much closer, and she showed better form and skill than half the guys her age, and that was enough for Jeb," he says.

"Why haven't I heard this version before?"

"Because it was so long ago, and it always angered your grandfather. He was not a man who liked to be wrong," he says. "Also, don't tell your mother, but I agreed to take on some personal coaching for free to smooth over the rift and keep dating her. Sweetened the deal for him a bit."

"You never told her?"

He looks up mischievously, does a hand motion that mimes zipping his lips.

Ethan nods, smiles. "Why exactly are you telling me this now?"

"Figured you could use a reminder that good people are worth fighting for," he says with a knowing nod of the head.

"I appreciate it," Ethan says. He doesn't go into it all. He doesn't say that it doesn't matter now, that he was ready to fight for Taylor, but Taylor said he didn't have room in his life for Ethan.

Maybe next time he won't give up as easily.

If there ever is a next time.

Twenty-Four

TAYLOR

Running on the fragmented sleep he got on the plane and the three hours he got in his own bed back at his apartment, Taylor greets the sunrise from the sand on the beach. He dons his 4/3 wet suit and booties. His surfboard is cradled under his right arm.

When life goes wrong, the waves go right.

At least that's how it's worked in the past.

The onshore winds and wonky tide at Moonlight State Beach do nothing to deter him. Leaving his belongings in the sand, he wades into the surf. There's a nippy chill to the water, even though the midfifties temperature of the air feels downright balmy compared to what he left behind in upstate New York.

Lying in wait, stomach flush to the waxy board, the present month comes to mind: April. Spring is a shitty time for

SoCal surf, but early April especially. The short period and small swells make it nearly impossible to catch a ride.

Time passes interminably as Taylor rocks alone in the uncooperative waves with only his thoughts for company. Usually, surfing wipes his brain clean. Today, he's waterlogged, literally and mentally.

He shuts his eyes against the sun and prays to some higher power for something, *anything*. When he opens them again, the less than ideal conditions have grown worse as a dense fog rolls in around him.

Discouraged and depressed, he heads back for shore. He's not looking forward to his first full day of unemployment. What's he supposed to do with himself? Look for new positions, surely, but he's not ready to dive into that. And it's not like Amy's going to write him a glowing letter of recommendation, so he's got limited options. Those limited options become a tsunami. If he has no job, he'll have no steady pay, and he'll have to move out of his place, and yup, that settles it, his life is over.

Except, maybe that higher power was listening to him before because there on the sand on a towel beside his stuff is Sasha. She's dressed in a university hoodie, jeans and sandals. She holds up a greasy brown paper bag like it's a trophy. "I brought breakfast!" she shouts over the wind whipping at his ears.

Taylor has never been more excited to see someone, or avocado toast for that matter. "How did you know I was here?"

"Went to your place and your roomies said you were out. This was literally the only other spot I could think of you being," she says, passing him a paper container and a napkin that almost blows away. "Did you hang ten?"

Taylor rolls his eyes and licks a bit of stray avocado off his finger. "I was prepared to hang up my wet suit for good given how dismal the surf was. I was really hoping it would clear my mind, but instead my mind is as mushy as this avocado." He takes a big, gooey bite. It's the first decent sustenance he's had in twelve hours.

"Would talking about it help?" she asks, ever the gold star sister. She wraps a towel around his shoulders as he eats.

Since their phone call in the airport barely scratched the surface of the situation, Taylor breathlessly provides the play-by-play.

"You are such a hard worker. I can't believe she just canned you like that. Where in your employment contract did it say you couldn't fool around with her ex-husband?" Sasha asks.

He nearly chokes on the multigrain toast. "I think some things are just, ya know, implied."

"Well, still. It's not like she should have a say over your love life, or Ethan's for that matter." She picks off a sliced cherry tomato with a rankled expression and sets it aside. "She sounds like a total bitch."

"Amy's not a bitch," he quickly defends. "She just demands a certain level of professionalism and commitment. It's what's gotten her where she is today. Long story short, I failed her."

Sasha sighs, but places a comforting hand on his closest knee. "If you still admire her so much, why don't you start acting like her?"

Taylor bristles. "What's that mean?"

She shrugs. "From the time you were eleven, you were changing diapers and reheating meals and making sure nobody got grievously hurt in our household. Then you went on to become a personal assistant and, I don't know, your whole life became about other people's lives. You're allowed to have a life and a love of your own. She certainly lets herself have those privileges."

"I don't know," Taylor says, mentally wrestling with the logic and truth. Selfishness still doesn't sit right with him. He knows he's allowed it, but in what quantity?

"What is there not to know? You said in your voicemail to me that you didn't feel guilty for sleeping with Ethan. Is that still true?" she asks.

Taylor concludes, "I do feel guilt, just not over what I did. But more about how it went down and how I hurt people with my actions, with my selfishness."

"Selfishness?" she asks.

"Like Owen," Taylor says. Owen's name—rarely spoken and missing entirely from the sibling group chat—twirls between them like a baton of resentment.

"Like Owen? What does this have to do with—" Sasha's eyes widen. "How could you possibly think what you did compares to Owen practically disowning our family?"

"I always thought him abandoning us was the ultimate act of selfishness. I vowed to always put those I loved and cared about before myself because I never wanted anyone to hurt the way I did when Owen left me in a scramble," he says.

Sasha sighs. "I'm studying to be a PT, right? I don't know much about the brain and the emotional centers that live there, but I do know about injuries and injuries hurt, obviously. Hurt happens to all of us. It's unavoidable. Sometimes we cause it and sometimes we receive it, but there's no way to seal ourselves off from it unless we stop living. I promise, hurt heals with time and the right exercises."

"That sounds too neat to be true," he says.

She clicks her tongue at him. "It's my client's job to accept responsibility for their care, to show up to sessions and to want to get better. It doesn't matter whose fault the accident was or where the pain started. I know Owen never apologized for leaving you to be the de facto parental figure in our family, and that sucks. But you're not Owen. You know the value of an apology. And once you apologize fully for not being open about what was going on, it's on Amy to do the work to figure out why she reacted the way she did and how she's going to tend to herself in the future," Sasha says, staring out at the ocean. "I'm not saying she's required to forgive you. Just like you're not required to forgive Owen. If Amy chooses to hold on to the hurt, that's her prerogative. That's her pain to carry, and you shouldn't inflict more pain on yourself because of it."

"I wish it were as simple as some exercises, though, to erase it all." He sets his food aside, stomach no longer engaged or interested.

"Exercises don't fully heal an injury. They retrain and strengthen the hurt muscles. Your heart hurts now. But that doesn't mean it will forever. I listened to your voicemail again this morning and, I don't know, it sounded like you really like Ethan. Is it possible you broke something that didn't need breaking?" she asks.

Taylor digs his fingers into the sand and pulls up a shell, chipped at the edges. Still beautiful. Ethan's voice is clear in his mind: *"Peace isn't a mural. It's a mosaic."* If he didn't take on Amy's pain and he forged ahead for a new job, could he and Ethan pick up the shards of what they had a week ago and glue them into something equally beautiful?

"Maybe," he says contemplatively. "Maybe."

She places a gentle hand on his knee. "Do the exercises. Take the steps. Want to be healthy, Taylor. Want something *for yourself* for once. You deserve it."

Twenty-Five

ETHAN

Early the next morning, Samara shows up at Ethan's cabin asking after a heart-shaped waffle maker from childhood.

"I'm sure it's around here somewhere," Ethan says, still wiping the sleep crust from his eyes. The door stands open, allowing the warming day and the fresh air in. Nana barks behind him, trying to get around his thick legs to get to Samara, who is all too happy to give her the pets she craves. "Why do you ask?"

"I want a waffle," she says like only a sixteen-year-old can—like this should be abundantly obvious and he's an oaf for asking.

"You have a final brunch with your friends in two hours. There will be waffles there," he says, confused but stepping aside so she can come in.

"Okay, and? I want *your* waffle from *your* heart-shaped maker so I can spend time with *you*," she says, exasperated.

"Jeez, I didn't know I needed to write an essay just to spend time with you."

This jolts him awake. "No! Gosh. I'm happy you're here. Waffles, coming right up."

In the kitchen, he throws on his apron, grabs the mix from the pantry and then goes hunting under the sink for the desired waffle maker. There are dozens of unused cooking appliances under there, and he regrets not decluttering when Amy and Samara moved out.

"What's this?" Samara asks from the living room where she's plopped herself down on the couch. Nana rests beside her, head nuzzled onto her lap. Samara holds up *Grimm's Fairy Tales*.

"A book," Ethan says, holding the waffle maker, which is red and smaller than he remembers it being.

"Yeah, no duh. Where did it come from? I never had a book like this as a kid," she says, flipping it over and reading the back. "These sound dark."

Ethan snorts out a laugh. "They are. We had a bit of an eventful story time that day. Um... Taylor bought that." He plugs the waffle maker into the outlet by the fridge and begins mixing the batter in a metal bowl on the island.

"I'm assuming this is Taylor's, too, then?" Samara asks, kicking a sock Ethan hadn't seen before across the carpet. It must've been trapped under the couch and Nana dug it out. Ethan's about to deny it when she says, "It's a little small to be yours."

"Turn sixteen and suddenly you're a public defender, huh?" he asks, laughing nervously. While he and Amy may not see eye to eye all the time, they still run everything by each other when it comes to parenting Samara. Telling Samara about his houseguest-turned-something-more seems like a line he shouldn't cross without consultation. Though that would be difficult when Amy isn't speaking to him. He focuses back on the batter.

Samara crosses into the kitchen and plops down on the chair at the island. She's wearing a white fleece zip-up with black koi fish swimming across it. Her hair is pulled back in a ponytail, and there's a hint of her makeup from last night still shimmering on her upper eyelids. "I texted Taylor this morning to say that I hoped everything was okay with his family and he immediately texted back, 'What do you mean?' Then sent, 'Oh, yeah. All good now.' Which leads me to believe that Mom lied to me."

Ethan sprays the griddle, then pours his batter into the mold. Shutting it, he sighs. "Shouldn't you be grilling your mother about this?" If only he could train Nana to use the coffee maker so he could down a scalding, caffeinating cup right now. He's not alert enough to field these questions.

"I would've, but then I remembered the way you two were looking at each other over fish and chips. Then the way you were looking at each other during archery. Then how grumpy you looked all through my party last night and how awkward Mom was when she lit his candle." Seriously, if this girl weren't so good at photography, she could have a career as a prosecutor. "Factoring all that with the book and the sock and the blush creeping up your neck right now..."

Ethan slaps at his neck like there's a mosquito there. Christ, he's in uncharted territory here. "This visit had nothing to do with the waffles, then?"

"Oh, no. I'm mainly here for the waffle," she says. "Syrup?"

"In the pantry."

With her head strategically ducked inside, she asks, "Do you have a thing with Taylor?"

Ethan nearly burns himself by reaching directly for the finished waffle instead of using the spatula. He saves himself at the last second and says, "I'm not sure we should be discussing this."

She slides the fancy bottle of Vermont Maple across the island. "I'm sixteen now. I've been around the block with a boy or two."

"What boys? What block?" Ethan asks, protector mode ripping through.

"Ha! No need for your teddy-bear-with-a-head-cold voice, Dad. Two boys, both Mom-approved, and I've done nothing more than kiss. Promise," she says, giving him a Scout salute. It's her even-keeled maturity that winds him down from high alert. She's self-assured and strong. No boy would dare take advantage of her. "Let me rephrase my question—do you *like* Taylor?"

"Christ, I didn't realize I was on trial. Should I return the camera and get you LSAT prep books for a gift instead?" he asks.

"You wouldn't dare," she says, drowning her waffle in syrup. "I've just been watching *Legally Blonde* a lot. It's my comfort movie. Don't avoid the question."

"Remind me what the question was again?" he asks just to rile her up a little more. They've always had an easy back-and-forth ever since she learned the full power of her charming sass.

"Do. You. Like. Taylor. Frost?"

Worn down, he relents with a sigh. "I do. Does that bother you?"

After a big swallow of no-pulp orange juice that he's poured for her into a tall glass, she says, "Not at all. I like Taylor, too. I like Taylor a lot!" She sets her fork down and looks at her lap. "Honestly, I don't really like the way Mom treats him. She gets stressed out and then she gets snippy, especially with him, and he always smiles through it, and like, yeah, obviously I love Mom, but as a boss, she's, uh, not the best."

"Don't say that about your mother," Ethan says, using the last of the batter to make himself a waffle, too.

"You don't see her in action every day like I do. She is so go-go-go that I barely see her. I spend more time with Taylor than I spend with her, and if I've cracked the case like Elle does with Chutney's perm, then Mom fired him!"

Ethan squishes his eyes shut, flashing back to the confrontation outside the Snow White cottage. "She did."

"Ugh. I knew it!" She pushes her plate away. "Just because you two hit it off? Like, she's seeing the resort photographer now. Why does she care what you do?"

Hearing this from his daughter's mouth forces him to consider it further. "It's a matter of principle, I suppose."

"I'm just saying, you *both* deserve to be happy."

"I am happy, Sam," he says while once again almost burning his fingers off because he's too distracted by the bold-faced lie he just spouted. Taylor's presence in the cottage gave him so much—confidence, comfort, joy—but it also showed him a harsh truth: he's lonely. And even the most solitary of people can't be entirely happy when they're constantly secluded. Emotionally shut-off.

"Fine, whatever. Let's say for the sake of this argument you are happy—" she cocks a dark, threaded eyebrow at him "—Taylor makes you happier, yeah?"

He sets his plate down on the island, dumping the remains of her waffle atop his own to create a syrupy tower that mirrors his emotions: runny, messy and, like his father said, *sticky*. "I guess…"

"Dad, come on. This isn't the open-ended writing portion of the SAT. It's a simple yes or no."

"Have you been prepping for the PSATs? You know if you need, I can hire you a tutor," he says.

"I've got it covered. Mom won't let me forget. Now, focus. Yes or no. Don't think too hard."

He holds up his hands in defeat. "Okay. Yes."

"Thank you! Was that so difficult?" she asks, reaching for his plate and splitting the distance between them as she grabs for a bite of his fresh waffle, leaving him with her semisoggy leftovers. Obviously, his vulnerability has resuscitated her hunger. "Happy doesn't need to be the default. *Happier* could be nice for a change. When I think about you out here at the resort, all alone with only Nana, I don't know, I get sad."

He bites the inside of his cheek with shame. "Hey, I'm the dad here. It's my job to do the worrying."

"Yeah, right. Because that's how worry works. Thanks for the psychology lesson." She swipes a napkin across her mouth. "I miss you. I know we have our calls and our regular trips and visits and I know you're good at being on your own and you have Grandma and Grandpa nearby, but…ugh, with Mom breathing down my neck about college and her obsessing over the California location of Storybook Endings, I'm scared."

Despite her age and displayed maturity, he can't help but hear the echo of the eight-year-old girl who, on their first night in the cottage, stood in the dark beside his bed holding her stuffed rabbit, sniffling.

"What's wrong?" he'd asked, sitting up immediately. Amy stayed fast asleep.

"I hear noises in my room," she said in a hiccupping mumble. "I'm scared."

His heart melted in that moment. He took her by the hand, brought her back to bed, and pulled the tiny chair away from her desk. Sitting down beside her, he grabbed her hand again. "I built this house just for us and this room just for you. This is our kingdom, and this room is your royal chamber, Princess. Nothing's going to harm you here. There's nothing to be scared of." If he'd had to dig a moat around the cottage and fill it with the gnarliest crocodiles to make her feel safe there, he would do it. Christ, he'd do anything for this girl.

He sat in her room until she fell asleep and even for a few moments after, watching her sleep peacefully beneath the painted lanterns on the wall and the stars on the ceiling.

He watches her now with the same awe, the same tears rimming his eyes. "What's scaring you, Princess?"

For the first time in a long time, she doesn't cringe or stick her tongue out when he calls her that. He apologizes anyway, and she waves it off. "I don't mind. I really felt like a princess last night. Thanks in large part to Taylor." She beams, then confides, "I'm scared that our trips are going to get pushed aside for college visits, and that Mom is going to be so consumed with her new location that she won't let me come see you."

"Sam, we'd work all that out," he says.

"Yeah, I know. I guess I'm just saying I'd probably worry less if I knew you had someone like Taylor looking after you," she says.

The response at the top of his mind is: *I don't need anyone to look after me.* Which is a true statement. However, what is it she just said? *Happier could be nice for a change.* His needs may be met, but he does have more love to give, and if someone wants to give him love in return in the form of looking after and care, well, he'd be a fool to inhibit that.

Which would be a beautiful revelation if Taylor hadn't left by saying he had no room for Ethan in his life. Maybe that had always been the case. They hadn't discussed it. His mind could've run away on a jet fueled by fantasy.

"That's a nice thought," Ethan says. But he doesn't let himself snuggle up inside it this time. It takes two to tango, and Taylor dropped the rose from between his teeth and stepped on it when he left the resort. "It's sweet that you feel that way. Thank you for sharing all of this with me. I miss you, too. We'll do whatever it takes to make sure we get our time together."

"All right," she says, greedily stealing the last of the waffles for herself. He shakes his head. "What? You can have some at the brunch, too!"

"Get cleaned up while I go change or we'll be late," he says, smiling to himself as he exits the kitchen. Happy that even though she lives on the other side of the country, even though she's sixteen now she's still his little girl, forever his princess. Thankfully, just not one that needs saving.

Twenty-Six

TAYLOR

The tide doesn't change for Taylor.

Every morning, aching for renewed purpose, he goes out to the beach in his wet suit with his board. The first two days, he paddles out, waits and breathes and tries to soak up some shreds of vitamin D. Still nothing surfable rolls in on the SoCal coast. It's better than sitting alone in his bed, wallowing and watching crappy TV, but not by much.

On the third day, he camps out on the sand and just watches the waves. His board falls from its staked upright position with a clunk as if even it is tired of this repetitive nonsense. He goes back to his apartment with his many roommates and his tiny room, shuts the door and fires up an online search for a new job.

On day four, restless from writing a million cover letters, he leaves the surfboard strapped to the roof of his car and quietly sits on the beach, curious if this might be one of those umbrella-versus-the-rain situations. If you bring one? Sunshine all day. If you don't? Torrential downpour. This method proves unrewarding.

By day five, he doesn't even deign to bring a board at all. In his tie-dyed hoodie and his Birkenstocks, he trudges out onto the beach, sits crisscross, places his hands on his knees and breathes in time with the whooshing winds that stroke his cheeks and jostle his hair.

Minutes pass. He enters a meditative state—a serene room previously locked up in his mind—where he asks himself all the questions that have been keeping him up at night.

Do you regret what you did?

No.

Do you miss Ethan?

So much.

Do you miss Samara?

Yup.

Do you miss Amy?

Actually, yeah.

Do you wish you could have your job back?

An answer to that one is harder to come by. Instead of digging for a response, he tunes into the crashing of the waves, sniffs at the fresh briny scent in the air. He can't recall when he's had this much free time before.

What do you want to do?

Considering his situation more closely, he's not destitute. Thanks to smart planning, he's got a sizable amount of savings. If need be, he could always ask his siblings to float him, to be paid back with interest later. It's the least they could do after he'd sewn Halloween costumes and administered medicine for them over the years.

What do you want to do right now?

His brain goes blank, but his shoulder muscles respond, stretching back and down. His hands float up from his kneecaps and take aim midair. Before he can second guess the impulse, he's walking back to his car and firing up an internet search.

Twenty minutes later, he's entering an archery and fencing studio not far from where he lives in Encinitas—the land of murals and smiling dogs. He must've passed this place dozens of times but never bothered to look closer. Today the swish of the door swinging open signals a fresh start.

He texts his sister: I'm signing us up for archery lessons

She's excited when, two days later, he drives them to the studio for their beginner class, equipment provided. She's wearing bright pink leggings and a stretchy headband that pulls back her brown hair. "Here, I brought an extra," she says, slinging a matching one at him as they take their spots among a bunch of teenagers.

He really should get a haircut, but every time he goes to make an appointment, he stops. Ethan ran his hands through this hair. Something about shedding it feels wrong, and yes, that's ridiculous, but so is the polka-dotted headband he slides on in preparation for class.

The instructor is not a tall, burly man, but rather a young, slender woman with brown skin and a warm smile. Good, he'll focus much better this way. Just getting the bow and arrow in his hands snaps him back to those moments out on the field at Storybook Endings, how free and safe he felt under Ethan's watchful gaze and how at-home he felt on those grounds.

At the end of the class, when it's his turn to shoot his shot, he does so with gusto. Every teenager and Sasha's jaws are on the floor when he hits just shy of center.

"Well done," the instructor beams.

Taylor beams, too.

ETHAN

A week later, Ethan's hand is finally healed. He can't say the same about his heart.

The damage inflicted upon his physical body while Taylor was around has vanished, but that book and that sock still sit on his coffee table, placed there by Samara. He looks at both of them and resolves to do something about them. Mail them back or get rid of them—those are his options.

Yet both seem infeasible.

Christ, it's not like he's about to start a shrine to the guy. It's just that he sort of wants to keep the illustrated book of fairy tales as a token of remembrance and it would be ridiculous to mail back a single sock. Taylor's probably just thrown away its match by now.

Thrown away its match. Is that perhaps what Taylor did when he walked out without fighting for them? Sure, they'd had no discussions about feelings or longevity, but there's no doubt in Ethan's mind that Taylor could sense his intentions surging through the air with every word, every touch.

Five years he's lived alone in this cottage that he built for a family that has dispersed. Five years he vacuumed the carpet, fed Nana, pruned the garden out front and made dinners for one. A king inside a castle that's not quite crumbling, yet it no longer holds the magic or fortitude it once did.

It may be time to abdicate the throne.

Out on the archery field an hour or so later, an acute wave of loneliness crashes over him. Teaching solo has always been most comfortable to him. Assistants just get in the way. But Taylor was more than an assistant in that week. He was an eager student, a positive presence, someone who balanced out Ethan's more spacey qualities.

Before a new crop of young guests at the resort arrive, he braces against the chilly wind and tries to take on some of Taylor's more sociable qualities.

Whatever his reserve, it's freeing to reunite with the bow in his hands, the trusty one he's kept since his late teens. The resistance in his shoulder blade as he draws back is an ache he's missed. The tension builds and builds to a pointed release that he'll never grow tired of, never stop wanting to share with others.

Not long after returning to the cottage, still puzzling over the Taylor memorabilia on permanent display in his living room, *Facetime Samara* blinks up onto his phone.

When he accepts the call, Amy's face in her home office takes up the full screen.

"I was worried if I called from my own phone you wouldn't pick up," she says by way of greeting.

There's no use rebuking that, so he sits down on the couch and pops in his earbuds. Nana comes up onto the couch, poking her head into the frame. The dog gets a warmer greeting than he does, but no use pouting over that. "I don't have long because I think Samara will combust if she goes without her phone for more than an hour, but I'm calling for two reasons."

He makes no comment about how she's acting like she's running down an agenda at a business meeting, a habit of hers that he's grown used to but only barely.

She connects the phone to what is surely a standing ring light on the edge of her desk, folds her hands in front of her face and sighs. "First, I want to say I'm sorry for the way that I acted toward you. I shouldn't have spoken to you that way nor accused you of trying to hurt me. I realize now that I was hurt, and it was easier for me to make your intents malicious than acknowledge that maybe there was something true happening between the two of you."

Ethan clears his throat. "I'm sorry, too. We—I—should've been up front with you. Sneaking around made us look guilty. No wonder you were hurt."

"I'll admit that hoodie wasn't a brilliant disguise," she says, a knowing smirk shifting to the left of her face.

"You get caught up in someone, and suddenly even the worst ideas seem like gold," he says.

"You must have real feelings for Taylor," Amy says after a practiced, loaded beat. Ethan struggles to find something intelligent to say. Even when they were together, they weren't well-versed in openly sharing. Perhaps that should've been a bigger red flag, but when you're young, in love and starting a family and a business, there's only so much time to talk. Now, five years gone, Ethan is still speechless over the wreckage of who they used to be.

"It's okay. You don't have to respond," Amy says, sounding borderline wistful. She runs a tentative hand through her silky hair. "I'm sorry if I've been distant for the last year or so. It's not easy trying to prove yourself as a woman in this industry. It didn't even occur to me that I'd be treated differently in meetings once we divorced. I'm working hard to make this business everything it can be."

"You will," Ethan says. Their relationship may have ended, but his belief in her and her vision is limitless.

She smiles. "Once the Lake Tahoe resort is opened, I'll be taking a long break. Samara and I will move up there for the summer to oversee launch and then be back in time for her to start her junior year."

"That's amazing." And he means that. Sincerely.

"Thanks. It'll be a nice change. A good change, I think."

Nana huffs a bit, her head resting on Ethan's thigh. It forces him to look around, inspect Taylor's book and Taylor's sock and the walls and the chairs, investigate the feeling sitting heavy in his chest. "I think I could use a change, as well," he says, surprised to be confiding in Amy of all people.

Her eyebrows shoot up. "Anything I can help with?" He can tell the offer is genuine.

He nods slowly. "Maybe."

"What did you have in mind?" she asks.

He takes a breath, whips up some courage and launches into the plan that's been brewing in his mind for some time now.

Twenty-Seven

TAYLOR

On a Tuesday near the middle of April, Taylor's at the tiny desk in his bedroom, working on a job application, when there's a knock on his door. One of his roommates—Thad, an older man with thick eyebrows yet a plucked slender mustache—pokes his head inside. "Package for ya," he says, tossing a padded envelope into Taylor's waiting hands.

Ethan's address is postmarked on the front.

Immediately, he tears it open.

Inside is the copy of *Grimm's Fairy Tales* he bought from the indie bookstore in Calico. He turns the envelope upside down. Not even a card.

Confused and upset, he flings the book onto his dresser and goes to make himself lunch.

After his third archery class, a text is waiting for Taylor with an unexpected invitation from Amy.

Hi, Taylor. I apologize for bothering you so late. Would you be available to meet me at Coffee-cita tomorrow around eleven? I'd love to speak with you. Thanks in advance.

At ten-fifty, dressed in the slacks and polo Amy preferred him in when he was her assistant, Taylor enters the establishment. He's welcomed by the scent of a bold roast and freshly baked scones. The walls are painted white brick with murals by community members laid over top. A metallic sign above the counter says DRINK. EAT. BE. The letters are made up of marquee lights.

A skyscraper of a man, not much older than Taylor, with dark skin and twist high top hair juts his chin out in greeting toward Taylor as he tries to get out the door. Taylor might be mistaken, but he thinks he's seen that man before at some reception or other he accompanied Amy to.

Taylor wanted to be early so he could choose his drink and table before Amy showed up, not needing to play the awkward dance of who pays for what and floating around to find a place to sit. Turns out, his ten-minute buffer didn't allot him enough time. Amy is already there, stuffed into the two-top in the corner, computer and tablet fired up. A medium whole milk latte in a large black mug sits on a saucer in front of her, growing colder the longer it remains untouched.

Taylor takes a breath before approaching. There's a chance she's going to reprimand him again. There's a chance he'll need to stick up for himself—do a better job of it this time. But when she glances up and catches sight of him through the rims of her scarlet-colored reading glasses, she flashes a smile with apology sketched across it.

As he sits opposite her, he gets a good look at the résumé open on the tablet he returned to her outside the Snow White cottage. Rodney Carmichael is the name typed across the top. He matches the name with the face of the man who just left. Rodney was working then as a second assistant to an even bigger name in hospitality than Amy.

A pang of fear should be dancing through Taylor's stomach right now, yet it never steps out from behind the curtain.

Amy thanks Taylor for meeting her there and asks what she can get him. "Oh, don't bother. I'll go get in line."

"Nonsense. You're here on invitation. Is it still the same matcha latte with oat?" she asks.

He's surprised she paid any attention to his drink order. "Yeah, thanks."

She's back ten minutes later with the latte and a plate with two almond croissants on it. "They were the last two. They looked too good to leave there in the case."

He takes the closer one, breaking off a tiny bit of the edge and stuffing it in his mouth, waiting to find out why exactly he's here when she's clearly been holding interviews for his replacement. But he swallows and, unable to stand the silence between them any longer, says, "I'm sorry for not telling you about what was going on with Ethan sooner. It went against my better nature. I'm not sorry it happened, but I am sorry it hurt you."

Amy purses her ruby red lips together and taps the tips of her fingers. "I'm sorry, too. I said some things I wish I hadn't and made a rash decision. I wish I hadn't done that, either. I was imaginably unprepared to run my daughter's birthday party, which… I'm not sure what that says about me, but I'm sure it's not anything I'd put in a bio."

Taylor opens his mouth to defend her, but she shakes her head resolvedly. "You're no longer on my payroll. No need to give out undeserved compliments."

Taylor doesn't know what stings more, the fact that she had to remind him of his unemployment or that she thought he'd been such a yes-man all these years. "I can promise I never did that," he says.

She smiles kindly. "I think I meant *under*deserved. You were a superstar at your job. If there was something higher than above-and-beyond, that's how far you went to make sure my life—and most definitely Samara's life—was easier. So easy, in fact, that I don't think I ever stopped to consider just how much you were doing on any given day, proven now by how impossible it is to replace you."

Taylor hikes his thumb back toward the door. "Rodney seemed lovely when we met him last year at that expo. I'm sure he'd be a great choice."

Recognition dawns faintly over Amy's face. "I knew he looked familiar. I'm surprised he didn't say anything during the interview."

Taylor's not. Sure, he wasn't carrying around a binder full of acquaintances like Anne Hathaway in *The Devil Wears Prada* (one of Samara's comfort movies they would watch together), but he did at times feel like an external hard drive where Amy kept her digital date book. Faces and names came easily to him. Regardless, he shrugs at her.

"Nevertheless, I think I've found fault in everyone I've interviewed across the last several days because none of them are you. Over the last three years, as Samara pointed out very astutely and not at all sassily—" she rolls her eyes "—you have become like family. I believe that's why I reacted so poorly when I saw Ethan coming out of the cottage. It felt like the call was coming from inside the house, so to speak. I was terrified I'd lost you as not only my assistant, but as a nephew of sorts. I realize now that I didn't pay you nearly enough to play all the roles I demanded of you."

Taylor quirks a brow, slides his hands away from his mug. "I played them happily."

"I know, but when you started this position, I promised you advancement," she says, eyes flicking away from their table. Possibly out of guilt.

"It's okay. People forget. Things fall through the cracks." He's attempting to make sure she knows he still sees the best in her because she did take a chance on him. She was good to him.

She lets out a lengthy sigh that nearly harmonizes with the hiss of the nearby coffee machine and the flush of the toilet behind them. A whistling, unsettling symphony. "The truth is, Taylor, I didn't forget. I just didn't want to have to do this." She gestures down toward the tablet. "That was selfish of me. Your skills are honed and perfect for hospitality. Judging by Samara's party alone, not even to touch on your three years of solid work, you have leadership and vision. I think you could have your own chain or an award-winning B and B someday. All of this is to say that I won't be offering you your job back."

There's a mixture of relief and disappointment churning low in Taylor's gut alongside that croissant he decimated. Unemployed isn't his favorite job title, yet still, he can't see himself returning to his old post and his old ways. His time with Ethan cemented the fact that he'd outgrown both. "Okay, I understand."

"I'd like you to consider applying for activities coordinator for the Lake Tahoe location," she says. "You wouldn't be reporting to me directly. There is a hiring committee currently interviewing internally, and I want to put your name into the mix."

"Wow, thank you."

"You're destined for greater even, but it's a good place to start I think," she says with an air that suggests the job is as good as his if he wants it. However, he's thrilled he'll have to go through the whole process to earn it.

Now that she's not his boss and won't be directly in the future, he's compelled to ask, "Is everything okay with Ethan?" That name on his tongue again tastes as delicious and earthy as his matcha latte.

"It is," she says after sipping her drink. "He and I have talked, but I know that's not what you're getting at. I'd say he's taking some time for himself to work out what he wants and needs from life right now."

"That makes sense."

Amy's gaze lasers past him toward the door before flashing down to her watch. "I hate to cut this short, but I do have an eleven-thirty. I think I see her waiting by the sugar bar over there."

Taylor can't help himself. He looks back to catch a slightly younger tan-skinned woman with dark hair and light eye makeup, wearing a dressy casual blouse and black pants. She carries an attaché. Even from across the room, he can tell by her energy that she really wants this job.

Taylor stands and offers up his hand to shake, but Amy, ignoring the gesture, pulls him in for a hug. It's not a heart-melting hug, the kind you could settle into for minutes and never want to leave. There's still a sheet of professionalism plastered between them, but it's sweet all the same. "Thanks."

"And I know it might not mean much or anything at all even," Amy says, still holding on, "but you have my blessing with whatever you may choose next. Both professionally and otherwise."

Taylor levels up their hug, leaning into it. He squeezes his eyes shut, thankful.

With Amy's quasi approval buzzing in his ear, Taylor can't sleep.

Even before his coffee meeting with Amy, he's been itching to reach out to Ethan, rescind his statement about not having room enough in his life. He's certain Ethan would be excited by his new pursuit of archery. But there's the matter of the book, returned with no fanfare, no note.

If Ethan's made peace with them going their separate ways, then maybe he has to, as well.

Though, didn't Amy say she'd talked to Ethan?

No matter how many sheep he counts, he tosses and turns, until the restlessness is overwhelming. He sits up and turns on the light. The book on his dresser catches his eye. In child-hood, he'd read aloud from a similar volume to his siblings to get them to doze off. Maybe he can trick himself into the same.

The trouble is, when he opens the book, the inscription on the cover page shocks him fully awake.

Every time I open this book, I hear your voice reading the stories as if we're in the same room. I hope we will be again someday.
All my care,
Ethan

Before he can second guess himself, he pops in his earbuds, opens his voice memos app, and turns to the first story in the collection. Using the character voices and a calm whisper, he reads the story aloud, pausing for effect in many places. His heart settles into a much slower rhythm.

When he's finished, he adds the story title to the file name, plops the audio note into his mired text thread with Ethan and sends it off.

Twenty-Eight

ETHAN

The voice message must be the Gen Z version of a butt dial.

That's all his mind can supply as he avoids listening to Taylor's message through brushing his teeth, making himself toast, letting Nana out back to pee. Frankly, he couldn't stomach listening to Taylor driving in the car and singing along to one of Samara's playlists or talking to one of his many siblings about his joblessness.

Yes, he sent the book away with an inscription about Taylor's dulcet tones, but that's the thing. He can already manifest Taylor's voice in his mind at will. *Against* his will sometimes! Hearing the real thing on accident would be an extra blow he couldn't recover from. Taylor already didn't respond to the book gesture, which felt deeply personal.

To torture himself, he goes through his whole workday without listening, which turns out to be the wrong move.

He spends the day distracted—sending housekeeping to the wrong cabin, misspelling names on over-the-phone reservations. Everything is fixable, except one major thing: *he doesn't want to be here anymore.*

For the first time in a decade, his brain has caught up with his emotions. The restlessness and discomfort that have been pounding away at the door of his subconscious have finally been let in.

The timeline still needs fixing, but he's on a path toward a different tomorrow.

"Youths today. Always staring at their phones," says Gabriel, coming out of The Thirsty Goat where he reupholstered some of the booths. Ethan noticed them fraying a few weeks back during that big dinner by the fireplace.

Ethan sets his phone in the drawer he usually keeps it in and sighs. "I got a weird message from Taylor last night at four a.m."

"You got a 'You Up?' text. Damn, when did you get so hip?" Gabriel teases, flashing a good-humored smile.

"He's on the other side of the country..." Ethan remarks with a shake of his head.

"There's this newfangled invention. I don't know if you've ever heard of it. It's called sexting and—"

Ethan holds up a hand. "It was a voice memo with no context."

"What did it say?"

"I haven't listened to it."

"Then how do you know it's weird?"

"Good point," he says, realizing latently how wishy-washy he's being over his feelings. They are alien—that's probably why. All the people he's dated since the divorce have been rest stops on a long road. Suddenly, Taylor showed up and the big green Welcome to Your Future sign appeared out of nowhere, catching him completely off guard.

Gabriel sidles over. "Why don't you let me listen to it for you? If it's a mistake, I'll delete it for you. If it's real, I'll give you the SparkNotes, and then you can decide how to respond."

Ethan readily agrees, passing his phone across the counter. He needs to be rid of this electronic torture.

Gabriel is gone longer than expected. Ethan paces behind this plank of wood, hands digging so deep into his pockets that they might funnel right out the other side. His heart is a missile the moment Gabriel returns. "Well?"

His face contorts in what appears to be confusion. "I think it's best you listen to it yourself."

"That bad?" Ethan asks, taking his phone back.

"No, but it's weird. You had that right. That's for sure."

Ethan intends to hit Play, but Gabriel stops him. "Maybe wait until you get home. Before bed." Ethan opens his mouth to ask follow-up questions. Gabriel just shakes his head. "Trust me on this one."

If there's one unfaltering thing in his life, it's his trust in Gabriel, so he suffers until he's in his sleep pants, tucked under the covers, with Nana in her dog bed across the way, to finally listen.

"Little Red Riding Hood… Once upon a time there was a sweet little girl." Ethan's heart jolts up into his throat as he's thrust back to the night they first kissed. Preserved here, complete with a husky, suave wolf voice, is Taylor's interpretation of this classic tale for Ethan's ears only.

Well, Nana's, too. Her head bobs and her ears perk up at the sound of Taylor's voice. To not disturb her sleep or confuse her further, he pops in his earbuds, shuts out the light and listens until the end. He's not sure how many times he replays the voice memo, but it gets into the double digits before he's letting out yawns, which are bordering on wolfish howls.

Come morning light, Ethan decides he needs to record his own.

On his lunch break, he jets into Calico to procure his own copy of the collection. That evening after dinner, he sets himself up on the couch in his coziest pajamas and a mug of tea. He even warms up his voice the way he learned to do in a public speaking class in college before choosing "Briar Rose" to share.

Unable to listen back to his own voice, he selects his third take, which was the most natural thanks to knowing the story better, and sends it off with one simple red heart emoji.

An hour later, his phone pings with a text: **You make an excellent prince**

Those five words are enough to make Ethan break out with an inextinguishable blush.

Hours later, Taylor sends him "Pinocchio" to enjoy.

In a way, these voice memos of words by the long-dead Grimm Brothers say more than any specific communication could.

At the end of his recording of "Rumpelstiltskin" Ethan says sweetly into the microphone, "Good night, Taylor."

For a moment, he imagines kissing Taylor's lips again.

Two weeks go by trading voice notes. They come to the end in the children's volume, so they send links to different fairy tale collections back and forth. They settle on a chunky, complete edition replete with sketchy, borderline creepy drawings. From this, they start again.

A month goes by.

Still, they've not reached the end of their story-sharing, each growing more confident with their character choices and silly background noises. Ethan swears he could become a Foley artist for movies at this rate—clanging pans, rattling change in a can and getting Nana to bark on cue.

Between voice notes, they send life updates.

Did I tell you I'm taking archery lessons? Taylor includes a video taken by his sister of him practicing in a studio somewhere in Encinitas. Ethan's heart takes on the quality of the raindrops pitter-pattering against his windowpane.

The next day, he has Gabriel video him shooting archery, as well. He captions the video: Back in action!

Taylor writes, And looking good doing it.

The ducks! They've arrived! Ethan types some weeks later, embracing the June sunshine along with a photo of the pond. He sends the same one to Samara and asks: Which one do you think is Donnie Ducko?

On stressful days, Taylor will send: Rough one. Nana pic, please?

Ethan's whole camera roll is photos of Nana sleeping, fetching, walking and one very silly picture of her tongue lolling and her head tilting when he tells her who the picture is for. Taylor makes one of them his lock screen and sends Ethan the proof.

Their connection, regardless of distance, revives itself in the digital sphere, becoming resplendent and near constant.

Ethan goes to bed with a smile on his face after saying good night to Taylor and wakes up with a grin on his face, thinking about the story he's going to read aloud later.

By late June, Taylor calls with exciting news, "I'm the Storybook Endings Lake Tahoe location activities coordinator!"

They celebrate over FaceTime, each with their own bottle of the wine that Ethan stockpiles in his garage. No glasses necessary. The virtual cheers they do is satisfying, except for the fact that Ethan wants to haul Taylor up, wrap his legs around his waist and kiss him silly for this amazing accomplishment.

"We're opening right after the Fourth of July. Will you come?" Taylor asks softly. It's obvious he doesn't want to burst the bubble of what's developed between them since they've been apart. Maybe it's best kept pixelated, intangible.

Ethan hears the emotion underpinning Taylor's question and says, "Wouldn't miss it for the world."

He marks his calendar, he books his flight, and the night before, he packs his bag with new clothes, plenty of sunblock, and a new collection of fairy tales for Taylor.

After dropping Nana off with Gabriel and Giselle, he heads south toward New York and then west toward the formerly impossible.

The plane touches down at the Reno-Tahoe International Airport just shy of 6:00 p.m. PST. Amy texted to let him know she arranged a car for him, which was a nice gesture. They've been keeping up a friendly text thread—mostly about Samara—but they've settled on biweekly calls to discuss life, business and the major change Ethan is pursuing. The one he can't wait to tell Taylor about in person.

With his suitcase rolling behind him to the pickup area, he may not have to wait long at all. A familiar tie-dyed hoodie sticks out among the crowd. A smiling, floppy-haired guy holds a whiteboard that says *E. Golding*. Taylor's freshly bronzed skin makes his teeth look impossibly white, and he's ditched the socks with his sandals out here. No joggers, either. Just a pair of borderline scandalous running shorts. He hopes this reunion goes as smoothly as he's been dreaming because he can't wait to slip those off Taylor's waist.

"Are you Mr. Golding?" Taylor asks, playing up this chauffeur charade.

"I am he," he says. All those hours in recirculated air made his throat go dry. Though maybe that's just the effect of seeing Taylor again after all this time.

"Right this way then, sir," he says.

Ethan preens at the word *sir* as he follows Taylor out to the short-term parking. Taylor pops the trunk on his car and stows his luggage. "No, no. Allow me." He gets the passenger door for him.

As they pull out, robotic directions chirping from Taylor's phone, Ethan grabs the handle above the door, needing the support to start this conversation. Yet as soon as he opens his mouth, Taylor beats him to it. "You're probably drained from travel. We've got plenty of time. No need to talk now."

Ethan confided over text that he doesn't sleep well on planes, so he's grateful to be let off the hook here. He unstraps his neck pillow from his backpack, tunes into the Samara-made playlist and dozes until they reach their destination.

He wakes up just in time to see the replica of the ONCE UPON A TIME… sign leading up to the lakeside resort. For once, he concedes that the high density urethane was a good move.

As they venture past The Castle, around the back where the staff parking is, Ethan wakes up fully.

"Don't I need to check in?" Ethan asks as Taylor leads him away from The Castle.

"Already done. Your chamber awaits," he says.

Ethan stumbles a tad as he stands before a faithful recreation of the Snow White cottage. As Taylor turns the key in the knob, he swears he catches a smirk ghosting over his face in the front light.

The inside is painted with lighter shades and the kitchen is faintly larger. There are mint Milanos and a bottle of his favorite wine on the counter, and on the nightstand is Taylor's copy of the fairy tale collection they've been working their way through. He thumbs the pages. "In case you need a bedtime story," Taylor says, so innocently he must not be aware of how much of an innuendo it comes across as.

Heat spreading through his body, Ethan hauls his suitcase onto the luggage stand and sets his backpack down. "I have something for you, as well," he says, unzipping his bag.

"Hold on to that thought," Taylor says. "I thought I could light a fire for us."

By the time Ethan makes it outside after unpacking, the fire is roaring, and the wine is flowing into glasses. Taylor sits in the glow of the campfire, under the stars, looking like perfection made manifest. Ethan hands him a wrapped present with a bow tied around it. "For you."

"Thanks," Taylor says, setting it in his lap so he can hand Ethan some wine. "I wanted to wait until we were together in person again to say this, but I'm sorry for telling you I had no room in my life for you. I thought it might be easier for us to move on, then I realized, at least for me, there's no moving on from this."

"Me neither," Ethan says, nervously swirling his wine. "Open your gift."

Taylor peels the wrapping with care as if he plans to save it for reuse at Christmas. He sets the bow on the ground by his feet. His face shines like the sun invading this milky purple night when he lays eyes on the fairy tale book. "Perfect. We'll have a book ready and waiting for when we finish that doorstop inside."

Ethan shakes his head, amused. "Open it up."

Taylor palms his forehead. "You know, I didn't do that at first when you sent me the original back. Would've saved me a bunch of heartache if I had."

Ethan smiles warmly at him. "Go ahead, then."

Ethan watches Taylor's perfect lips as they mouth the words he inscribed there:

Care to write our own?

It's his cheesy way of asking Taylor to be his boyfriend. He's forty. Is he too old for boyfriends? Is *partner* a better, more mature term? None of that matters because Taylor launches off his seat and into Ethan's lap, answering him with the best kiss he's ever received.

"I'd love to," Taylor whispers while running his fingers gingerly through Ethan's beard. His forehead presses into Ethan's temple. What a tableau they make for the other guests strolling by. He couldn't care in the slightest. "Does this mean you want to do long distance?"

"For now," Ethan says, ready to show the hand of cards he's been holding close to his chest for weeks.

Taylor tilts back. "Are you moving out here?"

Ethan shakes his head. "I couldn't up and leave my parents, nor the resort, like that. But…if you're interested, I happen to know in about a year and a half, a general manager position may be opening up at the Catskills location."

Taylor's mouth drops open. "You're retiring?"

A chuckle bursts forth from Ethan's throat. "Christ, how old do you think I am?"

"You know what I mean!" Taylor punches him lovingly in the meat of his shoulder. "I meant from hospitality. What will you do next?"

"I've been looking into opening an archery camp for kids and teens," Ethan says. "Not just archery—hiking, fishing. A camp for outdoor kids. I love teaching, and I love what I do at the resort. This seems like the best of both worlds. Building longer term relationships and teaching skills and discipline."

"You'd be amazing at that," Taylor says.

"Thanks. I've got a long road ahead of me with locations and certificates and inspections. Amy is going to help me with all of it."

"That explains the secrecy she's had about me seeing her laptop screen," he jokes.

"If in a year and some change, you're looking to move up and across the country, I know a guy who'll put in a good reference for you." He casts his gaze down and intertwines their fingers on Taylor's lap. "That's far from now, I know. I just wanted you to be aware that I believe in your potential and your future. Just like I believe there's strong potential in a future for us."

Taylor toys with the one curly hair constantly flopping onto Ethan's forehead. "Me, too. I already said yes."

"I just wanted to hear you say it again," Ethan retorts.

"I'll say it a million times. I'll say it 'til you get sick of me."

"Never," Ethan says, leaning in for a wine-tinged kiss. The heat from the fire infiltrates his body and grows unignorable in his pelvis. "So, Mr. Activities Coordinator, what do you have on the agenda for us?"

Taylor's eyes go soft and dreamy. "For tonight? You—" he kisses Ethan's sensitive neck "—me—" he kisses Ethan's scruffy jaw "—bed—" he kisses Ethan's waiting lips "—now."

Gallantly, from sitting, he hoists Taylor up into his arms like a princess plucked from a tower and carries him across the threshold of the cottage, eager for their first night banked toward a sweeter tomorrow.

And as he lays Taylor down on the cloud-like bed and kisses Taylor's lips with everything he has, he's okay that *ever after* isn't guaranteed because everything that happens next, every moment with Taylor, will be a moment captured *happily*.

Epilogue

TAYLOR

Two Years Later

Three months into his new position, he's still not used to the view behind the reception desk at Storybook Endings Catskills. Who thought it was a good idea for him to start right before summer? On this Friday afternoon in July, the front door of The Castle is constantly propped open, a flood of eager families crowding inside for a slice of easy living.

The biggest comfort underpinning the learning curve is that every floorboard that creaks below him as he crosses for a key on the wall is a floorboard that creaked for Ethan. Every drawer he opens to retrieve a ballpoint pen from has a handle that Ethan touched a million or more times. Even though Ethan doesn't work at the resort any longer, his presence remains embedded in the space.

Ping.

Not that Taylor could ever forget about his fiancé when they send voice notes to each other all throughout the day.

When the family of four—with twin daughters, each wearing their own fuzzy tiara—happily waddles away with their welcome packet, Taylor shimmies into the break room to listen.

"The archery exhibition for the first session went really well. Twyla's mom cried. I guess she's never stuck with an activity before. It's going to be tough saying goodbye to this first crop of kids, but I'm glad another one will be here next week. Seeing them get excited about sharpening their skills is... It's something else," he says before a pause. Taylor imagines his burly future husband going misty-eyed with passion. It's one of Taylor's favorite sights. Ethan's throat clears. "Anyway, I'm just glad the rain held out so we didn't have to move inside."

Taylor loses his focus for a second, switching over to the weather app himself. A nervous gurgle sounds off from his gut. Looks as if the storm system is moving quickly, bypassing them completely. Excellent. Taylor would have his own score to settle with Mother Nature if she begrudges them with lightning and thunder tonight. Though, he supposes given how their relationship started—him soaked to the bone while banging on the door to the cottage he now calls home—it would be on-theme.

Sasha, Samara and his parents emerge from How Do You Brew with to-go cups of iced beverages clattering and sweating in their hands. "Hey, we were thinking of taking a walk on one of the trails before the day gets away from us. Are you sure there's nothing we can do to help set up?" Sasha asks. She and his parents all came in last night and are secretly staying in the Rapunzel cottage together. Sasha wasn't thrilled by the prospect of having to share quarters with their parents, but it was a necessary evil given their aversion to being where they're supposed to be when they're supposed to be there, and this trip is all about Taylor, so she yielded to his wishes.

Once he knew his relationship with Ethan was one for the long haul and he'd 99.9 percent be taking over Ethan's job at the Catskills location, he made an effort to zip down from Lake Tahoe every other week and reconnect with his parents.

Meeting Ethan's family illustrated a long dormant thought: as he grows older, so do his parents. Ethan's weekly dinner trips—which have become Ethan and Taylor's weekly dinner trips together—with Mr. and Mrs. Golding aren't about reconciling childhood or airing old grievances. They are about honoring the people who raised you, faults and all. Taylor decided to adopt that model.

"No, thank you. My staff has it all covered."

My staff. Two words Taylor never imagined himself saying when he applied for the position with Amy Lu. This shift in professional perspective is strange. His whole life, he's lived in service of others, and in a way, in hospitality, he's still doing that. But now he has a whole team operating alongside him, lightening his load.

"Here. Take a map," Taylor says, passing a paper over to Sasha. "Reception can get spotty the farther you go."

"I think you're forgetting I grew up in these woods," says Samara. She arrived earlier in the week. In a little over a month, she'll be a full-time photography and sociology student at NYU. Ethan is thrilled to have this time with her and that she won't be too far away once the semester starts.

"Just be sure to make it back in time to get ready."

"Can I take Nana?" Samara asks.

"Please do, but don't forget to wash her paws when you get in."

"You got it," she says with a smile.

And he loves this little family unit they've created.

He can't wait to make it official tonight.

ETHAN

The cottage is quieter than it's been since he did those renovations last year and since Taylor moved in five months ago.

Where is he? Where's Samara?

He doesn't even hear Nana's nails tapping against the new floorboards. The only sound is a light wind rapping against the walls.

After dropping his bag and bringing his personal archery equipment into the garage, he wanders into the bedroom, following the light of a lamp accidentally left on. On the bed, there's a book he's never seen before set out beside his suit, which is in a dry-cleaning bag. A single red rose lies diagonally across the two.

The book is a hardcover with a matte finish. The script title reads: *The Two Lost Princes.*

The story goes:

Once upon a time, there lived two princes—Prince Ethan and Prince Taylor—with kingdoms on opposite coasts. One day a fierce, independent Queen sent Prince Taylor on a quest across the country...

As he flips the pages, taking in the colorful, blocky illustrations of two men laying down their armor and falling in love, he tears up. His heartbeat takes on a completely new tempo and his cheeks warm to the touch.

When he gets toward the place in the book that mirrors where Ethan and Taylor are now in their relationship—sharing a castle—he grows confused. There are more pages.

More story.

More—

One of his bright yellow sticky notes with Taylor's handwriting on it draws his attention.

Stop! Don't read on. Put on your suit and meet me at the barn at 7:30 sharp.
All my love,
Taylor

Feeling light on his feet and anxious with anticipation, Ethan showers, grooms his beard, fixes that one pesky lock of hair with a bit of pomade and then dons his suit. Whatever romantic gesture Taylor has in store for him is worth his best tie, which is purple with a gold checkered pattern. Another gift from Samara "because it looks like that flannel you never stop wearing no matter how many times we tell you it's too ratty."

For a change, he doesn't let his mind run ahead of his footsteps.

Music and soft light spill out the open doors to the barn. Underneath the guitar, there is laughter, chatter. Ethan zeroes in on his breath, the sensation of his hands unfurling inside the satiny pockets of his blazer. His engagement ring holds new heft when he turns the corner and peers inside, knowing that it will soon be replaced with a wedding band. The second and last one he'll ever receive in this lifetime.

Gathered there before him is everyone he loves—Amy, his parents, brothers, sisters-in-law, nieces and nephews. But his eyes swing right to Taylor at the end of an impossibly long aisle, hair tamed and cheeks pink. The music switches to more of a march. Samara, appearing beside him, takes him by the hand. "Come on," she says, tugging him along when he doesn't step in time with her to the music.

Amazement clamps his feet in place for a beat.

Amazement that he could love and be loved by a man who knows him this well. Well enough to know that planning a second wedding would've been an intolerable task for him.

This intimate, surprise ceremony is cozy and beautiful and everything he didn't realize he wanted when he proposed to Taylor all those months ago.

When he stands in front of Taylor now, the first of many tears fall. "Hey," Taylor says, gently brushing them away, "no crying yet. I haven't even said my vows." Everyone in the room laughs, including Ethan who, quite frankly, couldn't care less about tradition.

Instead of waiting for the customary "And you may now..." part, he takes his about-to-be-husband's gorgeous face between his vibrating hands and kisses him as they turn a fresh page together.

★ ★ ★ ★ ★

Acknowledgments

Once upon a time…there was a young boy ravenously reading books in a well-loved beanbag chair who desperately wanted to be an author one day. Today, he's writing the acknowledgments for his seventh (!) published novel. There are so many people to thank for setting him on the right path and helping him on the daunting quest.

His awesome agent, Samantha Fabien, and her colleagues at Root Literary.

His insightful editors, John Jacobson and Stacy Boyd, along with the entire publishing team at Afterglow Books by Harlequin.

His parents, John and Theresa Janovsky, and his entire family.

His prince, Robert Stinner, and his fierce friends, Melanie Magri, Kelsey Scanlon, Julie Matrale, Tarah Beth Jordan Hicks.

His fellow scribes, Alison Cochrun, Gina Loveless, R. Eric

Thomas, Andie Burke, Susie Dumond, Mae Bennett, Xio Axelrod, Helena Greer and many, many more!

His book pals turned confidantes, Stephanie Kersikoski, Kasee Bailey, Simone Richter, Laynie-Rose Rizer, Hannah Walker, Matt Chisling, Sara Quaranta, along with the countless other bookstagrammers and BookTokkers who have interacted with him over their shared love of storytelling.

You, dear reader, for taking the time to engage with his work. Out of all the books in the world, you chose to spend time with this one, and for that he is exorbitantly grateful.

And, of course, they all lived happily ever after.